BILL RANDALL

Born and raised in Aylesbury, Bill has always found time for the creative arts. Starting his career in finance, he travelled to London in the evenings and at weekends to study sound engineering. He then spent ten years in another sensible career, while also playing bass in a London-based band. He tried his luck as a full-time musician, which lasted six months before the birth of his daughter clarified the need for a salaried post. He currently works as a training manager in the energy industry.

Alongside writing, his passion is playing guitar as a session musician, both on the road and in the recording studio. Experiences within the music industry aligned with his long-standing love of crime fiction and inspired the themes for his first novel.

www.billrandall.com

To June,

Happy reading!

PROTECTION SONG

BILL RANDALL

BYTHEBOOK.PRESS

First published in 2025

Typesetting: ByTheBook
Print Management by Biddles Books, King's Lynn, Norfolk PE32 1SF

A CIP record for this book is available from the British Library

ISBN 978-1-917625-01-2
e-ISBN 978-1-917625-10-4

For Erin

Prologue

Oxford • December 2015

He runs in the late evening when it's tranquil. When he can be alone. Besides, he's discovered he can run further later in the day. He likes to stretch himself. It's his third lap of the meadow, the pathway snaking into the trees now. There's a ditch on one side of the path and a narrow section of the river on the other. His legs are burning; his back is sticky with sweat. Sucking in the cold air is somehow encouraging. He's thinking about his girlfriend again. There's cloud cover blocking most of the moonlight and in here, amongst the trees, visibility is worse. The wildlife rustles. He doesn't worry. As usual, Danny de Vries is focused entirely on the good in his life.

He draws level with the tree. Something catches his eye. Something that wasn't there the last time he passed. He slows, then bounces on the balls of his feet, unsure whether to keep going or turn back. He puffs out a long burst of air and spins around. As his head comes up, it's too late to react.

Chapter One

Ian • London • August 2018

Sofia appears perfectly in control. Her hair and makeup are immaculate, of course, and her posture too. But she chews on her lower lip as her gaze settles thoughtfully on our guest's empty place. Ellie, a young singer-songwriter whose demos I'm currently producing, has just excused herself from the table.

'What do you think?'

Sofia takes a breath. 'I think I should check the brownies.'

'Come on, don't do that.'

'Okay, I think it's a lot of shit,' she says, the last word emphasising what's left of her Italian accent. 'I think she wants attention.'

'Shhh, she'll hear you.'

Sofia just tilts her head to the side and raises her eyebrows. Why did she put so much effort into inviting Ellie if she finds her so annoying? Even the dining table is beautifully laid, with candles and folded napkins. That's a first.

'It sounds iffy to me too, but let's hear her out.'

'Who would want to harm the little small-town girl? What's so special about her?'

The bathroom door opens, and I motion to Sofia to be quiet. Ellie returns to her place at the table. She's fixed her mascara, but her eyes are still red.

'Dessert, darling?' Sofia says. She's smiling, and she rubs Ellie's arm as she gets up.

Ellie nods, and her head drops again. She's fiddling with her dessert fork.

'If you're that worried,' I begin, 'you should sleep here with us. We've got a mattress.'

'I like the studio,' she says. 'I just wanted you to know about it, like... just in case.'

'But that's just it, Ellie. You won't tell us about it. Who is it you're scared of? Why?'

She closes her eyes. 'I can't.'

I lean in closer. 'Could it just be overthinking? How long have you been in London?'

'It's not that. Wish I hadn't said anything now – can we forget it?'

Sofia calls from the kitchen, 'Is it Yannis?'

Yannis is Ellie's manager. I've worked with a lot of his artists, but Ellie is the first young female. I know where Sofia is coming from.

'He's nasty,' Sofia adds, pulling a tray out of the oven. 'Ian, tell her about the awards night.'

I shoot her a look.

She returns the glare. 'Ellie needs to hear what he's like. He's disgusting, and lucky I didn't do more than throw a drink over him.'

Ellie's hands fly up to her face. 'Please... don't. Yannis is a creep, but this is something else, I promise.'

'Has he tried anything with you?' Sofia looks up from the countertop, hands on her hips.

Ellie buries her head in her arms and rests on the table.

Sofia continues, 'Because sometimes these men just can't

control themselves,' and stares hard in my direction.

I signal for Sofia to shut the hell up and turn to Ellie. 'It's complicated, coming to a big city like this. I know. Especially when you're on your own. A little paranoia is probably helpful, to be honest. Well... awareness... that's a better way of putting it.'

Ellie sits up, and I reach over for a friendly hug.

'Here we are.' Sofia drops plates of vegan chocolate brownie and ice cream in front of us. We eat in silence. Sofia finishes half of her dessert and excuses herself.

Ellie drags her fork through a pool of melted ice cream. She looks up.

'Can I tell you what I really want?' she asks.

Chapter Two

London • August 2018

Yannis is throwing his arms around. It's just the two of us, but he's projecting his voice as if he needs the whole of North London to hear his bigshot plans for the music industry. He draws a diagram in the air, so I can appreciate the future trajectory of Ellie Beck's career. He jabs at me with his forefinger to make sure I understand how the demo recordings I'm doing for her are going to create a ravenous dogfight between all the top A&R guys at all the top labels.

'This'll be massive for all three of us, Ian. Stop worrying about the extra ten percent.'

'I'm not worrying,' I say.

'And she's only twenty-two,' he goes on. 'She's got it all. For fuck's sake, mate.'

I've stopped paying attention, but he carries on. He swears more than he needs to. I guess that's to show me how relaxed he can be in business situations. I notice that, sometimes, with managers like Yannis. They see me, the producer, as more in sync with the young artists than they are and ramp up their sweary, outlaw side. It's embarrassing. I'm no angel, for sure, but the truth is, a record producer needs to be the most sensible one in the room.

'Forget about the ten percent,' I say. Yannis nearly chokes on his coffee and can't stop the grin from spreading across his face. He's won.

'I heard the talent straight away,' he says. 'The later stuff she sent me was all wrong. Trying to be too clever. Just her voice and a guitar in the bedroom – that was the real magic. Throw in some hip-hop beats and you're done.'

It's difficult to escape an idiot when your unit only has two rooms in addition to the studio. But I go to the kitchenette and pour us both another coffee. It's a strategy I use in sessions, when a musician should really consider what they've said, before I reply.

I drop back into the leather sofa, opposite Yannis. He's probably in his early forties, like me. We're dressed similarly in dark t-shirts and jeans. He doesn't seem to have reconsidered his comment that my value consists of simply throwing in some hip-hop beats. But then, Yannis isn't a musician, and it's not my place to share Ellie's private plans.

I want to tell Yannis that Ellie isn't going to take-off into the pop stratosphere like the rocket he's been drawing in the air. That we're no longer treating the recordings as a mapped-out marketing tool. That, instead, we're crafting the most emotive and rewarding songs we can. Showcasing the art, not the performer. Ellie wants to be a songwriter, not a star. I want to tell Yannis that that's the reason I let that ten percent go. That I'm all in with Ellie on this. Not for my career... but because I admire her self-awareness.

I study Yannis, who is all chat and smiles and charisma. There's some aggression in there somewhere. Ellie's new plan might just force it to the surface. Money can do that if everything around it suddenly drops away. Like a clock with no hands, the motor has no value anymore. You shouldn't put money at the centre. Operating like this makes it a struggle to keep the studio and the flat. It's a risk, but it's the only way to make art, and my conscience is clear.

Ellie validated the philosophy that night at dinner. She spoke about the anxiety Yannis was causing her. Everything she thought she knew about breaking into the industry was turning gradually from dream to terrifying nightmare. She wants no part of it; no part of Yannis either. She talked about song-writing and her first experience of getting those tingles as a child, identifying with a song her dad was playing in the car. She understands music and connects with it on such a deep level that I instinctively knew she was making the right decision. I told her so and, in that moment, I saw the tension fly out of her.

I bond with all artists I work with. I won't work with anyone I can't relate to. After our conversation, I am aligned with Ellie Beck like no other artist before her. But her plans have changed… and Yannis, her manager, doesn't know.

The door opens, and Ellie enters, clutching a carrier bag from Suresh's Grocery. She pushes sunglasses up into her black hair, which is tied back because of the heat today. Yannis notices the fair skin at her navel where her vest top leaves an inch exposed. He stares a little too long before rising.

'Here she is, come here, girl,' he says, embracing her in a bear hug. Ellie pats him on the back and gently pulls away.

'Careful… eggs in here,' she says and takes her bag over to the kitchenette. Yannis is watching her walk as he whispers to me from the corner of his mouth.

'She still sleeping on the couch?'

'Yep, Sofia said she's welcome at the flat, but she says she's happy here.'

'Insurance risk?'

'Shut up, Yannis,' I say, keeping it light-hearted. I want to tell him that she wouldn't buy eggs. He should know his artist better than this; and she shouldn't be uncomfortable greeting her manager.

'She'll be fine here,' I say, although I'd much rather she stayed with Sofia and me.

Yannis heads to the door. 'That Rasta still coming round?'

'He's not a Rastafarian, Yannis.'

'Got the dreads, hasn't he?'

'Haven't seen him since. But I'm the one who should have the issue,' I say, jabbing a forefinger into my chest.

'As long as my girl's safe,' he says, and rubs his hands together, signalling the end of our meeting.

The meter levels on the console jump and fall, but I'm focusing on the lead guitar fills Ellie is intermittently throwing in. My back is to her because I don't want her to see my concentration; I want her relaxed. I don't need to be watching the levels because there's a little compression on the signal to keep it in check. I'm blocking out everything but the performance. There's a faint reflection of Ellie in the computer screen. She's hunched over the '58 Tele I loaned her after I heard her own guitar buzzing and rattling. When I told her which 90s grunge legend had left the guitar here, she didn't show any excitement. And it wasn't because of her age. That name-dropping stuff simply doesn't mean anything to her.

'How was that?' she asks. The headphones rattle as she takes them off.

'Come and have a listen.'

I start the track, and Ellie pulls up a chair at the console. I leave the metronome click in because I want to hear her timing. My percussion loop rises gently out of the monitors and is joined by a bar of low synths. Then Ellie's guide vocal comes in. It's only there for reference – we'll record it again later, when the track's done – but it's haunting. There's beauty in her delivery. When the lead guitar comes in, it is understated, subtle, yet adding new shades to the singing voice. This is Ellie's power; she has the gift of instinctive accompaniment.

'It's perfect,' I say.

She smiles.

'Can you make the acoustic guitar light?' She crosses her palms across her chest, like asking has made her vulnerable.

'We can try anything.'

'And push it back onto the horizon?'

I switch my focus to the acoustic guitar. It's doubled and panned wide open, and I roll off most of the lower frequencies, leaving just the light high-end. Then I sculpt the reverb to push it back onto the horizon. I love how Ellie describes it. I always like to find a language with an artist; everyone's different. Ellie doesn't say how many cents she needs the reverb tail pitched to. She doesn't tell me the guitar should be more like that of another musician. She uses landscapes. When we were talking percussion, she led me out to the carpark and laid out traffic cones to illustrate her stereo picture. The glitches out here at ten o'clock, the shaker at two to balance it, the timpani more forward. A teenager on a BMX started dodging in and out of the cones, cigarette dangling from his mouth. Ellie shouted at him that this wasn't some bloody cycling proficiency. Even he found it funny.

When the track ends, I turn to her. It's her dark eyebrows that convey the seriousness, I decide. She looks pragmatic. Yannis would've seen her potential to inspire as well: a face with that timeless wisdom and a natural beauty; the holy grail for photographers. She meets my gaze, and a huge grin breaks out across her entire face. Now, she looks energised.

'I love it. Can I add some violin?'

We pull the absorption panels across, and I set up a microphone close to where her violin's front face will be. It'll give us more of the scratchiness I know she'll appreciate. She warms up with some classical phrases, and I set the gain stages, allowing for the dynamic performance to come. I'm not disappointed. She begins by doubling the chorus melody on the violin, before launching into a soaring assault into the outro. Her fingers slide to the highest notes, her bow sawing across the strings in a burst of energy. It's mesmerising, descending into noise: beautiful, tonal harmonics that could only be made by a violin in the hands of an artist who knows its rules, and then pushes further.

'Let's do one more,' I say, when the track ends.

She's mature enough to know why I'm asking her to do it again, but the first performance will probably make the final mix.

Ellie Beck is an alternative artist, no two-ways about it; a talented singer-songwriter. But pop fans will love her music too, because of her sense of melody. There are melodic hooks, not just within sections of the song, but within individual musical phrases.

Getting on for midnight, we take a break, each lying on a leather couch, staring at a ceiling which is in desperate need of fresh paint.

'Okay?' I ask, without turning my head. She sits up and spins round on the couch to face me.

For my entire career, from struggling beginner through to working with artists at the top of their game, the clock has been arbitrary. I just finish when we reach a natural break.

'I'm okay,' she finally says.

She looks absent, like there's something else. 'I'm sorry I didn't open up about it sooner.'

'I get it. Yannis doesn't exactly create a safe atmosphere for sharing, does he?'

She looks away. 'Can you promise me something, Ian?'

I pull some stupid grin at the ceiling. 'I'd have to hear it first.'

'Can you keep these songs honest? No studio tricks, like Yannis goes on about.'

My throat suddenly feels dry, and I turn to reassure her. I can see how much it means to her. 'Absolutely. Don't worry about Yannis, either. I know how to handle him.'

'I know I don't need to tell you,' she says. She raises a hand to rub her neck, which has flared up. 'I'm just not used to anyone understanding.'

'Look, I'll make it work.'

'And...'

'There's something else?'

'Can you help me get this music out into the world? Get it heard?'

'I'll do everything I can.'

'Promise?'

I nod slowly. 'Of course.'

The shift in her demeanour since opening up at dinner is remarkable. Like a new Ellie has stepped out. Less guarded, more emotional, yet more determined. I'm glad she hasn't mentioned anything more about being scared. I suppose I was right about the new city paranoia.

'Let's call it a night. In fact, come home with me. Sofia's giving me a hard time about you staying here alone.'

Ellie just gives me that look and shoos me off with her hands.

'Bolt the door behind me,' I shout over my shoulder.

Chapter Three

London • August 2018

A closing door jolts me awake. Sofia crosses the flat to the kitchen, switches on the coffee maker. She's wearing running shorts and a black vest. Her athletic figure is much the same as I remember first seeing ten years ago. Only her eyes are thirty-five. She loosens her long, dark hair and re-ties it, neater.

'You're on the couch in your... boxers,' she says. I sit up and look about me in mock surprise.

'I am. Couldn't sleep... so I came out here.' She has dimples when she smiles. They appear further up her face than you'd expect.

'I told you to bring her back here.'

'I tried... Is that the time? I need to get to the studio.'

'No, you sit,' she says, and pushes me back into the couch. She returns moments later with a tiny cup of espresso and hands it to me. She sits beside me. 'I know clocks don't matter in music projects,' she says, and gazes through the window at the view across Islington. 'But when you're here, they do.'

Sofia's not afraid to speak her mind, but I haven't seen her this insecure since – let's call it a minor blip – she was at Saint Martin's, and I was busy at AIR Studios. We'd literally just met.

'Is this about Ellie?' I ask, after a long pause.

'Of course, not,' she says, too quickly. She's still sweating from her run and bends to wipe her brow with the bottom of her vest top. 'I need to take a shower.'

I follow her into the bathroom and join her for a moment under the water. I brush my teeth on my way into the bedroom and throw on some clothes. On the bed is a Bible.

'What's this?' I ask, as I hear her behind me.

'It's a Bible.'

'I can see that. It's just that you... don't read much.'

'I read all the time.'

'Yeah, JavaScript code... design magazines... It just surprised me, that's all.'

'I'm Catholic, Ian.'

'I know... but not...'

'Not what?'

I turn and she's still naked; vulnerable-looking.

'Nothing, it's cool... let me know how you find it.' I mean it, really, but she looks disappointed. 'I gotta go,' I say, grabbing my bike and opening the front door.

It's cooler this morning, but the wind on my face is still welcome. I weave between black cabs and honking cars, hopping onto the kerb to bypass a fight that's broken out between a white van driver and a Deliveroo guy. They're blocking the whole road.

Ellie will have been ready to start over an hour ago. We're on schedule; one track almost in the bag, just the final vocal to redo and it's there. Two more tracks, then we can start mixing. Sometimes it's helpful to have fresh ears, so I often get other people in to mix, but Ellie was keen for me to take it all on. I'm glad, because it's my favourite part. But first, the next two songs need recording. I'd usually do rhythm tracks, at least drums and bass, for all three songs first, but Ellie was adamant; first song in its entirety before we tackle anything else; and when an artist

I admire is that sure about anything, I go with it. One time, I ran a mic lead right into the lounge, because a singer wanted to record upside down on the couch. Tucked into the vocal booth, he couldn't get the emotion out. And the sonic imperfections were easily fixed: the recording studio's a magical place.

I pull into the business park, and glide across to the studio door. I lean over the handlebars and turn my key in the lock, but it's still bolted from the inside. It's ten o'clock. I feel my pulse quicken.

'Ellie! Can you unbolt the door?'

Nothing.

She must be asleep. I dial her number, but her phone's off. I ride up to Suresh's Grocery, but he hasn't seen her this morning. I race back to the studio and head around the back, jumping on a few Biffa bins and dropping down into the rear yard. I still can't see in. The glazing is frosted, and there are bars on the windows. I had them installed myself. I call again for Ellie to unbolt the door and press my ear to the glass, listening for a toilet flush or anything to calm the fear that's building inside me. Nothing. I tap on the window, listen again. Then I bang several times. Nothing.

I climb back round to the front and hammer on the door once more. The worst scenarios play out in my mind. I turn the key in the lock and lean on the door with my shoulder. There's creaking but it won't budge, although the top corner gives a bit, so I grab my bike pump and jam it in the gap, trying to lever it open. The pump snaps under the strain. There's a garage further down the road; I could grab a crowbar from them. But my body is charged, and I crash my full weight into the door again. Somewhere, the wooden frame is splintering. I throw myself at the door again and the top hinge busts off. A few hard kicks and the door twists inwards. I scramble between the bits and into the lounge.

Ellie's sleeping bag is rolled up on the couch. I notice there are no dirty coffee mugs or plates. My heart's beating out of my chest. She could still be okay. I call out. No answer.

The bathroom's empty, so I push open the heavy studio door. A quick glance around. I check the cupboard at the back and then move over to the sound booth. It's mostly glass, but I pull the door open anyway.

I move back into the lounge and perch on the sofa, head in my hands. It makes no sense. Calling Yannis is the only thing I can think to do. Maybe he's heard from her? I go to my recent calls list, but as I hesitate and glance up one more time, everything comes to a sudden halt. There she is, behind the second couch. Her face is white, eyes open and fixed on the ceiling. Her mouth is closed.

I drop the phone on the sofa. Instantly, I feel the world disconnect, but I manage to move awkwardly over to Ellie's body and check for the pulse I know will not be there. All I can do is sit down beside her.

Perching on a low wall, across the carpark, I survey the scene. There's been a lot of activity. A good deal of time must've passed. I've spoken to police officers and a paramedic and exchanged utterances with people I didn't even glance up at. A tall man strides towards me; he's wearing a suit and stretches out his hand long before he gets here.

'DI Scott Hannan,' he says, and shakes my hand firmly. 'How are you holding up?'

I just nod, pushing slowly up off the wall.

He doesn't say anything but seems to be assessing me. I imagine he's seen even worse scenes than I witnessed.

'Chipped paint on the ceiling,' I say. 'The last thing Ellie saw was a failing of mine. Something else I'd been putting off.'

'None of us are perfect,' Hannan says.

'I wanted her to stay at my flat. I shouldn't have left her on her own.' The guilt is going to cling to me for as long as I allow it to.

'I'm sorry?' I say. Missed what he said, wrapped up in my own mind.

'My apologies. I was asking about her manager. You mentioned to my colleagues that he might have a motive to harm Ellie. Can you tell me about that?' His mouth turns down slightly when resting, and it adds some warmth to his professional manner. He seems trustworthy.

'I don't know. It was just the first thing that came to mind when they started talking about suicide.' I can hear bits of his response, about how the investigation might play out, but I'm struggling to focus, looking down at the tarmac, at my legs that are still rattling. I look up at Hannan. 'We were making plans. She had a direction for the future. Why would she kill herself?'

Chapter Four

Free-wheeling down Camley Street, I pull up outside the Coroner's Court and throw my bike inside an iron gate, taking the steps three at a time. People are already filing out; I'm too late. Breathing heavily, I squat down against a railing in the leafy gardens, swearing under my breath. I wanted to be here for the inquest. It's taken weeks to get to this point. I've given statements, describing everything as accurately as I could, including my personal opinions, which, of course, had not been asked for. But I wanted Ellie to be well represented. They didn't call me as a witness, but I should've been here. It's Sofia's fault, starting another one of her rants and getting hysterical about the whole Ellie thing. I argued back this time, and it got ugly. These past couple of months have been hell.

I loosen my tie and crick my neck. Yannis spots me and storms over. I've been actively avoiding him.

'You win some, you lose some,' he says. 'But I won't forget about you, you twat.'

'Come on, there's more important –'

'More important than fucking up my business? Conspiring behind my back with my talent. We heard all about it in there, everyone looking at me like I was some sort of dickhead.'

'Ellie wasn't cut out for your world, Yannis.'

'Makes sense now, some of the questions the police were asking. You told them I had something to do with it, didn't you?'

'I told them the truth! But don't you feel even a little bit responsible for Ellie? I do.'

'Serious? You should've told me what she'd been saying. I would've known something was wrong. Could've stopped her topping herself.'

My jaw grinds. 'Did you even know Ellie?' Usually I keep a cool head, but now I have to battle the urge to retaliate.

'She's dead, dickhead. You don't seem to have accepted that yet. But I *knew* her, yeah,' he spits, his skin starting to redden around his collar. Strands of his dyed black quiff are sticking to his sweaty brow, and he pushes them up with a flick of his wrist.

'She talked endlessly about her new direction. She cared about the songs we still had to record, more than anything. There's no way she killed herself,' I argue.

'A tonne of barbiturates in her system. And the court just heard all about her history in there. It was suicide. If you'd told me what she was saying, I'd have seen through it.'

'This history from a reliable source, is it? Or did they not really know Ellie either?'

He looks at me like he's ready to kill me. 'Her cousin. I imagine she knew Ellie better than you. Although, apparently, they didn't like each other.'

'A cousin?' Ellie had told me that her father was ill, and her mother had died when she was young. I'd got the impression there was no-one else.

'Her dad's in a nursing home. Must be where all the family money went.'

I hate Yannis for saying that.

'Where's the cousin? Can you point her out?'

'Gone. Straight out the door at the earliest.'

'So... that's it.'

'Ellie was in a locked unit. She was unhappy. And you turned her against me.' He's jabbing a finger in my face.

I know all this, and it doesn't feel right. There must be more to it. The way she spoke about becoming a songwriter, a *good* songwriter; it was a clear path in her mind. After she opened up to me, there was a clear change, like a weight had been lifted from her shoulders. If she was struggling before, this was her way out. She talked about us working together in the future.

'I'd have stopped the sessions if there had been any sign of this happening,' I say. Yannis shrugs. 'But there wasn't,' I add, raising my voice.

'Ten percent of nothing's nothing,' Yannis suddenly says.

'What?'

'Your extra ten percent that you were pushing me for... feel a bit silly now?'

I want to punch him. It would be for Ellie, not me. Her memory deserves more respect than this. I want Yannis to feel how I feel. Like watching a tiny bird flying free, before being caught under the wheels of a car, her life and dreams snuffed out in a moment. But Yannis has hardened his heart. I turn and walk away without another word.

I collect my bike from the gate and, as I'm about to get on, I feel a gentle tap on the back. I turn and have to tilt my head to look up at a tall journalist with a camera around his neck. Long arms convince me he'd have the reach advantage over his colleagues for the best shot. I won't give the vultures anything, but he speaks first.

'You showed good restraint there,' he says, without a smile. He's older than me, sixty maybe, shaved head.

'Know Yannis then?'

'Enough.' He looks at the floor for a moment. When he raises his head, he avoids eye contact. 'I'm Glen Crane. Ellie and I were friends.'

Fifteen minutes later, we are seated at his scruffy kitchen table, with a couple of mugs of strong tea. Beneath the shyness, I can see he is as keen as me to talk about Ellie. He seems the kind of man who puts everything into his work, his photographs; not so much into his home. He must live alone here.

'Thought you were a reporter. I didn't know Ellie had any friends in London,' I say, and worry I've offended him. 'How did you meet?'

Glen smiles weakly, his eyes sad. 'I took some pics at her gig in Hoxton a few months back. Tagged her, and we talked online. I drove her to most of her other gigs, helped with the loading in and stuff.'

'That was cool of you,' I say, draining half my mug of tea.

He slides me a glossy photographic fanzine with his name on. 'Took early retirement and get to as many gigs as I can. I like to help musicians. Well, used to...'

'You don't anymore?'

'I can't,' he says, and looks away.

His pictures are incredible; mostly monochrome, inspired by the grit of punk and the glamour of new wave. His shots of legends sit comfortably alongside some young faces I don't recognise. But they seem famous already.

'So, she didn't mention me?' He shows me an image of Ellie, her outstretched arms perfectly lit by a stage spotlight. He must've anticipated this shot before it happened; it's too good.

'We mostly talked about the music,' I say, and his shoulders slump even further. 'To be honest, she was very private. I never met any of her friends.'

Glen nods. 'Me neither. But it wasn't like she was embarrassed or anything. People thinking she'd brought her dad along. More like she was... I dunno, it's difficult to know why.'

'Was she unhappy?'

'Only in the pictures.' He gestures at the exclusively moody shots across his fanzine pages. 'Serious, not unhappy.'

'So, you wouldn't have expected her to take her own life?'

'No.'

'It's hard to tell, though, isn't it? She had a vulnerable air.'

'Even so.'

'What do you know about Ellie's cousin? Did she speak in court?'

'She did. Emma Tate. She came across as very impatient.'

'Seriously?'

'They didn't get on. Seemed to begrudge all the hassle of the hearing. She was pretty derogatory about Ellie.'

'Wow! Really?'

'She said Ellie gave up her studies at Oxford at the first hurdle.'

'What was that, then?'

'Oh, nothing much... only that her boyfriend was murdered.'

'What?!'

There's a long silence as I try to process the new information. Maybe I'm wrong about Ellie; maybe something like that could drive her to suicide? But I keep coming back to her enthusiasm for her future plans.

On the ride back, I think about Yannis' mention of Ellie's family being well-off. That wasn't the impression I'd got. Yes, she'd had formal musical training, and she spoke well, and was eloquent;

but it didn't scream privilege. She said she'd been to university but hadn't elaborated on it. Didn't seem to want to discuss much except the music. I still can't bring myself to believe she'd leave the project unfinished.

I'm nearly home, but at Highbury I suddenly take a sharp turn. It's late, but I need to go to the studio. Sofia will be asleep, anyway. I want to hear the work again, connect to Ellie, to the vision we were working towards. I've been at the studio most days, after I was allowed back in by the police, but I haven't been able to bring myself to open Ellie's sessions. Now I hope that they'll help me make some sense of the tragedy. I promised to share her work with the world.

Still astride my bike, I fumble for keys. I still haven't taken the old key off the ring. As I wiggle the new one in the lock, I hear something behind me. I check over my shoulder, but there's no-one there. A rustling sound now, further away. Conifers run the length of the car park, behind the low wall, and it could be coming from back there. I prop my bike against the door and creep towards the hedge, narrowing my eyes to focus. Shadows obscure large stretches, and I can't see. But now the noise is closer. Someone is inside the fence. I force myself to take a few more steps forward, straining my eyes, blinking several times and staring hard again. I fix on a point in the trees. That's it. I'm in two minds, shuffling back and forth, bad thoughts rushing to the surface. Everything seems to slow down, and a figure bursts at me from the bushes. A gold tooth, black skin, grey hoodie. A slim kid I don't recognise lunges right past me and breaks into a sprint up towards the gate. He's gained a huge distance in seconds and already I've given up.

'Get out!' I shout, and it's all I can manage.

The kid turns as he reaches the gate and then he's gone.

I hope he's just a trespasser, but I'm not taking any chances. I head home.

The sun streams through the big windows. I massage my eyes with a flat palm and ruffle my hair. 'Sofia?' I call, padding barefoot across the oak floor. She's not here. But there are several new emails on my phone. One full of abuse from Yannis: no surprises there. He says he'll make sure I never work again in the music business. No problem. I wouldn't work with him anyway. But it's what he says next that bothers me. I hadn't thought much about the effect of Ellie's apparent suicide on my future clients. I was still too emotionally involved, I guess. Yannis asks why any self-respecting record label would ever risk sending their young act to a tainted producer, when there are plenty of safer options. He has a point. I wonder whether any of my so-called industry friends have been waiting for the coroner's verdict, and when I scroll through my other emails, I find out. All of my upcoming projects have now been pulled. I get it. There's already a huge risk for anyone investing in music talent these days. Of course, they'll immediately remove any new potential risks. A couple are honest about not wanting to be associated with my studio; others cite new scheduling issues and touring commitments. Bullshit.

I sling the phone down on the counter, next to a piece of notepaper. I grab it with one hand, flick the coffee machine on with the other, and read: *Meet me for a coffee... I want to tell you something.* I turn the machine off.

Why can't she talk to me here? But she's always particular about coffee. She gets it exactly how she likes it down the road. I won't shower; a quick wash will do. I need to talk to her about this new nightmare, anyway.

She's at a small table, tucked away in a corner beneath an ornate lamp and clusters of framed portrait prints. The whole place has an Ottoman style: terracotta walls and dangling trinkets everywhere. She's all in black; a button-down blouse suggests she means business. I hope that's not for my benefit. Her hair is down and wavy, and she looks up from her laptop, greets me with a smile. I want to know why she's being so formal, before I give her the bad news, so we make awkward small talk and I order a Turkish coffee.

'You wanted to tell me something?' I say, when I can wait no longer. She closes her laptop, and leans on it, folding her hands.

'Yes, in a little bit. I was thinking about a bird I saw once... a while ago. I still remember her.'

'A bird?'

'A pigeon. You know, we call them vermin because they're dirty. But I watched one, properly, for at least a half hour from the window. She caught my eye as she came down from out of the tree. She'd found a safe place in the canopy and needed to collect sticks to build her nest.'

'Okay... is it the female who builds the nest, or the male?'

She ignores me.

'But not just any old sticks. She'd take them in her beak and bounce them up and down to test them. Only the right kind would do. The first took her five minutes to find. I watched the whole thing: bobbing around, finding a stick with potential, struggling to grab it in her beak, testing it, rejecting it, and moving on. This was one stick, about ten centimetres long, the first of many she'd need; would it really make that much difference? But it had to be right. Well, she found it eventually, and flew with it back up into the canopy. It took her a while to push back into her spot, the leaves were quite dense; there was a lot of clattering, hovering, flapping, but she did it; she placed the first piece of her home.'

'How long did it take, the nest?'

'I don't know, I only watched for a half hour.'

I sip my coffee.

'You said you watched the whole thing.'

'The whole process... of choosing her first sticks... her method.' Sofia has a frown that causes her brow to bunch up consistently every time, the same peaks and troughs. It always makes me smile, which makes her frown all the harder. But she's clearly taking her nature-viewing seriously, so I tuck in my lips and concentrate. 'How long would it take to build the whole nest?' I say.

'I don't know... a week?'

'How much of it did you see get built... in the half hour?'

'I didn't see the nest at all. I told you – the leaves were dense. I only saw her take four sticks up that she was happy with.'

'That's slow work.'

'The first stick was the hardest for her. After she'd placed it, she came down to the ground to search for the next...'

'Great.' I don't ask how she knew it had been the very first stick. But Sofia's not even frowning this time. She's telling all this to herself now, like I'm no longer needed.

'... the next stick,' she continues. 'But there was a rustle of leaves and her first stick fell to the ground.'

'I get days like that. So, she picked it up and put it back?'

'No... she left it.' Sofia is staring into space. 'After all that work and effort, she just left it and moved on; chose another.'

She picks up her coffee cup in both hands and takes a long, slow sip. She keeps the cup there, by her face, and gazes into my eyes. She looks beautiful today, as always. But her dark brown eyes are pensive.

'So, what was it you wanted to tell me?'

'I bought us tickets. We're going to Rome for a few days, to see my family.'

I exhale sharply, and a strange, grunting noise comes out. 'I can't go to Rome. Not now.'

She smiles, her high dimples breaking out around her full lips. 'We need to get away, Ian. You've been through so much with Ellie; she's pushed us apart.'

'That's not fair. I've been justifying your fits for longer than Ellie's been around. Just leave her name out of it, will you?'

'Wow! So that's how you really feel? You finally said it.'

'I'm sorry, it's been rough. I just need time to straighten things out, okay?'

Sofia tilts her head, mirroring my movement, and takes my hand in hers. Our fingers interlock.

'I need to go,' she says. 'I'm going mad, cooped up alone at the flat. You know how big my family is, how we used to talk and laugh and eat... all the time... look how skinny I've become.'

'Sofia... all my work has been pulled.'

She freezes, her eyes wide. 'What? You're kidding, why?'

'I'm now associated with the suicide of a young woman. Why else?'

The revelation hits her as hard as it hit me. She takes a moment. 'Can they do that? You haven't done anything wrong.'

'It doesn't matter, does it? There's no loyalty. If my studio's a possible risk, they're not going to chance sending their acts to me. Simple as that.'

'Will we be okay?'

I shrug. 'You might need to go back full-time.'

'Seriously? See what happens? You pick these silly little jobs because you don't care about money.'

'I'm not an idiot, Sofia. Yannis had good plans for Ellie, but I couldn't support his agenda. Not when I found out what was going on.'

'We can't live on my salary. What about your other income streams?'

'Everything's tied up in the studio. It's what I do, Sofia. There's no money in the other bits anymore, things have changed. You know that.'

Her palm slaps down on the table and she half turns away, rubbing her face.

I lean forward. 'Look, I really don't think Ellie killed herself. But, even if she did, if I can find out the real reason behind it, maybe I can salvage my reputation, you know?'

'Well, you better, or we'll lose… everything. What will you do? Try to prove it was nothing to do with you, that she was planning it for a long time?'

'If she killed herself, then maybe she was forced into it somehow. There's something going on here. The girl I knew was not ready to die.'

She dabs at her eyes with a napkin, turning her head to each side and making an O with her mouth. She screws up the napkin into a ball and reaches across the small table. Our fingers interlock again, both hands.

'I need to go,' she says again.

I'm the guy who knows how to deal with tricky emotional situations. I speak when it's appropriate, listen in silence when necessary, sometimes just stay silent without listening at all; and I always know which option to take, because it's what I do.

But here I sit, looking into her eyes, and nothing seems good enough. I don't know how to react; it's like my brain has gone to sleep. Something isn't working properly. So, I do nothing. I just stare as she stands, shoves her laptop into her bag, and leaves the café.

Back in the studio, in front of the console, I regain some control. It's taken a good twenty minutes, thinking about how unreasonable Sofia's being, before I feel ready to start. Now I'm hesitating again, unsure if I'm ready to hear Ellie's work.

I pull up the session, and the waveforms fill the large monitor screen; green, pink and yellow visual representations of her sounds. I decide I'll come to her voice later; ease myself back in gently. I'm not sure how strong I am anymore. I listen to the whole track several times, with the vocals muted, then go to work where I always start: the kick drum.

Yannis had come in on day one of the sessions and listened to the drums we'd been working on for hours. 'Great, but it's just drums,' he'd laughed. A friend, who also happens to be a highly successful producer, once told me that a great pop song was mainly about the drums and vocals. Another fail for Yannis.

I listen to the relatively inexpensive mic we used to capture the kick drum, and it's good. I EQ the signal, giving it a boost at 60 hertz and making some low-mid cuts. It starts to sound a little boomy, missing the 'click' that's needed higher up. I add in a drum sample to handle the attack portion of the sound that the original live drum is lacking, and check for any phase issues. The beauty of digital recording is that you can now see everything about the sound on screen. When mixing, the trick is to ignore all that visual information and just listen. Nobody listening to music in their car is ever going to see what the sound looks like; but if it doesn't feel good, they'll soon be reaching for the tuner. I was lucky; I learned my craft in the days of tape machines. I had to rely on my ears; decisions were made on the spot, and we committed to them; no going back and trying different sounds and effects later. You'd printed the idea to tape, and that was the sound you built everything around. Just like Sofia committed to me and my lifestyle; she can't go trying different things now, after all this time: religion, running off to Italy. Maybe that's a cheap shot? I ponder for a few moments, and grab my phone, dial her number. There's no reply.

I spend another couple of hours perfecting the rhythm tracks: drums, percussion, bass and acoustic guitar. We did well in production, and Ellie's performances were excellent. I'd played bass guitar and, of course, handled the samples and programmed elements. Now, all I was doing was controlling how these disparate sounds worked together, creating a soundscape that was new, yet uncontrived. I just hope that doesn't amount to the studio trickery Ellie warned me about. The thought makes me smile. Most of all, I need balance across the instruments, and a place right in the middle for Ellie's voice to tell the story. If this was any other session, I would have put the lead vocal in from the start, referencing it against the slowly growing mix; muting it to zoom in on individual elements; compressing, gating, effecting sounds, always with the vocal idea at the forefront of my mind. After all it's the vocal that everyone, except maybe musicians and producers, listens to first.

Now, much too late, I have the courage to listen to Ellie's wonderful voice again: the quick guide vocal we intended to re-do later. I'm not concerned; it is as perfect and full of emotion as any final take I've ever recorded. But as I scroll to the track, my eyes focus on the waveform and I see it's not right. It's much lower in volume; not something I would've recorded. My palms start to sweat, and I rub them on my shirt. I grab the mouse and hover over the button for a few moments, before clicking in the vocal and starting the song. The intro is typically modern in its brevity, but my mind holds onto it for an eternity. Then Ellie's voice enters. And it's not her original recording. I sit, stunned, with my head in my hands, as the whole track plays. And when it reaches the end, I play it through again. She has recorded over her original track with a brand new vocal: it's the same melody, but gone are the nice-but-definitely-pop verses, and in comes a tear-jerking lament on a feeling I can barely fathom. I'm picking out lines about a mother's death, uncertainty and having 'the force of two'. The pre-chorus is an almost crooning, drawn-out 'underneath Philippa's tree'.

This is not pop, not even alternative pop. But it must be what Ellie wanted to share with the world. She had some home recording experience; I'd heard some of her tracks online. And she watched me closely. I love it when artists do that; it shows me how likely they are to have success. She knew what she was doing. What it boils down to is that Ellie intended to wipe the original vocal. This wasn't an experiment; she wanted this new song to be heard. I'd left the microphone set up in the booth, so her sound is good. Luckily, in the digital realm, I can deal with her signal, which is slightly lower in volume than I would've liked. But that's just detail. What I have here is a wonderful, soulful singing voice. I start switching in the plugins I need to complete Ellie's track, that I'm now calling *Under the Tree*. It's late afternoon, but if it takes all night, so be it.

I keep my promises.

Chapter Five

Aylesbury • October 2018

I'm shaken out of a deep sleep by the vibrating of my mobile phone. I find myself on a couch in the studio, raising a hand to block the morning sun that's adding to my disorientation. I wriggle to release the insistent phone from my jeans pocket.

'Ian, it's Glen Crane.' After a pause, he helps me with, 'The photographer.'

'Of course, sorry, I just woke up.' He tells me it's mid-morning. Then his tone changes. I noticed that yesterday. His mouth barely opens when he speaks, and his voice is monotone. But when he wants you to hear something important, his pitch rises slightly. The mouth stays thinly open.

'I did some digging on what I heard at the hearing.'

Suddenly, I'm fully awake and bolt upright.

'I know which nursing home Ellie's dad's in.'

'Let's go see him,' I say, already heading for the bathroom.

Aylesbury is only fifty minutes from Marylebone, but I've never been here before. I'm aware of the town's music history, though. It hosted some big gigs in the 60s and 70s. Bowie debuted *Ziggy Stardust and The Spiders from Mars* at the Friars Club in 1972, and the town's cobbled market square may or may not have inspired the opening lines of his song *Five Years*. Glen and I leave the station and head towards the nursing home. According to Google Maps, it should be just a ten-minute walk.

My phone buzzes and it's a text from Sofia; she's flying to Rome today. It's a sweet message and ends with a kiss. I won't miss the grief she's been giving me, and it'll do her good to see her family and unwind. I ponder her crazy pigeon story again; I'm sure it was a dig at me. I hadn't had the heart to point out it was the male who rejected the stick. The female would've been up in the tree, waiting for her man. I reply with a nice message.

Glen has stopped to take pictures of a tall building from interesting angles. It's funny watching some of the stances he works his wiry frame into. He tells me the ugly, grey building that rises above the town is actually fascinating brutalist architecture, and that, apparently, Stanley Kubrick shot some scenes around here for *A Clockwork Orange*, though he's not sure it isn't just rumour. Glen's been here several times and remembers Friars well. I get the impression he's been most places with a camera round his neck.

We continue along a main thoroughfare. I turn to Glen. 'Appreciate you bringing me along. What's the pull for you?'

He exhales a long breath. Looks at me and away again.

'I'd like to say I'd do the same for anyone,' I say, when the silence becomes awkward. 'But that's not true. I don't feel like I have a choice.'

I can tell I won't get the full story yet, but he's as keen as me to dig into all this.

'I drove her to a gig a bit further afield once: Croydon. She was tired of the trendy venues, she said, wanted to play for normal folk.'

'What's normal?'

'She wanted to play to people who wanted to listen, not

people who were checking out her style, I guess.' He gazes into the distance, like he's remembering the night. 'Trouble was, only one guy at the front was listening. Ellie was there with an electric guitar and tiny amp, and the whole place was talking over her. Football songs, arguments, all of it. This guy at the front finally lost it. He grabbed Ellie's microphone and berated the whole pub.'

'Smart.'

'It turned into a bit of a bundle, pint glasses everywhere, and scantily clad women pulling their fellas out of it. I got loads of good pictures that night.'

'Is this it? The nursing home?'

We're approaching a modern three-storey complex that could just as easily be an office building. The smart reception area opens onto clean corridors and several lifts. The smell is slightly clinical, but nicer than I'd prepared for. My grandad spent his final years in a home, and the stink still sticks in my nasal passages. But this place is a class above. Ellie's family must be well off, as Yannis said. This is the sort of place I want to go to, if the time comes. We sign the book, under Emma Tate's name.

I raise my eyebrows. 'Smile and she might be nice to us.'

'There she is now,' Glen says.

Emma Tate is walking with a member of staff. She's giving the poor girl a dressing down by the sound of it. Emma looks in her early thirties. Her figure isn't as good as her posture.

She glances at Glen as she finishes with the girl, and I seize my opportunity.

'Emma, hi. You probably recognise my friend from Ellie's hearing?'

'What are you doing here?' She carries on walking, and we fall in step with her.

'My name's Ian. This is Glen. We were good friends of Ellie's.' We follow her up some stairs like we're being marched to a job interview. She has long, dark hair, scraped up and held with a clip at the back. Her skin is fair, like Ellie's, but she's disguising it with fake tan.

Suddenly, she turns, and raises her voice. 'Look, I don't know you. I'll call security –'

'Please, just a few minutes,' I say, intentionally keeping on the lower stair. 'We were hoping to talk to Ellie's father, but maybe you can help us?'

'With what exactly?'

'I was the producer working with Ellie, I'd like to hear a bit more about her... make some sense of what happened.'

'I thought you must be *that* Ian. You know what happened.'

I shrug my shoulders.

'Well, there's no way you're seeing David, so come with me. You've got two minutes.'

She leads us to a kitchen area and a table by the window overlooking a manicured lawn. It's left for Glen to put the kettle on.

'Thanks for this,' I begin. 'Ellie was our friend.'

'She never liked me,' Emma says quickly. 'Resented my success I suppose. Proper job, a career.'

'She got into Oxford, though,' I say.

'To study music,' Emma says, like that discounts everything. 'She couldn't even finish that.'

She's looking straight past me. She speaks in short bullet points, like she's trying not to waste too much time on me.

'There was a reason for that, though, wasn't there?' Glen asks, as he puts down two black coffees and a water for Emma.

'Well, I suppose so. She got close to a boy, and he was killed.

Danny, he was called. From a family of low-lifes. '

'Poor kid. Her boyfriend?' I say.

'So they tell me. I expect they came together after everyone else at a party hooked up and they were the only two left.'

Glen and I glance across at each other.

'Please tell me Ellie didn't find his body,' I say.

'No, he was found outside in the early morning. Ellie was asleep at St Peter's.'

'And his killer was never caught?'

'No. Look, I think I've said enough now.'

Glen says, 'This was three years ago, wasn't it? Ellie was nineteen?'

'Yes,' Emma says. She didn't go back after Christmas – said it was all too much.'

'Her father... how was he at that time?'

'Your two minutes are up.'

She makes for the door, as a Filipino guy in a white uniform appears. He has tattoos up both arms and smiles warmly at us.

'Do I recognise you?' he says.

'Probably not,' I say, 'unless you're a hardcore music fan. My name's purely for the small print. Ian Wren.' I shake his hand.

'You did some articles for *Sound on Sound* magazine last year,' he says. 'Hardware sequencing.' He beams at me.

'You're a musician?'

'Bedroom producer,' he laughs. 'It's a hobby. Wow, pleasure to meet you, Ian.'

Emma glares at him. 'Quite finished?'

'Sorry,' he says. 'David's ready for you in the library now.'

'Hold on,' I say. 'Could I just play David something Ellie recorded?'

'Goodbye,' she says, and marches off down the hall.

I catch the guy's eye, and he shrugs. 'Wait downstairs,' he whispers, and jogs after Emma.

Outside, Glen kicks at some loose gravel on the tarmac. 'What a bitch.'

'Let's wait for the carer. He might give us a chance,' I say.

Glen shoves his hands into his pockets, looking as frustrated as I feel. 'Want anything from the garage? I'm gonna grab a chocolate bar or something.'

I shake my head.

I take a wander around the basic, but neat garden. After a few minutes, I turn back towards the front door and see Emma Tate leaving in her car. The carer is waiting for me in reception.

'I can't believe she wouldn't let you play Ellie's music to David. Oh my God!'

I laugh. 'Some people, eh?'

'Come with me,' he says, and heads towards the stairs.

'I don't want you getting into any trouble.'

He turns to face me. 'Look, music is great for dementia patients. That's enough justification for me. Besides, everyone knows what Emma is like.'

'Did you know Ellie?'

'A little. She was lovely. David came here when she went to Oxford. She'd been looking after him at home before that, with help from carers.'

I follow him down the corridor, and he taps a security code into several door-locks before we reach the library. It's more of a sunroom, glazed roof and nice furniture, walls lined with dark bookcases. A lot of the books are Bibles. Doors open onto a veranda, which is where I see Ellie's father for the first time.

David Beck is sitting in a wheelchair, a soft fabric strap

helping to keep him upright. It's difficult to judge his age, but maybe late sixties. He's smiling broadly. His face has that Parkinson's mask that seems to stare at you. I approach and shake his hand, introducing myself. He has a strong grip and it's difficult releasing my hand. He just stares up at me, smiling away.

'Sorry,' says the carer. 'The Parkinson's just freezes him up.' He giggles and places David's hand back onto the arm of the wheelchair, where it grips on tight again. He still has most of his hair, which is grey and parted to the side. He's dressed in a smart white shirt, with a small ketchup stain down the front.

'Hello, David,' I say, gently, pulling up a chair beside him. 'I'm so sorry about Ellie, she was a very good friend. And an incredible musician.'

He carries on smiling but does not speak. It's a wide, uninhibited smile, maybe unlocked by the Parkinson's dementia, removing all the inhibitions that worldly things can stack up on your character.

'I worked with Ellie on her music. She wanted to be a professional songwriter.' David's face scrunches up; a cross between confusion and sadness, but then his smile returns. I wonder if his condition is a blessing, protecting him from the distress losing a child can bring. Maybe it's true that his condition was a contributing factor to Ellie's depression and eventual death. I ask David some questions, but he can only shake or nod his head, and the delay makes me wonder how much of them he even understands. It's too much to expect anything useful.

'Can I play you one of Ellie's songs?' I say.

I have to repeat myself, but then he nods slowly, scratching at an itch on his forearm.

There's a portable stereo in the corner and I plug it in, loading the CD. I have it on MP3 as well, just in case. David seems distant at first, but as Ellie's voice comes in, he appears to be listening. His brow furrows, as he strains to focus on his daughter's singing voice. He's tapping his foot to the beat; I've read that music's helpful for Parkinson's and I intend to leave the CD with him. By the second verse, he's tapping his chest.

'My poem,' he slowly drawls.

'I thought so,' I say, turning and smiling at the carer behind me. When I lived with the new lyrics for a while, I felt they might be from a single father's perspective. The song ends and I press play again, listening to his story.

The shifting lines that ride around and show and hide
Pull into the deep and open up to light and leaf
Underneath Philippa's tree...
In the knots already tight so very few years into your life
That changed the day your mother died
Underneath Philippa's tree.

That's the bridge that brings it together – the heart of the sentiment.

There's only me to set the rules, to lay it down, the force of two,
to know exactly what to feel, I never did, I never will.

David has written this poem, about them, and about a tree that belongs to his dead wife? Where he broke the news to his daughter? When the song finishes, I try to formulate a gentle way to ask David about it. But it'd be too much for him. His eyes are closed, and he's emotionally spent.

'Philippa was his wife,' the carer says. His eyes are moist.

'I thought so.'

'She had stomach cancer. David used to visit her every day in the John Radcliffe, while Ellie was at school. Ellie told us about it when she first brought him in.'

'How old was Ellie when she died?'

'Seven or eight, I think. We asked her to bring a memories book in, you know, like photos or letters we could use to help David. But she didn't get the chance, and after she came back from Oxford, we only saw her over Skype.'

'Really? She didn't visit?'

'She had real problems after everything that happened. One of her friends asked us to set up some Skype calls, so she didn't have to leave the house.' The carer suddenly notices David looking at him. 'I'm sorry, we shouldn't really talk about this now.'

I smile and nod. 'Thank you for everything.' I say goodbye to David and wish him well. He has the stereo and CD on his lap as the carer wheels him towards his room.

Chapter Six

Aylesbury • October 2018

'You could've waited.' Glen is annoyed I went in to see David without him. I follow him up through a cobbled churchyard into Aylesbury old town. Georgian buildings, which look to have been converted into flats, sit opposite a museum on the narrow street. Take away the cars and road markings and you'd be right back there in the seventeen-hundreds. Glen swings his rucksack off his back and grabs something inside, deftly fixing a new lens to his camera and rattling off a few shots of the ornate windows. Some guy's grumbling at us as he passes, shielding his face with an arm. Glen doesn't seem to notice.

I'm searching the Oxford Mail website on my phone as we walk, and soon find an article with the headline: *Murder Probe After HIV Victim's Body Discovered.* It reports initial details of a young man's body being found in Christ Church Meadow and an appeal for witnesses. Somehow the reporter had discovered that the victim, Danny de Vries, was HIV positive, which surprises me. I'd have thought the police would have wanted a detail like that kept out of the press in the early stages. There are a couple of links to later articles on the murder investigation, which reveal little, apart from further calls for witnesses and a mention of the body being discovered by a rough sleeper.

We go into an old coaching inn-turned-pub, order two pints

and settle into a sofa. I ask Glen about Christ Church Meadow, not at all surprised to hear he's been there with his camera.

'It's next to the college,' he says. 'A bit of greenery between the Cherwell and the Isis. There's a footpath around it, full of tourists, office workers, mums with pushchairs. Quite picturesque, but I wanted pictures of the trashings.'

My eyebrows raise.

'The end of Finals,' he continues. 'Students spray each other with shaving foam and silly string and slap each other about a bit. All friendly. I got some nice colourful shots. And the vomit-art on the paths.'

'Danny was HIV positive,' I say.

'We knew that… Emma said.'

'I don't think so.'

'Maybe it was said at the hearing then, sorry.'

He ducks as I aim a smack to the back of his shaved head. For a moment, I wonder if he understood the playfulness. But I'm glad to have him with me, sharing the load a little. He seems to care for Ellie as much as I do and probably shares the same guilt at not having picked up on the signs.

Glen pays the taxi driver and joins me on the pavement. There's a large, detached house before us, protected by gates at the front, walls and firs to the sides. It was a quick four miles from the town to the village of Weston Turville. We edge down the side of the property, using a narrow public footpath that flanks the long high-walled garden. Not much can be seen, but it's worth a try. The path reaches a stile into a field, and we step over into undergrowth, tracking around the rear wall of the house.

'Give us a hand,' I say, and Glen bends down, interlocking his fingers.

A quick burst upwards and I'm resting my arms on the top of the wall, peering into a wild garden. The grass is too long, the beds choked with weeds. The firs are straggly, in need of a trim. I can't see what I'm looking for. And I don't know what it is.

There's a dog growling somewhere behind me, getting nearer. Low snarling, followed by loud, threatening barks. Glen shouts, and I look down through my arched arm. We're penned in by a huge German Shepherd. The owner has its lead short, but possibly not short enough.

'Come down, or I'll set the dog on your friend here,' he shouts.

Glen drops his hands and I shield my face from the brickwork as I come down.

The man is older than Glen, bald and stocky. He reaches into his Barbour wax jacket and produces a treat for his dog.

'This is private property,' he says, keeping the dog between him and us.

'I can explain,' I say, and he stamps his Wellingtons on the ground. He's not used to the tone he's using, I decide, and he seems relieved when I respond politely. 'This house used to belong to a friend. I just wanted a quick look round. Sorry if I startled you.'

'Your friend's name?' he asks, keeping up the front. His broad Bucks accent doesn't lend itself to intimidation.

'Ellie Beck, and my name's Ian,' I say, offering to shake his hand. He ignores the gesture.

A voice calls out from the garden, behind the wall; younger, female. 'Tell me something about Ellie.'

I think for a moment, then call back, 'I'll tell you something about yourself.'

'Okay...'

'You weren't allowed to meet her other friends.'

'Bring them round, Dad, it's alright,' she says.

The man brings us to a side-gate. The padlock jumps into his palm at the turn of a key, and he leads us to a brick patio.

He says, 'I bought the house from Ellie's father. There's still plenty of work to be done, as you can see.' He gestures to the unkempt grounds before us, and a green-windowed orangery to the side of the patio.

His daughter appears, throwing her father a look. 'They had more pressing things to deal with.' She drops into a seat and offers us the oak bench, which looks like a newer addition to the garden furniture.

'Did Ellie tell you that?' she says. 'That I was kept away from her London lot.'

'She didn't really have a London lot, as far as I can tell,' I say. 'I think she probably met her friends individually.'

'We were friends since infant school,' she says. 'Looked out for each other. She was grieving and I... well, I wasn't the most popular girl.'

Gaynor is on the large side, but her blonde hair is well-cut and modern. Her dress is slightly mumsy and detracts from her efforts in the hair department.

'You seem like you'd have made a good friend,' I say.

She looks at the ground.

I tell my story, but Gaynor has already heard about my work with Ellie. She tells me she works for Thames Valley Police, which surprises me, but then it turns out she's behind a desk. She makes it sound important, glossing over the detail, but I gather she's part of the civilian support staff. They use civilians a lot these days; it's cheaper than using trained officers. Gaynor tells us she shared the Becks' house with Ellie, when she returned from Oxford after Danny's death.

'I just assumed when she went to London that I wasn't good enough to visit. I don't know why... insecurity, I guess. But we never mixed with other school kids, so not overly surprising she kept herself to herself.'

'She didn't have a permanent place to stay in London anyway. She was kipping on my studio couch for a while. You didn't miss out on anything.'

She smiles, wipes a tear away. 'Her music helped, after Danny died. She spent all her time at her laptop, recording ideas. Never sang around the house though.'

'I heard the stuff she put online; really great,' I say.

'The music she kept for herself was better. Those songs were important to her.'

I wonder if *Under the Tree* was one of those songs.

Glen says, 'Did she have any other devices she might've left here?'

'The police took them.'

'Do you know a song mentioning "Philippa's Tree"?' I ask.

She shakes her head. 'No, why?'

'I was looking over your wall earlier to see if I could answer that. I think there's a tree that meant something to her. The song talks about gnarls and knots and majesty. Do you have a cherry tree, something like that, here?'

Gaynor's scanning the garden, as her father appears with a tray of hot teas.

'Definitely not, just birches and firs. Not even an apple tree.'

This is a man that clearly knows the outdoors, so I don't pursue it.

'I still can't believe what she did,' Gaynor says. 'I kept her room exactly how she had it, in case she ever came back. I still can't bear to mess with it, even though... well, even now.'

'It was a surprise to you as well, then?' Glen says.

She nods. 'I was shocked. But when you line everything up, it... I don't know... maybe it was inevitable?'

'Could I see her room?' I ask.

Gaynor glances at her father, and then at Glen.

'I can stay out here,' Glen says. He winks at her.

We climb the stairs, a proper staircase with a decorative banister. The decor of the house is classic, all oak and oil paintings of English landscapes. The landing has a balcony off it, overlooking the garden. To the right is Ellie's room.

I push the door open and at once the vibe changes. From the formal elegance of the house to a child's bedroom; at least that's my first impression, but as I take it in it becomes less obviously childlike. Yes, the dresser and wardrobe seem like a younger girl's; there are fairy-like carvings in the feet; and there are some nice, framed drawings around the room. But the walls and carpet are neutral shades of magnolia and blue, a young woman's touches. Ellie kept things simple. I believe this is close to how she'd have had the room, apart from the now missing laptop and recording peripherals. I check my surmises with Gaynor.

'Yes, this is pretty much how it's been for a long time. Before college, she was busy with her dad's care. When she dropped out... sorry, after Danny, I should say... she only really had her music. There wasn't much else.'

'Her guitar and microphone came with her. They're still at my studio,' I say, remembering the laugh we both had comparing Ellie's rattly guitar to the Telecaster I loaned her.

Gaynor gestures with her hand as she turns around. 'I think the bed's the original.'

I turn and see a low, single bed, more suitable for a child than a young woman. A double duvet has been folded to fit.

'The framed drawings are nice,' I say. They're mostly black ink sketches of fairy-tale landscapes with a cast of characters I recognise from Enid Blyton's children's books.

'Ellie's mum drew them.'

'Philippa was an artist?'

'An accountant. But drawing was her hobby.'

I scan the rest of the room. It's nice to see how Ellie lived, but there's nothing more to learn here, so we head back downstairs. As we make to leave, I try one last time.

'Are you certain Ellie never mentioned a song talking about Philippa's tree or a poem?'

'I'm sure,' says Gaynor, looking concerned.

It seemed to have meant a lot to Ellie. But she didn't mention such a special poem to her best friend? Maybe it really was a secret father-and-daughter thing.

Chapter Seven

Ellie's Diary • November 2015

Is it too soon to be in love? Danny is <u>the</u> perfect guy. Even though I didn't trust him at first, I always felt so comfortable with him, so, deep down, I knew he was right for me. Maybe I've just got used to bad things happening? Mum dying, caring for poor Dad. Hate myself for agreeing to put him in the home, but I know it was the right thing for him. He looked after me. God, sometimes he went over the top, wrapping me up in cotton bloody wool. People usually look back at their childhood and long for that carefree innocence again. I hear that a lot, but I never felt it. Too much stress too early. It's not surprising I'm not the most sociable of people. I've struggled with sociability ever since. The immediate responsibility for Dad has lifted, but my character's set now: Ellie, the chronic introvert. The only version of myself I've ever known.

Deborah Harvey pulled me aside today. I was obviously looking like crap. I told her I was nervous about the compulsory papers and worried I wouldn't pass the preliminary exam. I said I owed it to my dad to do well here. I even shed a tear, but it was all a lie – except the bit about owing Dad. Truth is, I feel a bit stifled by the topics already, and can't wait for the options next year. But who wants to admit they're a social outcast who can't enjoy a good drinking game now and again?

Freshers' Week – what a nightmare that was. Reliably informed it was an essential part of surviving the first year. A chance to mingle and meet people. Planned events and parties. Right! I tried, and St Peter's is supposed to be one of the friendliest colleges, and I guess there were plenty of smiles and waves. But it was just duty really, a quick drink in the bar, sitting on the periphery of the largest group I could find. I didn't feel comfortable. Until I met Danny.

Danny's a natural musician. He performed his first piano recital at the age of six. I can't believe how easy-going he is, with the HIV and everything. He's diligent about taking his meds. Even runs every day down Cornmarket and around Christ Church Meadow. Apparently, HIV can be controlled nowadays, and the virus stopped from replicating in the body. He's doing everything he can, doesn't touch alcohol or drugs, not even cigarettes. I guess we make a good team, with his broken body and my broken personality, lol. He's soooo fit though! And when he looks at me from under that thick black fringe, OMG!

He told me straight up about his brothers. Didn't want me hearing about it from anywhere else. He's nothing like them, though. He's always honest. I've never felt so trusted before. It was easy to tell him about my own life, and how hard it's been adjusting to Oxford. He just listened, and I couldn't even believe I was still talking. I told him how much he had helped me, and when I finally shut up, he kissed me. I didn't want it to end.

Chapter Eight

Ian • London • October 2018

Green hills rise and fall behind the train window. Footsteps come to a stop beside me. An older gentleman is looking directly at Glen, who's nearly asleep, his long legs across the seats opposite.

'Would you put your feet down?' says the man, smart in his suit.

Glen gestures with his arms at the virtually empty carriage.

'I don't need a seat. I want you to put your feet down.'

Glen stays where he is. 'Why?'

'Because you're not allowed to put your feet on the seats,' says the man, his pitch rising.

'I've taken my shoes off.' Glen closes his eyes and slouches further into his seat. The man huffs and strides down the carriage.

It's been a long day. After leaving Gaynor and her father, we stopped at a pub for something to eat, and tried to think of anything else that might be important. We drew a blank, and I wonder if Glen's frustration triggered his response just now.

He shakes his head. 'My father was like that guy. Give them an inch and they'll smother you with even more pointless rules.'

'Punk was too early for me,' I say.

Glen smiles. 'I couldn't bloody wait to leave home. As soon as I snagged a couple of part-time jobs, I was out of there.'

'I quite liked living at home,' I say. 'Sad, eh?'

Glen sits up. 'Mummy's boy, was ya?'

'She was cool, actually.'

'Maybe you should've stayed then,' Glen chuckles.

'I got out early. Left at sixteen.'

'Why, if you liked it so much?'

'This lad had it in for me... ecstasy dealer. Everyone said he was linked to the Essex Boys. He got me mixed up with someone who'd tried it on with his girlfriend. I think he realised he'd got it wrong but couldn't lose face, so he and his mates gave me a good going over.'

'Good for the ego, that.'

'I didn't trust that it was finished. They'd done worse to other kids round our way. I wanted to keep my mum and dad out of it. So, I moved into an older mate's flat.'

'Well, it made you the man you are today.'

'Maybe.'

Glen lounges back into his seat and closes his eyes – obviously had enough – so I don't have to admit how often I found myself back home for tea and a chat. I used to pretend it was for my parents' benefit, because they hated me moving out so young. But I just enjoyed seeing them. What happened later made a huge impact.

The view from the train window has switched from countryside to concrete. We're approaching Marylebone. The setting sun illuminates the base of a cloud and forms one of those long intergalactic vessels in my imagination. Revisiting my teenage years has got me thinking. I reckon getting beaten up that night heightened my empathy for any kind of vulnerability. Although I'm kind of at ease with crime in London – you almost expect it – I wonder where our moral code comes from if we're a product of chance and randomness. Surely, if the fittest survive, we should all follow the impulse to do the crime? We pass a stationary train on the other track, and it takes me a moment to realise it's my train that's not moving; the other train is rattling out of Marylebone. It makes me think about points of reference, having something unmoving as a benchmark for good. I shake Glen awake and we step out onto the platform. Maybe there is a solid moral law – but not everybody listens to it.

I take a slow walk home. I need the air. I was born on a snowy Essex day, and I reckon that's why I prefer the colder weather and spend all my time holed-up in an air-conditioned studio. At the top of my building's staircase, I stop. There's a thin iron gate that protects each flat's front door, and mine is ajar. It's always locked unless we're in. I push it further open – the hinges whine like an inquisitive puppy – and slip through. Lights are on. I turn my key in the lock and open the door just a crack. I don't hear anything. I wait another minute, summoning the courage to stick my head around the door. I wish Glen was still with me.

Finally, I look, and Sofia is sitting on the settee.

'Sofia… you didn't go to Italy?' I move towards her carefully, pushing her long dark hair behind her ears. Her makeup is a mess, and her face is scrunched up.

She breathes heavily and splutters, 'I'm sorry.'

'What's going on?'

She can't reply, letting out short gasps between tearful grunts. I sit beside her and put my arm around her. She's shaking.

'It's okay,' I say.

'No… no it's not.'

'Come on… what is it?'

She pulls away. 'Why couldn't you just come to Rome?'

'I told you why. You said you were going anyway – what's happened?'

'We could've put all this behind us, but you ruined it. Ellie killed herself, let it be.'

'How can you be so sure?'

Her emotion breaks through again. 'She left a note.'

'What?'

She buries her face, bending her upper body down into a protective cocoon.

'I took it from your bag.'

I am momentarily vacant. 'After she died?'

'The night you came home. The... last time you saw her.' She breaks down, pulling at her hair and I battle to stop her.

'Hey, it's okay.' My mind is racing, but I need to protect her.

'I was scared you and she...' she sobs. 'At first, I couldn't bring myself to open it, in case I read something awful. And then she died, and... well, she said in the letter she was going to kill herself. But by then it was too late. I didn't know what to do. But I can't take it anymore.'

My head is in my hands. I should tell the police. But what would happen to Sofia? Would this be classed as withholding evidence? It was my fault. If I'd spent more time with her, she wouldn't have had such ridiculous ideas about me and Ellie. I can't risk getting her arrested for a note that only confirms what everybody already thinks.

I lie down on the floor and stay there, the blood in my head pounding. 'Why tell me now, after all this time?'

'I didn't know she was going to destroy our livelihood by killing herself, did I? I wanted us to get over it, quickly. Go to Rome for a break and start over.'

'Where is the letter now?'

'It's gone.'

'God's sake, Sofia! What did it say... exactly?'

She looks away. 'I can't remember. I didn't really understand. She mentioned pills.'

'Think! It's important.'

'I... was only interested in making sure there was nothing between you two. I was devastated when she killed herself, but I just wanted to get rid of the letter. I knew I shouldn't have taken it. I didn't want to get into trouble.'

'She didn't say why she did it?'

'I'm not sure. I was just relieved you and she were not –'

'Oh, come on!'

'It wouldn't be the first time, would it?'

'That's not fair.'

'No?'

'Sofia, I said I was stupid, I said it would never happen again. It's different now, everything we have. We'd only just met, for God's sake, it was different. It's been years.'

'I'm sorry.'

'Okay, okay. But please think, Sofia. If anything comes back to you, I need to know why Ellie did it. It might help salvage the business.'

As much as I need to restore my reputation, there was – is – an emotional side to my relationship with Ellie. I can't risk Sofia continuing her stupid, childish worries about an affair, so I keep it to myself. But I know I won't be able to move on until I know the truth about Ellie. She had a hard life: the death of her mother, the responsibility of caring for her father, the murder of her boyfriend. How could she come back from that? I need to admit she killed herself. But was she pushed? I force the image of Ellie's empty shell away, running my hands over my face.

I can't decide if I should tell Glen about the note.

In the bedroom, Sofia is on her knees, her hands folded in prayer. Her eyes are closed, lips whispering something too low to hear. This is a side of her I haven't seen before, and I watch silently from the doorway. This isn't new to her, a prayer life, I can tell. I wonder if she came back to it recently, or if she just kept it private. All these years together, and I'm questioning how well I know her. I have to assume she's telling me the truth now.

I can't stop the will to help Ellie. I wasn't always like this, so dogged and driven. I used to stay on the sidelines. Everything changed when my parents died. A car crash took them both. I was at AIR studios at the time and grief hit me hard. Someone suggested I read Viktor Frankl, and I devoured his account of surviving the Nazi concentration camps. I liked Frankl's thinking. He knew the only way to keep inner strength in that terrible situation was to imagine a future goal. Limping back from a worksite in bitter cold, with sores over his feet, Frankl pictured himself in a warm lecture hall, sharing his experiences with attentive psychology students. It was a simple device, and I started to wonder if I could do the same. I settled on work as the answer. I imagined my own studio where I could devote all my energy to one artist at a time; pictured myself, like Viktor Frankl, using my potentially devastating situation to bring about something good for the next generation. It helped me start to recover, and I felt like someone had finally wound up the clockwork key in my back. Everything fell into place, and looking out for the next artist to help became an obsession. I can't turn my back on Ellie now.

I take a seat at the dining table by the window, and flip

open my laptop. Ellie had all the usual social media accounts; I checked them all after Yannis asked me to work on her demos. I tried to find a personal profile, where her real friends were, not the followers and fans who lurked around her artist accounts. I know now why I didn't find anything. I'm always as interested in the character of the artist as in their media persona. But all I had to go on for Ellie was the guarded – or what I took for intriguing – character on her social pages. She had a good number of followers, on the strength of the home recordings and videos she posted. I doubt many of these people actually went to her gigs. The ones that did and posted about them afterwards were an odd tribe; a mixture of photographers and commentators, all on the fringes of society. I scan the posts and these people don't interact with each other at all; they just comment, sometimes bafflingly on Ellie's posts. Like many successful artists, Ellie didn't get into threads with these people, just threw them a tune or a few words, or a moody selfie to whip up a frenzy. What I find interesting is that she didn't actively publicise her gigs. Yet those in the know came, like she'd played a magic flute or something. I bet they didn't stand together either. I click open some gig footage and confirm my prediction; I pick out some of the more recognisable characters: some fat, some thin, some with a pint, some without; but all standing alone. Ellie was their night out. Something about her spoke to these people.

Through the large window, Islington is still going strong into the night. So much going on. Is this what it was like for Ellie's fans, always looking on? I scroll through deep pages, looking for Gaynor, a proper friend. She sent some early supportive messages; no replies from Ellie. Her posts peter out. Ellie treated her old friend the same as everybody else; and she kept them all apart. *Under the Tree* keeps slipping back into my mind. Did

Ellie complete the project after all? Were the other two songs of her EP ever going to be finished? I close the laptop and without the light, I can see more of the city. It can take your life, or it can watch dispassionately as you take your own.

Chapter Nine

London • October 2018

I'm sprawled on the sofa, a guitar resting across my body. It's an old Martin acoustic; the strings haven't been changed for years and I like the almost rusty feel of them. I can't remember where it came from. Someone probably left it at a rehearsal one day, in the same way that I lost countless instruments and pieces of recording gear back then. I've always liked music technology and gadgets, but – I don't know – when we were younger, those things weren't so important. I only became so damn controlling when I started out on my own, I guess. Over the top of the guitar, I can see Sofia reading by the window.

I didn't sleep well last night; couldn't stop thinking about what Sofia had done, and the kick in the head that was accepting Ellie's death as suicide, and premeditated, at that. Sofia's been quiet all morning, sat through lunch without looking up, and approached me warily to take my plate. She doesn't believe I can forgive her. Was I so tired that I didn't hold my anger in? No, I acted properly: I looked after her, consoled her; forgave her.

She's resting her cheek on her fist, concentrating on her book. When I sit like this with a guitar, it's always playing around: little riffs that must sound awful to anyone listening. It helps me think. It's not fair on Sofia to have to listen to that stuff, so I play something 'proper': some jazzy chords from an old Al Green song. I play them lightly, but she looks up with a smile reaching across her face. It's the song we danced to when we first met.

'It's Saturday. We should go out tonight,' I say. 'Like we used to.'

'That would be nice,' she says, breaking eye contact like she's feeling undeserving.

I want to tell her how *I'm* feeling, but the phone's ringing. I want to get to know her again, aware that I've missed things about her lately, but the phone won't stop. Eventually I pick up.

I didn't recognise the number, but the professional voice is familiar, and I can almost see the downturned mouth as Detective Inspector Hannan says, 'Are you okay to talk?'

'Yes, sure, yes,' I answer, clumsily. Guilt, probably.

'A drug dealer called Robert Warrister... I believe you know him?'

Hannan has my attention. 'Yes.'

'He was arrested and released today. But he made some verbal threats towards you.'

He leaves a moment of silence for me to take it in. I wish he hadn't – I prefer to bury uncomfortable thoughts. Then he continues. 'In interview, I brought up Ellie's name – we never found out who supplied the drugs that killed her. Warrister suspected it was you who tipped us off.'

'We had a business disagreement,' I say, after a moment. 'He ripped me off, actually.'

'Well, I told him his arrest was unrelated, but I wanted to make you aware. If you see or hear anything from him, please call me straight away.'

Hannan gives me his number, but I have it in my phone still. Despite his warm facial expressions, he won't miss anything; I need to be careful what I say. I wonder about the kid who was hanging around in the bushes outside the studio. I don't mention it to Hannan. It probably doesn't mean anything and, frankly, I want to forget about it.

'Do I need to worry?'

'I think it was just bluster and bravado. But I thought you should know. Call me if you see anything.'

'Thanks, appreciate it.'

As he hangs up, it occurs to me that Warrister probably has bail conditions. Hannan would love me to call it in, so he can pick him up again. If I was the type to hold a grudge, I might just do that.

Sofia sits opposite me at the restaurant table. My mind is on when I should release Ellie's music. I forcibly shift my thinking back to Sofia; this evening out is about trying to rekindle our relationship. She's called the waiter over. It's a nice place, in Highbury; modern, but with a trattoria feel about it. The decor is simple and rustic, but the white table linen is immaculate. Another bottle of wine is just what we need to finish off the meal.

'Nearly as good as my mother's pasta,' Sofia says.

I tell her I'm sorry about how things worked out. 'We'll visit your family soon, I promise.'

'This place is a good start,' she smiles. 'Reminds me of home a little bit.'

There's a large window behind Sofia, and I'm glad I'm the one facing it. While she sees a little bit of home, I see a bus stop, a fried chicken place and the head-down, London-pavement-pounders.

I feel her hand on my knee beneath the table, and she purses her red lips at me, breaking into a huge grin at my surprised look. I desperately wish we were alone now. I think we're coming together again. She gives me another promising look, and stands up, making her way towards the restroom.

I watch until she is out of sight, then turn back to face the window. I sip my wine and, for the first time in a long while, I start to relax. I haven't stopped for so long.

I feel disconnected from the busyness in the street but, as a bus pulls up opposite and a crowd spills out, I spot a familiar, tall figure pause on the pavement to rummage in his bag. Glen. I go to the restaurant door and call across the street. He doesn't hear me, so I run over and slap him on the back.

'Hey, how are you?' he says.

We move into a doorway.

'I have to talk to you about Ellie. Can we meet, tomorrow or something?'

'How about now? What is it?'

I really don't want to do this in the street, rushed, but he says he's on his way to a gig; no, he doesn't have time to join Sofia and me in the restaurant. 'What is it?' he asks again.

I can't keep him hanging on now. I want to be fair to him; if it were me, I'd want the same. I take a breath and try to pull out the right words.

'I'm starting to believe Ellie meant to kill herself.'

Glen freezes, his eyes searching somewhere above. Eventually, after several false starts, he says, 'Why do you think that all of a sudden?'

There's no other way. I tell him about the letter Ellie left in my bag. I explain, as softly as I can, how Sofia couldn't be blamed for being too scared to come forward. It was difficult for her too.

'You could've stopped it,' Glen says.

'Huh?'

'If you'd seen the letter that night, you could have stopped

Ellie killing herself.' His voice has raised now, each word forced out, staccato.

'No, I wouldn't have looked in my bag until morning. It made no difference, mate. If I thought there'd been any chance, I couldn't live with myself.'

'What if she'd wanted you to find the letter that night?' He's fronting up to me now, pushing his chest against my white shirt. 'Did you think about that? It could've been a cry for help.'

I'm shocked at his reaction. 'No, mate. There's no chance I would've seen it in time… when someone wants to kill themself, there's no way of stopping them. I'm sorry, but it's the truth.'

Glen looks over at the restaurant and I track his eyes. Sofia is at the door. A red bus blocks my view for a second.

He storms across the road, long strides, making directly for her. I charge after him, grabbing at his shoulders, but he shrugs me off.

'What did you do?' he shouts at her, getting nearer, pumping himself up with rage.

Sofia steps back inside, pulls the door closed behind her. I reach Glen just as he gets hold of the door handle.

'What did you do, bitch?' he shouts through the glass, as the restaurant owner puts himself between Sofia and the door.

I grab Glen's arm and pull him towards me. I can explain, if he'd just let me talk to him. But his face is red, screwed up with fury, and he lands a heavy fist on my temple, forcing me sideways. I'm dazed for a second, and when I look again, he's gone.

I go inside and hug Sofia, hiding my own shock as best I can. She's crying and the most important thing now is to reassure her. The restaurant owner wants to call the police, but I won't let him. He takes us to a table at the back and brings over some coffee and a brandy each. He returns again with a bag of ice for my head.

At home, there's a voicemail message from Glen. I'm about to spare Sofia from any further abuse, but the message was left much earlier. Glen's voice is friendly; his manner calm, as usual. He explains quietly how he called Emma Tate about Ellie's funeral arrangements, so we could pay our respects. Apparently, she told him we weren't welcome – it was a small family arrangement – and it was scheduled for the morning. The wake would be private also. Glen wasn't sure if he should tell me the unfortunate news, but thought I'd want to know. I suppose he called the landline so there'd be less chance of me picking up. We'd swapped full contact details and addresses when we first teamed up in all this – a right dynamic duo.

I'm worried about Glen. Worried for him, and worried about him. What the hell was that tonight? Where was the reasonable, thinking man I'm listening to on my voicemail? I still want to talk to him, but I don't know whether it's safe.

Everything's changing.

Chapter Ten

Marlon • London • November 2018

Cassie tells me to cross the street when there's trouble. I could get stabbed for being on the wrong estate, even though I'm nothing to do with drugs and stuff. These guys both got hoods up and have that walk going on. I can feel that thing happening with my mouth again. Cassie tells me, 'Stop chewing the damn air, Marlon.' I didn't even notice until she pointed it out. That's what big sisters are for. It happens more when I'm scared. Maybe these guys will leave me alone. They won't want my phone, too old. At least it's daytime and other people are about. Oh, my days! I know these two. As they get nearer, I can finally take a breath.

'Marlon, what's that thing on your head? Dickhead, man!'

They grab my baseball cap and throw it between each other, slapping the back of my head every time I turn around. Then they disappear around the corner, and I pick my cap out of the bin.

I run the rest of the way, turn off the street and look for the hole in the wire fence. My hoodie gets caught as I duck through and I wriggle a bit, pulling it free. The big gates are open, but I want to stay hidden. Black kid like me hanging around, they'll be straight on to the police. I pull myself through and sit between the trees. I can see the studio from here. They fitted a new door after Ellie died. The studio was nice inside, the bit with all the gear in. The rest of the place was a bit messy. Cassie would've hated it. She's gonna go nuts about this ripped hoodie, as well. I might chuck it on the way home.

I know I shouldn't keep coming back here. I can't help it. I should be in town, making myself useful, but I quite like sitting here on my own. I wonder why those guys didn't like my cap. Coz it has a band name on? I go mental down at the front when bands play, and people start clearing away. But I prefer that music to the stuff the rest of my estate are into. I've never fitted in around Hackney. Mum kept me away from all the crime, took me to church and everything. I miss her still. It's Sunday today, but Cassie says we don't have to go anymore. I kind of miss that, too.

There are footsteps coming down the road. A man and woman, talking. I shuffle my butt back a bit and try to see beneath the branches of the tree. It's Ian, the producer guy that owns the place. Ellie liked him. He's cool, looks like he should be in a band, but smart enough to run a business too. That's what I'd like to do one day; prove all them teachers wrong. Ian's holding the door open for the woman, but she's staying outside.

'Thought you'd given up the smokes?' he says to her.

She makes a funny face at him. 'I need one, just today. One's not going to hurt.'

Ian heads inside and the woman lights her cigarette, wandering up and down the car-park. She's pretty. She holds her cigarette in her mouth and ties her hair back. She looks foreign. Sounded a bit foreign when she spoke too, but she seems nice. I think you should be nice to everyone, whatever country they come from. My mum's parents were from Nigeria, but I never heard anyone disrespect her, ever. She was strong, man. She could be polite to people and still get their respect. It's different for me. Ellie liked me though. Told me so. Helped me as well.

What's the woman up to, crouching down by the brook? I crawl up on my belly to get a better look. She's reaching under the flat little bridge that cars use to get over the brook to the car park. She's got one hand on the concrete, one foot on the bank, picking something out of the reeds. Looks like a bit of paper. She's got it on the floor now, pressing it out flat. Ian's calling her from the studio, and she looks surprised. She folds whatever it is, shoves it into her back pocket and goes inside.

I sit there for another hour, dreaming about music and thinking about Ellie. Eventually Ian and his friend appear at the door and lock-up. They disappear up the road. There's nothing more to see here. It's time I did some work. I'll hang around Camden, keep an eye out for anyone that looks promising. It's been a while since I found anyone new, and I need to keep my boss sweet.

Chapter Eleven

Ellie's Diary • November 2015

I'm so tired – but I won't sleep. I have to write this down in case I forget. In case the police ever come knocking. God, it was the worst, most horrible thing I have ever seen. As if I could forget.

I was coming out of Westgate, I'd just bought a waterproof jacket, cheap and a lovely dark green. I heard shouting from around the corner – the lane where the hairdressers is. I didn't want to look, but I thought I should – and it was Danny's brother, Jon. There was a taxi with its engine running and Jon was arguing with another guy who was twice the size of him. I wanted to get out of there but felt I had to stay – for Danny. But I was frozen tbh. Danny's other brother, Jude, was there too, but it was Jon the big guy had the problem with. Sounded like Jon had pinched the taxi off of him and his friend, who was keeping back. The big one looked like a proper gym boy – tracksuit, duffel bag. He was posh, though, calling Jon scum and some really horrible names. Jon was laughing at him and shrugging his shoulders. But he didn't get in the taxi, just leant against it. The taxi driver was trying to persuade him to get in, but Jon was still listening to the insults with a grin on his face. I wondered why Jude didn't pull him into the taxi. He was just hanging by the other door – didn't say a word.

Gym Boy suddenly lunged at Jon. His friend jumped in and managed to get his arms around him, and Jon said something like, 'You really want to go there, rich lad?' He was laughing at him. Gym Boy pumped up and slipped loose from his friend and charged straight into Jon, crumpling him into the taxi. Jon jumped straight back out. Now he wasn't laughing. He threw a punch and caught Gym Boy square on the jaw. It rocked him and seemed to take him by surprise. I wasn't surprised; Dad was the same size as Jon when I saw him overcome a bigger man. But that was a long time ago. Anyway, it didn't take Gym Boy long to get back into the fight and he kicked at Jon's legs. He seemed to know what he was doing, but looked like he had more technique than heart. He probably wished he'd just walked away.

For a moment he tried to back off, but Jon had a vengeful look about him. I couldn't catch my breath! I was so scared. Jude was telling him 'Enough', but Jon landed a big hook to the side of Gym Boy's head. He went down hard. Motionless. The taxi driver seized the opportunity and ragged out of the lane with the open back door swinging. I thought the guy might be dead. His mate was frozen. Jude was frozen. I wanted to call an ambulance, but before I dared, everything erupted again.

Jon began kicking the guy in the ribs, then the head, then he stamped on his crotch. Jude tried to hold him back but Jon just shrugged him off. Gym Boy began spluttering, turning his head, and spitting blood. I thanked God he was alive. Jon kicked him again as his head raised up. Gym Boy didn't make a sound. He looked entirely removed from the situation, like he'd already died and floated out of his broken body.

Then Jon turned to the other guy who was curled up on the floor, crying, and started threatening him if he thought about reporting what had happened, saying he'd come and find him in the hospital waiting room. I'll never forget the tone in his voice. 'You better start thinking about what you might say. And picture in your clever little head what you just saw happen here. Because if you start telling too much, you know exactly the level of shit that's coming your way.'

The guy just nodded, he didn't seem able to stop. Jon and Jude started to walk in my direction, and I scuttled out of sight, back down the lane, and when I was certain they'd gone, I called 999. My hands were shaking, and I could barely stammer out the location.

It's the sounds that will stay with me, I think. They were sickening. I can't tell Danny. I don't want to tell Danny. He is not like them. I love him. This never happened, this never happened, this never happened...

Chapter Twelve

Ian • Kent • November 2018

A high, wire fence encloses the entire farm-park. It's to keep the animals contained, but also to keep the likes of us out. I motion to Sofia to follow me to a corner, where a locked fire gate seems climbable. It's not dark enough yet, really, but I want to get moving. Besides, it's too cold to hang about. A slip; my toe snaps out of its foothold, but I straddle the gate and Sofia throws up the rucksack. As I drop to the ground, she's already over the top herself, starting to climb down gracefully.

The park is low-level, except for a children's helter-skelter in the play area. The animal pens are spacious and well-maintained. Nobody is about, but there are lights on in a couple of the cabins behind the entrance building, probably belonging to zookeepers or groundsmen. We move along the edge of the fencing, keeping off the gravel pathways that snake smartly around the attractions. I stop to check the contents of the rucksack and hear a crunch of footsteps. Sofia tugs my arm, and we tuck in against a pen. A voice crackles out of a radio in the near distance and somebody's moving towards us. My heartbeat quickens. The figure heads back the way he came.

I allow myself a breath and clamber over a low fence, towards the far corner of the park where grasses have been allowed to grow tall and conifers are no longer pruned. It's different but familiar. It's been a long time. I can't see the brook, but I know it runs behind the oak tree up ahead. Our caravan was on this spot. I was only young, but the place is bringing back the prickles on my skin from pushing through hedges to make camps. I loved opening the caravan door to an early morning scent of grass and dew, birdsong welcoming in the day. I was free here: no roads, no limits for my bike rides. It was somewhere we could be together: nobody at work, busy with housework, or off with friends.

Sofia takes the rucksack from my back and places it on the ground, carefully removing the box inside. She takes one clear plastic pouch and I take the other. Without a word, we slowly scatter the ashes, tipping the pouches up as the breeze catches the flow of dust to the ground. She's whispering a prayer, eyes closed. She always had time for my parents. It's taken me a long time to do this, but I can think of no better place, or person I'd choose to share it with. The pouches empty, we gaze at the ground, arms limp at our sides.

I hadn't allowed myself to stop after Mum and Dad died so suddenly. I was always moving onto the next thing, anything to keep my mind busy. Ellie's death was the first roadblock that finally slowed everything down. You can distract yourself for a while, until time clips the edges off the ache, but eventually you come face to face with the emptiness of it all. These days, I'm thankful for the images and memories that pop out of nowhere.

A voice breaks the moment, but I don't catch what it says.

'Sorry, I didn't –'

'I asked what you're doing – this is private property.'

He's scruffy in his untucked park uniform, and sounds like he'd rather not be bothering with intruders. There's a strong smell of cannabis, as he slides a vape into his pocket and scratches his ginger beard with a stubby knuckle.

'I was scattering ashes. This spot's special to my family.'

'Not creepy at all,' he says. 'Pretty sure that's not allowed, to be honest. How'd you get in?'

There's nothing he can do – we've finished our little ceremony – so I go with the simple truth. I'd written to the owner, asking for permission, explaining why it was important to me. I'd opened right up, only to receive a curt reply, disrespecting the memory of my parents in the process. I'd screwed up his letter and ditched it. But Sofia had retrieved it, and she hadn't liked it either.

'That would've been McKelvey, eh? He's a tit, mate.'

I laugh: a moment of relief. 'I don't want any trouble, we'll leave the way we came,' I say, but he's shaking his head, pulling the vape back out of his frayed pocket.

'Nah, I'll let you out the front,' he says, exhaling a large plume of pungent smoke over our heads. 'Take my number and you can come back anytime.'

Sofia's head lolls as I manoeuvre the Mini through a swarm of North Circular tail lights. My mobile rings and I tilt my hips so she can take it from my pocket. She turns the speaker on.

'Ian?'

'Yeah, who's this?'

'It's Steve. Steve Lewis.'

'Steve, how are you?'

'Good. I've got a problem here though and she knows you. Can you come over? Yours is the only name I can get out of her; she's mashed.'

'What's her name?'

'Gaynor something.'

'What's she doing in London?' I look at Sofia. She throws her arms up.

'Mate, I know nothing about her.'

'Can't you leave her somewhere to sober up?'

'Listen, she's had a bit of a fight, mate. She kept on asking for you.'

'Where are you?' I should at least see what I can do. If only for Ellie's sake. I shoot Sofia another look.

'Dublin Castle.'

Sofia says, 'Drop me off, I'm not going.'

'I'll swing by,' I say.

There's a crowd of smokers outside the Dublin Castle. I go in, and push past the bar to the rear of the building, where the live music's coming from. A woman sitting with a cash box at the door seems to recognise me, and waves me towards the backstage area, where it smells of broken plumbing. Steve meets me in the doorway and motions towards a girl slumped on a chair in the corner. There are guitar cases and drum boxes scattered around the room. Camden attracts all sorts, but still Gaynor looks out of place. She's tried, with black skinny jeans and T-shirt, but they don't suit her. Her blonde hair is sticking to her sweaty face. She raises her head and struggles to focus.

'Came on her own, I think,' Steve says. 'Only bought a few drinks. I wonder if she had a little something else as well?'

'What happened to her face?'

'She was talking to a few lads, telling them she was police, going on about it and everything. They didn't take her too seriously, but one of the girls got a bit offended. When she saw 'Support Staff' on her ID badge, she punched her in the face.'

'You got any coffee?'

'Tried that; she's had a couple.'

'I meant for me.'

Steve ruffles his blond mop, smiling as he leaves. He's a good guy; I'm not surprised he took it on himself to get Gaynor sorted. I squat down and try to get her attention.

'What's this all about then, eh?'

It takes a while, but she drawls, 'I just wanted to do what Ellie did. She never told me what it was like.'

I laugh, in a nice way, and chase her gaze with my eyes. 'Well, now you know.'

Steve's back with the coffee and I drain it quickly enough to scorch my tongue and throat. I need the caffeine hit for a round-trip to Weston Turville. I gave it some thought on the way over. I couldn't get Ellie's face out of my mind, the look she'd be giving me if I ignored her old friend. All I can think to do is to throw Gaynor in the car and take her home. It'll probably be quicker than waiting for her to be fit enough to leave on her own, anyway. But she's fallen asleep, her seated body sliding down the corner wall. Steve takes her legs, I take her shoulders and we lay her down, grabbing a coat and rolling it into a pillow. The rest will do her good, but we'll keep an eye on her.

'Did you know Ellie Beck?' I ask Steve. 'She told me she'd played here a few times.'

'Yeah, I put on most of the gigs here now. Terrible, what happened.'

'What did you think of her?'

'She was quiet. I liked her music, and I think I'd have liked her if I'd got past her guard.'

'Would you say she looked depressed?'

'Withdrawn, maybe? She'd always have a few friends in the audience, though. Odd bunch.'

Steve rolls his shirt sleeves up. The heat, even at this time of night, even at this time of year, is uncomfortable. The walls are pulsing from the loud music in the room next door, where the ceiling will be dripping moisture back onto the crowd. He pauses, then shifts forwards in his chair. 'I saw her one night, quite hysterical. She was with a photographer bloke who used to help her.'

'Glen Crane.'

'Don't know his name, tall guy, older. Yeah, I stepped in when I saw them arguing outside, but turned out she was upset and just taking it out on him.'

We don't get any further with the conversation. Gaynor's starting to wake, and Steve's game for helping me get her out to the car, her arms around our necks.

We're soon on the M1, window open a crack to keep a flow of air. Gaynor's had another brief nap, snoring against the car window, and now seems a bit more with it.

'What was all that about, shouting around about being police?'

'Sorry, I couldn't help it. They reminded me of the bullies at school. Just wanted to show them I was somebody.'

'I'm not sure that's how it works, love. You can't go round threatening people with that. You'll get yourself killed.' I feel like I'm talking to a kid.

She's gone silent again, head back, mouth open.

Eventually, I pull into her gravelled driveway and lights come on in the house.

'Can you imagine,' she slurs, 'how hard it was for Ellie?'

'What?'

'Danny.'

'Danny's killing?'

'Not just that... what the murderer did to him.'

'How do you mean?'

'Like...' She's hyperventilating and can't finish, sobbing. And here is her father, approaching the car with a red face and an expression somewhere between fear and anger. I hand Gaynor over, like a used handbag at a jumble sale, and leave the explaining to her.

Chapter Thirteen

London • November 2018

Suresh has thrown a free extra bagel into my bag, bless him. We had a nice chat about Ellie; he still misses her polite manner. I'm ready to work on her song again today, see what I can add to it. I'm nearly back at the studio but stop suddenly. There's a black BMW parked outside, and I think I recognise it. Edging closer, I try to see inside, but the sun reflects off the rear windscreen. I come around the side of the car as the driver's door swings open. Robert Warrister. Dreadlocks swish across his green parka as he climbs out. We're chest-to-chest. A sickly-sweet smell of weed on his clothes.

'You gave them my name,' he whispers in my ear. Adrenaline is making me light-headed, but I won't try anything stupid. There's no way Robert goes anywhere without at least a knife, and that big, long coat is a perfect place to conceal it.

'Look, that business, I let it go a long time ago. It wasn't me that gave them anything.' I try to hold his gaze.

His bloodshot eyes widen, like he's deciding what to do with me.

I'm distracted by a movement beyond him, someone else coming from behind the car. I clench my jaw, ready to absorb whatever's coming. But it's Warrister he's going for. Arms reach around Warrister's neck, but he's the bigger man and he easily bats them away, dumping the figure on the floor. Warrister produces a machete and stands over him.

I get between the black kid curled up in a ball at the madman's feet, and the blade now raised above his head. 'Don't do it, Robert, don't! Come on!'

The stand-off lasts minutes, in my pulsing brain at least, and Warrister kicks the kid's head like a football. Then he backs off towards his car, climbs in, and reverses slowly. His eyes don't leave mine until he's out of the yard.

I throw open the studio door, then race back and hoist the kid up. Somehow, we reach the studio sofa in a tangle of arms and legs. I lock the door and grab a towel from the bathroom. The kid is wiping the blood away with the bottom of his t-shirt. I press the towel against his wound. I recognise him now as the intruder I chased out of the yard. Gold tooth and everything.

'I'll call an ambulance. I don't have a car here.'

'I'm okay.' His voice is soft and he's shaking violently.

'Thanks for helping me, but bloody hell...' I attempt a grin, but it turns into a grimace. 'I've seen you here before, haven't I?'

He murmurs and bows his head, his body still jittery with electricity.

'Why were you here?'

There's something not right with him, and I can't tell if it's shock or whether the kid's got issues. He's taken a good whack to the head, and he needs to see a doctor, whether he likes it or not.

'I'm okay,' he says again, waving his arm, as I put the phone to my ear.

'I'm calling a cab, it'll be quicker.'

I make him a cup of sweet tea and he takes small sips as we wait for the taxi. After a while, he looks over at me.

'That guy...' He's unable to finish the thought.

'I'm sorry you got involved, it's me he's got the issue with. You were brave to try.'

'I thought... he might be the one Ellie was... frightened of.'

A sickness rises in the pit of my stomach. 'You knew Ellie?'

A car approaches, and the taxi driver beeps his horn. The kid's looking vacant, and I help him to his feet, putting an arm around him as we go outside. I don't want him fainting on me and cracking his head a second time.

He signs into Accident and Emergency as Marlon Williams and is quickly taken in for triage. I sit among the cast of less-than-impressed patients who have been here hours already, agonising over what he said. He was quiet on the cab ride over. As if he'd said too much. My mind keeps going over that night at dinner – when Ellie told Sofia and me she was scared of someone. I put it down to paranoia, but ever since her death I've had an overriding sense of guilt. Marlon thought Warrister might be the guy. What does that mean? I exhale hard in frustration and all eyes turn my way. I stand and stretch my legs. Ellie couldn't have known Warrister, could she?

A door opens and Marlon comes over, his head bandaged. 'She said I'm alright, did loads of checks.'

'That's great, what now?'

'I have to wait to see someone else. Might need stitches.'

'Okay, mate. Let's go over there.' We move to a couple of chairs further down the hall, away from the staring multitude with nothing to hold their attention other than who might sneeze or clear their throat next.

'How did you know Ellie?' I ask.

'We were friends.'

'Is that why you've been hanging around the studio?'

'It's, uh… it's difficult,' he says. He turns his face away. 'Ellie told me not to say anything.'

'I think we're well past having to worry about that, Marlon.'

'She taught me the guitar a bit, was nice to me. Showed me how everything worked and –'

'You were in my studio?'

His eyes widen.

'It's alright, I just want to understand.'

'Sometimes, after you'd left,' he says. 'I didn't touch anything.'

'What makes you think Ellie was frightened of someone?'

Finally, he says, 'She told me. Someone killed her boyfriend and she found out later it was to protect her.'

I feel as though I've been hit. I stare at Marlon, wrestling with the implications. I don't want him to clam up on me, so I keep my tone calm.

'Ellie knew who murdered Danny?'

'Was that his name?' Marlon's head drops like he's being disrespectful. My worry is that he didn't truly grasp what Ellie was telling him. Then what chance do I have?

I ask again, 'Who killed Ellie's boyfriend?'

'She didn't know. Just said that someone killed him because he had a disease.'

My eyes widen. Worse by the second.

'So, someone close to Ellie, if they were trying to protect her from Danny's HIV. I doubt Robert Warrister ever leaves North London. Why did you think it was him?'

His face scrunches up.

'Come on… I need more than this.'

'That's why I was watching your place. To try and find out who it is.' He's crying now.

'If there really was someone hassling her, they're not going to be seen where her dead body's been found.'

He shrugs, his tremor returning, mouth opening and closing in rapid succession.

'No-one else knows about this. How come she told you?'

'She told me she had a plan. Wanted me to keep away. It freaked me out, and I wouldn't leave until she told me everything.'

'And this is everything…?'

He shrugs again.

'Ellie must've known this killer if they did it to protect her.'

Marlon stares into space like something's falling into place.

'She thought her dad might have got someone to do it.'

Detective Inspector Hannan leads us through to an interview room. It's sterile and bright, the sun beating through thin blinds. Marlon looks at the floor, touching the dressing on his wound.

'What happened to him?' Hannan asks. His suit is crisp.

'Robert Warrister. He did come to see me.'

Hannan shifts in his seat, and I tell him about the morning's events, culminating with the machete attack. He jumps up, returning a while later with an assurance that Warrister will be picked up today. I take a long, deep breath, and recount the story of Ellie's protector, motioning to Marlon at times, and getting nothing more than a shy nod in return. Hannan takes it in, his expression neutral, his focus as keen as an owl mantling. A female detective enters and Hannan stands.

'Marlon, this is Nikki. She's going to take a statement from you about the assault, okay?'

Hannan motions at me, and I follow his tall frame down the corridor to a canteen. The tables are all empty. He orders two coffees from an older lady, who seems pleased to see him, and we take them to the table furthest from the counter.

'What do you know about Marlon?' he asks, his mouth turning down.

'Only what he's told me today, and what I told you back there. I think he's got some issues.'

'Ellie Beck never mentioned him to you, or anything about this character who might've killed to protect her?'

'Nothing at all. Do you think it's likely... there was someone like that?'

'I'll need a list from you of Ellie's contacts. In case we've missed any. Can you put that together for me please?'

'It'll be a small list – you probably already have them.'

'Also, think about anyone connected to Ellie who may have travelled between London, Oxford and Aylesbury. An ANPR analysis will be done to throw up any vehicles appearing in all three areas, but it'll be a huge list. Anything to help us narrow it down would be great.'

'Glen Crane,' I offer, without hesitation. It surprises Hannan, and he presses me for more. He doesn't write any of it down.

'I'll pass your information to Thames Valley – they'll need to speak with you at some point. And coming back to your question... we hear all different stories and false confessions when somebody is murdered. Most of them we can filter out.'

'I noticed they didn't hold back the fact that Danny was HIV positive in the news reports.'

'Something else was held back at the time, but it doesn't seem to fit with a... 'protector' who's serving such a specific purpose.'

Hannan blows on his coffee and takes a sip.

Sofia's scared, her jaw tight, and she's grinding her teeth as I recount today's events.

'So, what do you make of it?'

'I'm just so glad you're okay,' she says, and takes my hand across the table.

'I meant all the stuff about Ellie and her protector.'

'I know, but you're the most important thing to me.'

'It was weird when I told you about it, the way you looked.'

She exaggerates a look of surprise. 'I don't... know. It's scary to think about.'

'Sure there's nothing else you want to tell me?'

'Ian...'

'I'm sorry.' I squeeze her hand. 'I feel like I let Ellie down. Maybe her protector should be coming for me next.'

Chapter Fourteen

London • November 2018

I've not been to the studio since giving Hannan the protector story. I've sat with Sofia as she works, dipping into Ellie's song with my home set-up. The production of the music seems less important than the truth behind it, though. I need to hear back from Hannan. I wonder if the real reason I've been holed up for three days is Glen Crane. I'm still shocked by his outburst. Whether he's capable of murder, of course, is an entirely different thing, and at the moment I can't see it being true. I've left several messages for Hannan to get back to me, desperate to know what they've found out about this protector story. Sofia smiles more now, but I've also a sense that maybe some distance is good for a relationship.

'Juice, in your favourite glass.' I place the tumbler on her desk. It says, 'My boyfriend rocks the spot!' with a picture of me pulling a face. I can't remember why I thought that was a good idea.

'Oh, my God! I forgot about that thing,' she laughs.

I leave, but peer back around the doorframe, and there it is, the roll of the eyes. I'll give her some space this afternoon.

My mobile vibrates.

'Ian, it's Scott Hannan. How are you?'

'Haven't left the flat all week.'

'We're not pursuing the lead from Marlon any further. Major

89

Crime at Thames Valley assessed it and we're in agreement that it doesn't stand up, given the evidence.'

'Marlon made it all up?'

'Maybe not. But if Ellie did tell him the story about a protector, we don't know why. Maybe she was keeping him away from the studio, so he wouldn't be the one to find her body. I've a feeling she mothered him a bit, from what he told us.'

'Well, he's been staking the place out ever since. He was definitely told something. And he went for Warrister.'

He changes the subject. 'Robert Warrister has been charged for the assault on Marlon. He's been released on bail.'

'Okay…what happens now?'

'You may need to give evidence, depending on how he pleads.'

'And Marlon? Would he cope with court?'

'There are procedures. I wouldn't worry about it yet. We also interviewed Glen Crane –'

'And?'

'We don't think he was involved, and his alibi checks out.'

A knot tightens in my stomach, a mixture of relief and disappointment. 'I'm glad about that,' I say, finally.

'He mentioned you'd had a disagreement. Anything more I should know about that?'

Good: no mention of the suicide note Sofia had hidden. 'Not really. It just blew up, all that stress. I'll give him a call. Did Major Crime know any more about Danny de Vries' murder.'

'The investigation's ongoing.'

'I can't believe there's nothing more to go on.'

'We'll keep on it,' Hannan says. I feel I can trust Hannan, but nothing seems to be progressing.

I lie on the living room sofa, gazing at the colour spectrum the glass lampshade has thrown across the walls. Wavelengths reflecting and refracting, just as sound does. It's time to put out the song and share Ellie with the world. I don't need Yannis or the labels he was eyeballing for Ellie's deal. I've got people that'll help. It'll be like a charity release: one song to raise some money for suicide and self-harm charities, a tribute to Ellie's life. Social media will carry it, and maybe new witnesses will come forward. Maybe we can identify a protector after all. I catch myself, wondering if my imagination is running away with me. But I made a promise to tell the truth. I spring off the sofa and through the door, bouncing off Sofia as she exits her office.

'Sorry! I've had an –'

'Hold on a moment,' she commands, and pushes me against the doorframe. We embrace and she looks up at me. Our eyes close and she slides her hands underneath my shirt, warm on my back and chest. Light as air across the floor to the bedroom, falling onto the sheets – connected and unavailable to the world.

A shrill buzz interrupts a blissful doze. Sofia's eyes are half-open, her face scrunched up against the light, as I stumble over to the intercom.

'Yes?'

'It's Glen… I've come to apologise.'

I turn to Sofia, and she pulls the bed sheets over her body. It's her call. After a few moments she shrugs, begins putting her clothes on.

'Come on up.'

Glen looks around as he ducks into the living room, checking for anything to use as a conversation starter. He's awkward, his thin lips tight together, and he's trying to make himself smaller. But it's not me he needs to apologise to.

'Sofia, I think Glen has something to say.'

She appears in the doorway and leans on the architrave. She won't come any closer.

'I was all over the place,' he says. 'I'm sorry. Wasn't thinking straight. Too angry. Sorry... to both of you.' He looks at us in turn, shoulders hunched, accepting of anything.

'Let's not mention it again,' I say, after clocking Sofia's relief. She goes to boil the kettle, and I motion for Glen to take a seat on the sofa. I perch on the edge of the arm.

'I understand why you gave the police my name.'

I just nod, and there's a brief silence.

'This story about her dad organising...' he looks off to the side, smacking his lips.

'What if it's true? Did Ellie ever seem scared of anyone?' I watch Glen closely.

'No, I don't think so.' He looks away. Maybe he's forgotten that night Steve told me about in the Dublin Castle. 'Oh, after the police spoke to me, I went to Oxford.'

'Yeah?'

'See if I could dig up anything on Danny de Vries' murder. Or on this protector thing.'

Sofia puts the mugs of tea in front of me, so that I have to pass Glen his, and disappears again. I drink slowly as he tells me about his trip to Oxford. He knew of some homeless shelters, off St Aldates, where drugs could be found. And with heroin, he says, comes desperation and disloyalty, so within a couple of hours he had an address for one of Danny de Vries' brothers.

'What was he like?'

'Jon, his name is. Doesn't like visitors, but I used Ellie's name to get his attention. Scruffy place: he had a metal bar to jam the front door with.'

'You shouldn't have gone on your own. The other brother wasn't there?'

'No, Jude is the other one, but I didn't meet him. Jon wasn't big, but sinewy – looked a bit of a nutter. One of his tattoos was Danny's name.'

'Could Danny's murder have been payback for a drug deal?'

'I asked him that – gently, of course. He said not, and I believe him. He wanted to know all about Ellie. He seemed to like her...'

Glen trails off, like he's considering whether to go on.

'What is it?'

'He mumbled about Ellie needing something to take the edge off the grief.'

'You think he gave her drugs?'

'He changed the subject, but I can imagine him giving her a good supply to take with her. Ellie wasn't a druggie, was she? But she could've accepted them not to offend and they came in useful later when she had to kill herself.'

'But Jon didn't confirm that.'

'No. He went on to grill me about the case, but I obviously didn't mention the protector theory.'

'I should hope not!'

'Yeah, he was surprisingly brazen about how he got some university kids to answer his questions. He wouldn't take kindly to a friend of Ellie's being his brother's killer.'

I'm guessing Glen would've wanted to get out of there as soon as he had something. And the way he's looking at me now suggests he got it.

'The inquest didn't give specific details about Danny's murder. But Jon said Danny had a cable-tie around his right leg. A tree near to where his body was found had scuff marks, like a chain had rubbed against the bark. There's a theory that the killer had wrapped a chain round the tree, then attacked Danny and cable-tied him to it.'

'Why do they think he did that?' I ask.

'So, the killer could take his time, beating Danny senseless until eventually one of his broken ribs punctured a lung.'

'He took his time…? And nobody saw anything? Where was this again?'

'Christ Church Meadow. Danny climbed over the gates at night sometimes, to run. This time someone was waiting for him on the footpath.'

'That's horrific.'

'And Ellie knew it. That someone had shackled her boyfriend to a tree, then smashed him to bits.'

We sit in silence. Then he says, 'So, the music then…'

It's a stretch to call it either an office or a studio, but the small room next to Sofia's study is my second workplace. The desk is a long kitchen-worktop with screw-in legs from Ikea, covered by a large gaming mat. On it sits my laptop and completing a triangle to my face are two expensive nearfield monitor speakers. Glen picks one up and nods at it.

'I don't know why, but I was expecting a lot more gear to go with these beauties.'

'It's the modern way,' I say. 'Working "in the box". Instead of using the large mixing desk and outboard racks of gear I have at the studio, everything is worked on digitally on my laptop's software.'

'Options. I like it.'

'I'm pretty happy with the final mix. I spent a lot of time on production, so blending everything in was straightforward. The difficult bit is knowing when it's finished.'

'I have the same problem with editing shots,' Glen says. He disappears into the hall and returns with a bag, pulling out a laptop, and nestling in next to me at the desk.

'This is all about speed,' I say. 'How about one of those online distribution services? Get it out quickly on all streaming sites?'

'They don't generate much of a profit, do they? What about the charity side of it?'

'We can sell downloads separately. They'll take a revenue share, but if we can push it well through social media, we might do okay.'

I'm going to need to pull in a lot of favours from industry contacts. The amount of incredible music that sits almost unnoticed out there in the streaming world is shocking to a producer who appreciates the amount of work that goes into the art. We set up an account with an online distributor I've heard good things about, and it's soon done. In a few days *Under the Tree* will be available to stream on the major services. It's a marketing disaster to risk such a short release build-up, but I want it out there quickly. And maybe it's the right time of year, just coming up to Christmas. Setting up the downloads service is equally easy, and we've soon set the pricing. The release date will coincide with the streaming services. Now begins the hard work of promoting it and telling Ellie's story. I won't let the protector theory drop, but it's not safe to share it yet.

'The video platforms are my domain,' Glen says, and pulls up a folder on his laptop dedicated to images and video footage of Ellie Beck. 'Give me the words to the song and I'll do a lyric video. Might be nice to narrate her story over some gig footage as well.'

'Perfect.' I already have Ellie's social media account logins from our original planning sessions at the studio. I can use her original profiles and access her network and followers.

'I think this is going to work,' I say, and we settle in for a long session of planning and implementation. I want to include Marlon somehow and I share the idea with Glen, so I don't forget about it.

Chapter Fifteen

Marlon • London • December 2018

It's a dirty job but someone's gotta do it. That's what the boss
always says, as he scrubs my head with his knuckles. Not today,
though. Today, I called him instead. Didn't want him to see my
head injury. I hoped my cap would cover it up, but the brim
catches where it hurts. They didn't stitch it at the hospital, put
those strips on it instead, so it's obvious.

He wanted me to come here, an all-day music festival in Bow.
They've set a stage up in the pub garden, with infra-red heaters
round the sides, and a blue plastic sheet to protect the gear. It
looks like a market stall, but the PA is a good one, well loud.
The band on stage are playing alt. rock; the girl singer has black
clothes, black hair, and even blacker eye makeup. The band are
crap, but she's good. There are more people inside the pub than
outside watching. It's all about getting hammered at this time of
day, when newer bands get their slots, but everyone will be out
later when the bigger bands are on. I push through to the bar
and order a pint of tap water. In the corner there's a drummer I
recognise from a famous band. His singer's always in the news,
but he doesn't get as much attention. He's talking loudly about a
snare drum he's got with him, trying to sell it; tells a good story
too. Seems a bit desperate, though. He looks like he's been up for
a week straight.

Ellie was just herself, and she had tons more appeal than that. She was honest too. The nutter looking out for her… there's no way that was a lie. I don't care what the police say, Ellie was scared to death – that guy is real, man. Now Warrister's been nicked, maybe they'll get something out of him.

I wish Ellie had told me more about the guy, what he looked like or something. I could've found him. She just wanted me away from it all: don't get involved, Marlon. That's why she'd only see me at the studio when Ian had gone home. She was like another older sister, even if she was younger than me. Only a bit, though. She was wise, man.

She tried teaching me the guitar. I didn't understand a word she said, so she just showed me some chord shapes and how I could move them around on the neck of the guitar. That made more sense. I was playing a few tunes after that by ear. Shapes and patterns are easy. Ellie knew, got it straight away. If I'd had a teacher like that at school, I reckon I could've done well. I told Ellie a story that I'd written at school, about an astronaut. My teacher told me that even sci-fi writers can't bend the laws of physics that much. But Ellie liked the conversations the astronaut would have with his memories. She smiled when I told those parts.

Here he comes, the boss's mate. Full of himself, he is; Cassie wouldn't like him at all. All hyped-up, better than everyone else.

'Make sure he gets it, yeah?' he says, giving me a lumpy envelope that's been folded in half, a rubber band around it.

''Course.' I shove it in the front pocket of my jeans.

'Pull your trousers up as well, no one wants to see your pants.' A couple of girls laugh, and he winks at them.

I push back outside and stand next to the soundman in the middle near the back. It's the best place if you want to hear properly. The band with the girl singer has finished and the next lot are sound-checking the drums. At the side of the stage, the singer is squatting down, packing up her gear, and I make my move. Maybe I can scout her for the boss.

'Great set,' I say, pausing before I reach her.

'Thanks.' She glances up and smiles. She looks even younger than she did on stage. Her hands are on her hips, confident.

'My name's Marlon. You've got an amazing voice. What's your name?'

'Kelly.' But I can tell she doesn't want to talk to me. She carries on packing up her gear.

'Do you always play with these guys, or do you do your own stuff as well?'

'That was my own stuff,' she says.

'Ah, okay. I really liked your voice, that's all.'

'And not the band?' She's standing square on to me again. She's got them shoes with massive soles, but she's still quite short.

'My sister says I should always be honest...'

'Yeah?' she almost shouts.

'...and I reckon you'd be better off going solo. You've really got something.'

She shoves me in the chest, spilling my water. Suddenly there's a scuffle, people telling me to calm down and stuff. They're shoving me and pulling back and I'm in the middle of them. I try and explain that I'm all good, but it's just a stammer, I can't get the words out. They seem to think I'm trouble. I try to leave but they're pushing me back towards the stage.

'Oi! Stop it or get out!' The boss's mate shoves them away and pushes me out to the roadside.

'Sorry, I didn't...' but he pushes me again, towards the station.

'Make sure Yannis gets it today,' he hisses.

Chapter Sixteen

Ian • Weston Turville • December 2018

Gaynor has a patio-heater out on the balcony, and it's welcome after my drive up on this cold, damp day. I clutch my coffee, gratefully. She's done with skinny jeans, back to mumsy dresses, and she seems quiet, gazing down across the unkempt garden, which does have some charm in its current state. Her father is tying back some rose bushes against the wall.

'Sounds great, what you've done,' she says.

'I wanted to fill you in on how it's all going. Saw you shared the posts. The single was released today, streams are pretty good already.'

'Exciting.'

'Samaritans and Mind were pleased to hear from us. We'll see what we can raise for them and a couple of the smaller charities as well, hopefully – if punters are as interested in physical CDs and vinyl as they are in the Spotify streams. Might have to do some merch!'

That makes her smile. 'Sorry, I was imagining Ellie's face on a t-shirt. She'd have hated that.'

'We wouldn't be that crass,' I laugh.

'They did a collection at her funeral. Emma dealt with it, but I don't know where the donations went to.'

'How was it, the funeral?'

'Well, it wasn't what Ellie would've wanted.'

'That's a shame.'

'I mean, everything was done properly, but it could've been for anyone. I didn't hear much in the eulogy that couldn't have been equally true about any other girl that had died. There was nothing about Ellie's troubles or suicide, like they just wanted to sweep all that awkward stuff away.'

'How was her father?'

'He wasn't taking it in. Everyone made a fuss of him outside the crematorium, showed him around the flowers, but I don't think he knew what he was there for. He's deteriorated so much.'

We sit in silence for a few moments. I don't want to make it too obvious that the conversation is settling on the real reason for my visit.

'What kind of man was David, before his illness?'

'The kind that gave everything to his daughter.'

'Was Ellie comfortable with that? I mean, some kids hate being smothered.'

Gaynor's brow furrows. 'Ellie was his entire world. And no, if you're insinuating Ellie resented his love, you're wrong. She didn't kill herself because her father was too suffocating.'

'I didn't mean... sorry, I was just interested in the dynamics. I can tell she was very fond of David.'

'She was.'

'I was just trying to put myself in David's position. I'm not a parent, but I'd imagine there's a primal instinct that kicks in when you're responsible for a child.'

'I wouldn't know.'

'David seems like a gentle man.'

'I still remember him the way he was.'

'How was he?'

'Let's just say he would have hated becoming so vulnerable. The dementia's probably a blessing.'

If the police didn't see the protector thing as a credible theory, then it's not my place to perpetuate rumours. And it would scare poor Gaynor to death. It's niggling away at me, but I'm not prepared to share it. Gaynor's still staring out at the garden, shifting in her seat and avoiding my gaze.

'Did I... say anything to you when you brought me home?' she asks, finally, though her focus is still on her father, working in the bare flower bed.

'Bits, you were asleep most of the time.'

'I mean, did I say anything weird?'

'Like what?' I hope to God she hasn't taken my help the wrong way.

'Nothing,' she says. 'But I woke up paranoid, trying to piece it all together.'

'You know some girl hit you?'

'Yes.' She touches her face, like she's trying to make sense of it all. 'Are you married?'

I put my empty glass down slowly on the table, giving myself time to think. I haven't given off any signs that could be misinterpreted, have I? She's looking right at me now.

'Not yet, but it won't be long. Sofia's my soulmate. We've been together years.'

'Don't worry. I can imagine what she must look like. I'm not stupid enough to try anything.'

I was too obvious. 'Oh, I didn't mean –'

'What I was trying to get at is... did you and Ellie... like, you know...?'

'Absolutely not.'

She reddens, and before I can say more, she's grabbed the

tray and disappeared downstairs. I pace around the balcony, moving inside onto the landing.

The door to Ellie's old room is ajar, and I push it open. Above the bed, one of Ellie's mum's framed drawings catches my eye. I rest one knee on the bed so I can see better. One of the characters is a human child. Her hair is long, and she's dressed in a nightgown, lying in the grass at the foot of a tree. It has nice detail in the bark and could be the one described in David's poem. That would make the child Ellie... under Philippa's tree? It makes sense; I can imagine her parents talking about it while getting Ellie off to sleep at night. A nice memory David Beck might write about after his wife's death.

I hear footsteps on the stairs and use my phone to take a quick photo of the drawing. As I stand, I notice an iPad on the bedside table. It's an old version, but it's the band stickers on the casing that catch my attention. Instinctively, I shove it into my waistband, pulling my t-shirt over the top. Gaynor told me the police had taken Ellie's devices, but those stickers were not of bands Gaynor would like. I straighten the duvet and wait for her at the foot of the bed.

'That tree with the child laid underneath...' I motion with my finger. 'Could that be the one from David's poem?'

'Maybe,' she says, without really looking at it. 'I told you... nobody ever mentioned it.'

She's upset with me, and as I try to conjure up an excuse to leave, my phone rings in my pocket.

'I've got to go. Thanks for the drink. I'll keep you up to date with how it's all going.' I smile and jog down the stairs and out the front door, pretending to answer, while secretly rejecting the call. It was Yannis. I fully expected to hear from him now Ellie's song is out, and I want to get well away before I speak to him.

A few miles down the A41, I pull into a layby and return the call.

'Yannis, what's up?'

'You prick, you know exactly what you've done.'

I can almost see his temples throbbing under the quiff.

'Look, we're just trying to tell people about what happened to Ellie. She deserves to have her work put out, and you weren't interested after she died, anyway.'

'That's not fair. I liked Ellie, and she was my bloody artist, not yours. You think you can just put out her record without talking to her manager first?'

'I'm not trying to get one over on you, Yannis, just sharing the music like Ellie wanted. Did she sign anything for you?'

He's silent.

'Prick,' he says again, after some thought.

He never gets anything in writing until he's onto a sure thing. He'd have touted Ellie's demo tracks around his contacts at the major labels and if there were no bites, he'd have dropped her without any legal messiness. And without a shred of guilt.

'Look, help us get the word out,' I offer. 'You were the one that scouted her from nowhere – you can take all the credit.'

'And the money?' he spits.

There's silence because I simply can't find the words. If he saw the *Under the Tree* single release online, the charity appeal would've been directly below it. After a moment's reflection, the best I can do is end the call.

Chapter Seventeen

Ellie's Diary • Christmas Day 2015

Christmas. The idea feels ludicrous. I couldn't even go downstairs.
Couldn't even get dressed. It's not actually the tinsel and canned carols
and good cheer I was afraid of, really. It's just that I know I'm not good to
be around. I'm not who I was. I don't even listen to music now, because
I'm scared of missing noises outside. I check the window locks every
hour, and then maybe I sleep properly just before dawn, and I wake with
a headache and a tense band across my chest. I feel sick with nerves.
I keep seeing Danny's attack as clearly as if I'd been there myself. If
someone can do that to him, how am I ever going to feel safe? Gaynor
is trying so hard to be kind. She leaves magazines on the dresser, but
they're not the sort of thing I'd ever read; I'm not really a crosswords and
agony aunt kind of girl.

This morning, I heard Gaynor and her dad talking about making me an
offer on the house. Apparently, he'll move in, and Gaynor and I can live
with him rent-free. I think they're worried I won't pull myself out of this.
I'd appreciate them if I could. I came back to my room, remembering how
Dad used to encourage me to sit under Mum's drawing. 'We'll keep your
mother alive in spirit,' he used to say. All I can do these days is just lie on
the bed, looking up at the drawing, wishing that one or both of them
were here to comfort me now.

Of course, Gaynor and Dennis couldn't leave me alone, not on Christmas Day. Gaynor poked her head around the door and even though I knew it would be her, I still flinched. I tried to pretend I wasn't crying, but she started welling up herself, so I guess my grin looked forced. She put her arm around me. It felt a bit weird, and she must have thought that too, because she grabbed me in a big bear-hug and started rubbing my back. We lost our balance, though, and somehow I ended up underneath her, and she struggled to roll off me. Awkward! And Gaynor's always anxious about her weight, so she was saying sorry in about a hundred different ways. I laughed, to make light of it, and that felt good for a moment, but then I was sobbing not laughing, and she scurried out.

She came back with her dad, each of them carrying a tray. Dennis had a red paper crown on his head. They pulled up chairs around my bed and started eating their turkey dinners. Mine was a vegan tartlet. It could have been cardboard. I balanced the plate on a cushion and tried to force the food down. I picked at it and managed a few mouthfuls. It was nice of them and everything, but I didn't really know what to say. Dennis looked like a student, with his knees together and his feet up on tiptoes to bring his plate high enough.

They drank wine. I couldn't stomach it, but I didn't mind them having some. I didn't hate that they were here.

Dennis got through his meal like a man possessed. He's a man who doesn't like silence. He started talking about Gaynor's training, how well it's going – she looked mortified, but he wouldn't stop. Told me all about the things she's learning, like definitions of burglary and robbery, and how to grade the responses to different kinds of incidents – kidnappings and assaults and the like. I pretended I was interested. I wouldn't have thought it was Gaynor's kind of thing tbh.

Just when I was thinking they might go and leave me in peace, Dennis twisted the conversation round and started telling me how lonely he was in his little house up the road. Gaynor hissed at him – it almost made me smile – and sent him off to get the desserts, and tried to smooth things over. She apologised, like she always does, and then started stuttering about wanting to talk to me, but maybe not now. I put her out of her misery – told her I'd heard them, and yes, I thought it was a good idea, and yes, freeing up some cash would be great, and yes, I could see it would do us all a favour. She looked so happy, I was glad I'd squashed down my misgivings. Anyway, it makes sense. I can't live on my own now, can I?

We agreed to discuss it in detail another time, soon, and then – bizarre! – she started to hint that maybe I might like to work for the police myself. Jesus! I mean, I'm glad she's enjoying her training, and it's great that she's feeling part of something, but it's definitely not for me. Besides, my confidence is blown, like forever.

I told Gaynor that, but she just spouted the same platitudes about how I made it through my mum's death, how I managed caring for my dad, how 'we'll get there'. She smothered me in a big cuddle and I collapsed into despair. I so want to see Dad, and Gaynor says she'll take me, but what if Danny's murderer's following me round?

Then I slept, maybe three or four hours. A respite from this deep sadness and vague sense of dread.

Then this evening Gaynor called me downstairs. Dennis's face told me there was something afoot, and Gaynor spun her laptop around with a flourish and a 'Look who it is!'. The screen was tuned in to Skype, and on the other end was Dad. He was wearing a lopsided Santa hat and he smiled and waved at me. I couldn't bear it.

Chapter Eighteen

Marlon • London • December 2018

I swallow. My mouth is chewing the air again. Gotta try and relax, look like I belong here, just passing through. Hope people round here don't have security cameras, or them new doorbell cams. The house I want should be a bit further up on the left, past the taxi place. I pull my hood over my cap as I pass the waiting room. Should have waited for it to get dark. But there's only one bloke in the window and he's facing the other way. There's not much to hide behind here if it goes wrong, just railings along the road and a few garden walls. Loud dance music suddenly bursts out from a window. Scares me. There's cheering and shouting. I keep my head down and keep going, counting the house numbers. There it is: ninety-seven. I slow down, just enough to get a good look. I think about doing a knock-and-run to see if anyone answers, but it looks dead inside. I know what I'm about to do is wrong. But someone's gotta do it.

I head over to the back where the car park is. Counting along, I think I've found the house I want. I push open the gate and, checking behind me, I slide in and pull the gate closed. The garden's a mess! I sneak up to the back door. I swallow and try to hold my breath, listening for any movement. All I can hear is the music from further up the street. The door is locked, but the windows are old-fashioned. Looks like the big one is raised by a pulley-type-thing, and the catch hasn't been put across. With a bit of jiggling, I push it up just high enough. I drag a plastic recycling box over and stand on it, throwing my left leg into the open window, and pushing off the window ledge to force the rest of my body through. I pull the window back down and squat for a few moments inside. I feel sick.

I wouldn't be here if it wasn't important.

I look around the house, stopping every few moments to listen. This isn't a family home. Cassie would go mad at the dirty pans on the draining board in the kitchen. There's not even a door from the kitchen to the lounge, just a brown curtain. I tread carefully up the narrow staircase. A small bedroom is full of junk, suitcases, books, leftover bits of wood, and a roll of carpet. I check the other bedroom, and it's a bit tidier. But it still feels unloved. A few gadgets and art books. Lots of vinyl stacked in the corner. A carving knife, still in the packet with a matching fork. What sort of nutter keeps a knife in the bedroom?

I pull open a drawer and flick through some papers. I dunno exactly what I'm looking for, but I reckon I'll know it when I see it. If this photographer bloke was the one who killed Ellie's boyfriend, I'll know it, I'm sure I will. I've heard all about Glen Crane, people talking about how he was with Ellie, how he was obviously after something, helping her out for free and everything. I don't trust him.

As I'm about to open the next drawer I hear something. I freeze but force myself to peer out the front window. He's back. I run to the top of the stairs but there's nowhere to go from here. All I can do is hide. The sound now of rustling bags and unpacking downstairs. If I can find somewhere good to hide, and stop the loud thumping noise in my chest, I might get out of this alive. In the corner, there's a rail with clothes hanging on it. I pull it out gently, squeeze myself in to the gap between it and the wall, and sit down. My breath is mad, and I struggle to listen. He is well noisy, so I'm okay for now. My phone pings and I grab it, hands trembling as I struggle to hit the right buttons to silence it. I keep telling myself I haven't done nothing wrong. If the police come, I'm looking into my friend's death. I might even have helped them. Cassie will be proud if it works out alright. Yeah, but this bloke could be a killer. It's sheeps and lambs, innit?

It's gone quiet, too quiet, no sound from a telly or nothing. Why can't he put a film on? Lord Jesus in Heaven, please don't let him come upstairs. Brings back images from church, Mum glancing over at me with a smile that says, 'I hope you're paying attention, darlin', this is good advice.' Well, if I get through this today, I'll make you proud, Mum.

I need to text Ian. He might be able to work something out. Someone will at least know what happened to me if it all goes wrong. I tap out a message, backspace it several times and finally click send. Now I have to try and protect myself. I push the clothes rail enough for me to get out. Tiptoe across the room, testing the squeaky floorboards, and soon I'm back in my hidey hole. I pick at the sticky tape and pull the knife out of the packet. I try a few different grips on the thick handle. Should I hold it like an ice-pick, or is it better to slash around with it? Cassie says people might leave me alone if I just puff out my chest and appear more confident. If I sit quietly maybe this'll all go away. Anyway, now if I need to do something, I'm ready.

Chapter Nineteen

Ian • London • December 2018

The streets are a blur until I hit traffic at Archway. Tapping the steering wheel, I think again about calling Hannan, but I'd rather deal with this myself if I can. What the hell, Marlon?

I got into the iPad on the fifth PIN attempt, having worked through the usual lazy options, the journey back from Gaynor's interrupted by several stops in laybys and London Gateway services to look through the content. It was registered to Gaynor. I was already feeling terrible, but Marlon's text has knocked that into a cocked hat. I undertake a couple of cars, who honk their horns, and move up through the traffic, pulling another illegal move to make the lights onto Junction Road. My ears are itching with anxiety. Dreadful images appear one-by-one, the reel of situations I might find when I get to Glen's. I've got to find a way of getting him out of the house. Options come and go for ideas I can use as excuses for the call, but it's difficult to focus on small details when the serious issues are crashing in.

I park badly and run up to the front door. I exhale sharply to remind myself to breathe and take a second to settle myself. I need to convince Glen that all is well, and that means acting as naturally as I can. Damnit, Marlon, what made you come here? I ring the doorbell. No answer. I try again, adrenaline surges through me. I hear a shout, someone telling me to come round the back. I force my body to steady itself. I can still sort this out safely. I run along the street and round to the back. Through the open door, I glimpse old-fashioned lino and a wooden cupboard at head height.

'Hello?' I push the door wider. Suddenly, all my forward planning is irrelevant.

Glen is sitting on the floor, with his back against the wall. His upper left arm is tied off with a blood-stained tea towel. Kneeling in front of him is Marlon, holding a carving knife to Glen's throat. Glen's head is thrown back against the wall, resisting the tip of the blade. Marlon's face is a frozen mask of panic, his eyebrows fleeing up into his scalp.

'I had to defend myself.'

'You broke into my house!' Glen's eyeballs roll up and towards me, like he just wants the whole thing over with. 'Ian, get this stupid kid off me and call the bloody police, would you?'

I kneel down beside Marlon, leaving the knife at Glen's throat. 'Why did you come here?'

Marlon lets out a gasp of air, like his actions have been justified somehow.

'For God's sake!' Glen's eyes are wider still, staring me down.

'He was too old for Ellie, he was too close to her, there's something wrong with him.'

'How did you know where he lives?'

'My boss.'

'Who's your boss?'

'Yannis. Didn't tell him what it was about.'

'Yannis? What the hell do you do for him?'

'Talent scouting. I found Ellie for him.'

'And that's all you have on Glen – he was close to Ellie?'

Suddenly, Glen's eyes shut tight, and he says, 'Alright, alright! I was in love with her! Is that a crime? I told her... she rejected me... that's it.'

'That's it?' I ask.

'Did I feel guilty? Did I worry it had something to do with her suicide? Yes... at first, I did. We'd argued about it – she felt betrayed – but I told her the truth, and we were good again after that. We were still friends when she came to work with you.'

Marlon's eyes fill at this, and I guide his hand away, taking the knife and sliding it across the floor. Glen's chin drops. Marlon slides back, leans against a kitchen cabinet, puts his head in his hands. I turn to Glen.

'When I went in to meet David Beck, you were off buying chocolate. Was that so he didn't recognise you? Please tell me you didn't know him. Please tell me you didn't take his money to do a job for him. You retired early. How did you afford a house in this street?'

Glen ignores me, sniffing and breathing heavily, hanging his head.

'Answer me.' I take his shoulders in both hands, pull him to face me directly.

'Of course not. My mother died. I sold her house so I could buy this.'

I believe him.

'The police spoke to me. At the time Danny was killed, I was at a media agency conference in Brighton. Twenty of us in the hotel bar.'

I hug him hard, forgetting his injury, until he cries out.

'We're going to have to get that looked at,' I say.

University College Hospital is close enough. I pull into a bay outside the red façade of the Emergency Department and help Glen out of the Mini, his good arm around my neck. We catch each other's gaze for a second as we separate, and he shakes his head in disbelief. I tell him to call me when he's been treated. Then I nod over my shoulder at Marlon to tell him to move into the front seat.

'What will he say?' Marlon asks, as we pull back out onto the Euston Road.

'He'll think of something. But don't try anything stupid like that again.'

Glen has apparently let it go this time, but I wonder how much of that is due to Ellie. So long as we're all committed to the same cause, he can hold back, but what if that common goal ended? Would we see the temper that caught me so off guard before? What else do I know about Glen? He's been the most proactive of the pair of us, making the first moves to contact Ellie's family, going up to visit Danny's brother. His guilt at making Ellie feel uncomfortable when he declared his love for her might've been his motivation. But none of this points to him being involved in murder or serious threats. If I can keep him on my side, he could help in getting to the truth about Ellie and Danny.

Marlon is humming softly.

'So, you discovered Ellie? That's how you knew her?'

'Yeah, she was lit. I'd taken people to meet Yannis before, but he was never interested.'

'How did you get into that?'

'Being around, going to loads of concerts.'

It seems uncharacteristically charitable of Yannis to let a kid like Marlon work for him, but I know him better than that. If he is giving something back, there's more in it for him. 'What does he pay you for the scouting?'

'Nothing.'

'Uh-huh.'

'But I do other stuff for him,' he says quickly. 'While I'm there doing my main job. He gives me cash for that sometimes.'

'Such as?'

Marlon looks out of the side window. 'Packages sometimes, picking stuff up, or delivering to people. I'm there anyway, so it's no problem.'

'Do you know what's in these packages?'

'No.'

'Marlon, you need to stop doing that for him, okay?'

'But –'

'Carry on scouting for him if you like, but I'm telling you to stop all that other stuff right now.' His jaw's going, and he clenches his teeth. 'But I appreciate what you did for me with Warrister, honestly,' I add. 'Take that determination and do something good with it.'

'Can I work for you?' He's stopped slouching in his seat.

'I work on my own,' I say.

'You don't need to pay me.'

'Listen, interning for a bit is one thing, but don't ever offer to work for free. You're worth more than that, okay? You could add value.'

He's grinning. 'If you ever have anything –'

'I'll ask around, see if there's anything that might suit you, yeah?'

'Thanks. My block's just there on the right.'

I drop him outside a block of flats. The entrance drive is flanked by broken bollards and walls missing most of their bricks. I can't help but feel for the kid.

Chapter Twenty

London/Amersham • December 2018

The events of yesterday play across my mind. Part of me is hyper-aware of time slipping away with so much still to do; the other part of me is resigned to thoughtless stupor. It's a miserable combination. It's like a nightmare, in which I am running and failing to put distance between me and the monster at my heels. I ricochet from the strain of negative thoughts to complete emptiness in a moment, and then back again, and I can no longer cope. Sofia appears at just the wrong time.

'Will you answer your Goddamn phone, please?'

I turn my head on the pillow and her hands are on her hips.

'Put it on silent.'

'It already is, vibrating away on the coffee table. What the hell does she want with you anyway?'

'Who?'

'Your Goddamn country girlfriend. She's called you non-stop for fifteen minutes. It's not enough that you drive her all the way home after she gets all pissed?'

'I don't know what she wants.'

'Just answer her, will you?!'

I close my eyes and remain a dead weight on the bed. At this moment, I don't care about anyone's feelings, or my own well-being. I want to disappear completely.

I sense Sofia leaving the bedroom and I remain on my back. I cannot speak. A few empty minutes pass, and I feel a jolt through my entire body. I'm weightless, dropping several feet through the mattress. I regain composure, but I'm left trembling and charged. What the hell was that? I try to shake the feeling out of my head, sitting up and bringing myself round. I drag myself to the bathroom and splash cold water on my face. I have to pull myself out of this. A slamming front door tells me Sofia has gone.

In the kitchenette, the sink is full of dirty dishes, and I fill the bowl with warm soapy water. Something mundane. Just do the dishes for a while, be normal, Ian. The water feels good, and I slowly wash the plates, searching for mugs or anything else I can use to prolong the task. With my hands busy, my mind begins to reset itself, and I take several deep breaths. I try to expel all my air, before breathing in quickly through my mouth and nose. It feels good. I allow the breath to settle into its own rhythm. I fold the tea-towel neatly on the rail, as my phone vibrates again on the table.

The train pulls out of Amersham, and I make my way across the bridge and out onto the street. Gaynor is there, as arranged. Meeting half-way was the compromise we reached. She hugs me lightly and I catch a floral scent of perfume. It catches me off guard, as she sounded annoyed on the phone, and she was already upset yesterday. I take a couple of steps back and hand her the iPad. A thin-lipped smile is my insincere apology.

'Thanks,' she says. 'Shall we get a cup of tea while we're here? There's a place round the corner.'

'I can't be too long.'

'Oh, me neither.'

I follow her around the corner and up the hill. She looks

dressed for high tea, not a cuppa in a greasy spoon. But she stops at a clean, white-fronted café, decorated for Christmas with lights and fake holly, and we take a table by the window. The waitress watches us closely, and I wonder if she's trying to decide whether we're together or father and daughter. We order, and from Gaynor's manner, I can't help feeling she's pushing the impression that we're an item. It's uncomfortable, but maybe I can use her friendliness. She rests her elbows on the table, props up her chin with her palms, bringing her face closer to mine.

'So why did you take it?'

'Sorry, I assumed it was Ellie's.'

'That doesn't mean it's okay,' she says. 'Even if it was Ellie's, I won't have people digging into her private life. There's been enough digging, alright?'

'But the police have seen it, though?'

'Why would they? It was mine.'

'Come on... those band stickers, it must've been Ellie's once?'

'Well, Mr studio techy man has probably broken into it, right?' She taps the iPad with her finger. 'And if there was anything interesting, you wouldn't be here handing it back, would you?'

She's pulled back now, crossing her arms.

'What are you hiding?' I say quickly.

'How dare you?'

I nod, raising my eyebrows, encouraging her to continue.

'Just stop all this. I've been nice to you, but there's nothing more you can do for Ellie. You promised to tell her story and put out her music and you've done it. Now, just leave it alone. I look after Ellie, always have, and she's not suffering anymore, alright? Just let it go.'

The waitress arrives with our drinks and Gaynor turns on her chair to the window. When she turns back, her hand is rubbing her forehead, trying to disguise the redness. I believe her when she says she resents all this digging into Ellie's private life. But I sense something more, and I need to get Gaynor back on side.

'Look. I need to tell you something. My partner, Sofia, she's jealous. Of you.'

'What? Don't be silly.'

'Seriously. That night I dropped you off when you were drunk; she hated that.'

'I'll be back in a minute,' she says, standing and looking for the bathroom.

I notice she's taken the iPad with her and, while she's out of the way, I go to the counter and pay the bill. I don't know how this meeting will end, but I want the option of a quick getaway.

When Gaynor returns, she sits forward in her seat and looks me in the eye. 'Would you have done all this for any other artist you worked with?'

'I don't know.' It's the honest truth, as well. The promise I made myself when I was suffering with grief over my parents was that I'd devote myself to my work and to new talent. But how far that devotion should go might depend on the circumstances. I know for sure I'd give everything I have to bring out the best in any young artist. But like a teacher, there's a line that shouldn't be crossed, in helping a student's learning and intruding on their personal life. I've heard Gaynor talk of Ellie as awkward, but when she came to London and found her voice, found like-minded people, she... must have been almost born again. I connected with her, and – I don't know – maybe I crossed that indistinct line.

'I don't think you'd have done it for anyone else,' she says.

Now it's me looking directly into Gaynor's eyes. 'How did you feel when Ellie went to Oxford?'

'It was her time. She had to start thinking about herself, for once,' she says, almost too quickly.

'I asked how you felt about it.'

'What's that got to do with anything? Nobody cares how I feel.'

'Were you worried about Ellie, going off on her own without you?'

'Of course, but... what does that matter?'

'Did you do anything about it?'

'Like what?'

'I don't know. Did you visit? Did you ask anyone to look out for her while she was in Oxford?'

She stares, open-mouthed, pushes her chair back and storms out. The waitress peers over at me, so I politely order another coffee and a mince pie. I didn't get to say half of what I intended, but it was clearly enough.

Chapter Twenty-one

London • January 2019

'That's it, find which way it naturally wants to go.'

Marlon is here at the studio, learning how to wrap audio cables. I like that he hasn't questioned me on why it's important. It may seem like I'm labouring the point, but when a cable goes dead and you're scrambling around on a dark stage to keep the singer happy, you can't be dealing with twisted mic cables. So, everything about running live sound starts with the basics of setup. Marlon is a good student – so far, at least.

'It'll get more interesting,' I say. 'We'll set up a live sound situation in the main room, exactly as you would at a gig. Boards, monitors, and go through some microphone positioning.'

'Thanks,' he says, but I can see there's something else on his mind. 'I thought Steve was just gonna use me to load in gear and stuff?'

'That's the plan,' I say. 'But let's get you ready to step up when the time's right, yeah? The best producers I know got their start by being available when someone else didn't show up.'

'Okay, cool.'

He's beaming, and I'm pleased to see it. I'm going to do what I can to get him up to speed. Steve Lewis and I had a good chat yesterday. He's seen Marlon around and he's willing to throw him some part-time work, mostly as a favour to me. I've helped Steve out with enough charity gigs. Mostly, I want to sever Marlon's ties with Yannis and give him something to focus on. I don't know how far he'll be able to get, but I want him aiming high. It's all about the dream.

'Did you get hold of Glen?' he asks.

'No, but I wouldn't worry about it. He probably needs some time to process what happened. Grab those tie-wraps off the desk, would you?'

He hands them to me, and I start hanging up the cable loops he's rolled. I don't know what Glen's thinking. He never called me to pick him up from the hospital, like I asked. And he hasn't been returning my calls. I'm going to assume he's taking some time to cool off. Besides, I've had a lot on my mind too. Sofia moved out just after Christmas. She's staying with her friend Simone, on the Holloway Road. She was calm when she told me she was going; just said she needed some breathing space. I had to believe her. She came by last night to pick up some stuff.

'She'll be back soon,' Marlon suddenly says.

'Huh?'

'Your girlfriend... you looked like you were thinking about her.'

'Right...probably.' The kid's sharper than he gets credit for. 'Okay, pull that wedge over. Pretend this area here is centre stage,' I say, making a box shape with my arms.

Marlon manoeuvres the monitor wedge, so the speaker grill points up and towards where the singer would be.

'Is this so the singer can hear themself?' he asks.

'When guitarists are playing a solo, they need something to put their foot on.'

He misses my lame joke, so I quickly follow up with, 'Yes, we can route whatever the singer needs to hear to this. They might just want their own voice, or they might want anything else from the rest of the band. If they can't hear properly, the show will be a disaster – so it needs to be right.'

'One time I saw Ellie play, and the crowd were all talking and shouting over her. I hated them. I got up on stage and shouted at them.'

'Was that in Croydon? Turned into a big fight?'

'Yeah.'

'That was you?' I can't help but grin. 'Glen told me. He took pictures of the brawl.'

'But she could probably hear herself fine through one of these,' he says, pointing at the wedge he's still examining.

'Yeah, but it's more about respect for the performer. I don't blame you for saying something.'

'No, I just thought she wouldn't be able to hear herself, with all the noise they were making.'

He's giving this way too much thought, so I suggest we take a break.

Marlon tucks into his cheese sandwich, and I sit across from him on the other leather sofa with a coffee.

'So, you must've met Glen at that gig – Ellie can't have been in London long at that point?'

'It was the second time I saw her. Went down specially… see if I could talk to her. I didn't meet Glen, though. Ellie took me outside.'

'She didn't like her acquaintances mixing. Everyone says the same thing.'

I pull up Facebook on my phone, find my way to Glen's page, and scroll down to posts from early 2018. Eventually, I find a pic of the brawl. Glen had posted it with an amusing caption. Marlon comes and looks at it over my shoulder. We can't make out any faces, just an arty collage of chaos. The comments are banal, but one of them catches my attention because the profile picture features Ellie's face. I click on it and am taken to the profile of someone called Andrew Raine.

'Know him?' I ask Marlon.

'No.'

I get why Andrew Raine has used this as his profile image. He's older than Ellie, and in the black and white shot, she's glamorous, against his own fat face in soft focus behind her. There are a few other pictures of them playing guitars together, but they're rehearsals – all in someone's house, rather than a gig venue. Maybe this was a brief partnership when she first arrived in London. The pics are dated January 2018. I make a mental note to find Andrew Raine and talk to him. He might be able to tell me about Ellie's early days in London.

Marlon returns to his sofa and slouches into it, his legs wide. He looks more confident now – I think the training is helping him already.

'You know Ellie's story about her protector...'

'Course.'

'It seems you might've been the only person she shared that with.'

'Probably – she did tell me to keep it to myself. I only told you because of Warrister, remember? I thought it might be him.'

I shake my head, staring at the floor, lost in thought. 'She told you she couldn't go to the police because this guy had started threatening her friends?'

'Yeah.'

'Well, nobody else knew about the protector until you mentioned it – so I'm wondering who was threatened.'

'I dunno.'

'Hannan wondered if she made it up to keep you away from the studio – so you wouldn't be around when she was found dead.'

Marlon's eyes widen. 'That's mad! She was telling the truth. Why would Hannan say that?'

'You're convinced Ellie was being honest?'

'One hundred percent. She was crying, telling me about it – we were right here.'

I reach over and put a hand on Marlon's shoulder. 'I'm just trying to work out all the possibilities. She may have been crying because she was planning to kill herself.'

Marlon's the one shaking his head now, probably grasping at all the possible truths. 'I didn't just pop in whenever I wanted, you know?' he eventually says.

I shrug. 'No?'

'You said she might've lied to keep me away? Well, I never went unless she called to invite me – after you'd left for the day – she always told me when it was okay to come.'

'Okay, that does make it unlikely she'd need to invent something to keep you away...'

'Exactly!'

'Know anything about a Gaynor?'

'Don't think so.'

'Blonde, largish girl, Ellie's age.'

He shakes his head.

'She kept a lot to herself, didn't she?'

He nods and takes his plate over to the sink.

By mid-afternoon, we've laid out a full rig, and I've given Marlon a run-down of each piece. Behind a small mixer, I talk him through one of the channel strips, starting with the input, working down through the EQ section and finally how to assign a signal to busses. I ask him how comfortable he is with the channel strip, and he nods enthusiastically, so I let him into a secret. I tell him the rest of the mixing board is mostly more of the same. It just looks daunting because of how many channel strips there are. He grins like a huge puzzle has begun revealing itself.

'You're doing great, Marlon. Honestly, we've covered way more than I intended today.'

His tucks in his lips, like he's trying not to look proud and nods his head energetically.

'How does your sister feel about all this?'

'Loves it – she's glad.'

'I wondered if she'd want you away from me, after Warrister attacked you,' I say.

He looks away, rubbing the back of his neck. 'I err... didn't tell her about any of that.'

'Oh, what about your head?'

'I said it happened in a mosh pit. I didn't want her to worry.'

I get it – but I should really introduce myself to Cassie at some point.

Chapter Twenty-two

London • January 2019

Nearly home. Climbing the stairwell, I feel a comforting ache in my hamstrings: proof of a good day's work, moving gear around with Marlon, and a brisk walk from the tube station. Things are working out well with Marlon. I just wish things were as good with Sofia. Even though I've been out all day, simply knowing that she's moved more stuff out is enough to make me miss her. I slow my steps, not relishing the anticipation of an empty flat. I wonder if that was how Sofia felt, when I was out working.

As I reach my floor, there's someone sitting by the gate. Gaynor. Propped against the wall, scrolling through her phone.

'What the hell are you doing here?'

Startled, she struggles to get to her feet, inching away from me like I've come on too aggressively. 'Sorry, sorry... but I need to talk to you. Please, I've been here ages.'

'How do you know where I live?' I ask, before remembering she works for the police.

'Voters' register... I shouldn't have looked you up, but I really need to talk.'

I want her gone, right now. I'm about to shout, but one of the neighbour's windows opens and I'm left with no choice but to get her inside quietly.

'Come on then,' I say, unlocking the gate and the front door, and ushering her in. At least she's not dressed like she wants to seduce me today – just trousers and a plain top. The perfume's still overpowering though, as she moves past me to the sofa. I nod to confirm she may sit.

'Something to drink?'

'Just a cold drink, if that's okay?' she says, placing her handbag carefully at her side.

I pour her a lemonade and wait for my coffee machine to warm up.

'So, what is it?'

'Do you know why I was angry in the coffee shop? Why I left?'

'Not really.'

'Because I was hurt. You asked me how I felt when Ellie went to Oxford, remember? Nobody ever asks how I feel about anything.' She starts to blush.

'I remember.'

'Well... it caught me off guard a bit... I thought maybe you cared about me. And you said your girlfriend was jealous.' She looks the other way and brings a hand up to her face.

'I'm sorry if I upset you... I –'

'But then you started insinuating I should've visited Ellie in Oxford – I wanted to; she wouldn't let me – and looked out for her, and all this stuff.' Her eyes are moistening, and her voice starts to quiver. 'That really hurt, you know?'

'I'm sorry.'

'But then afterwards, when I'd had time to think about it, I worried I'd misunderstood you. What if you thought I had actually gone to Oxford, and was somehow involved? What if you suspected me of causing Danny's death or something terrible like that?' She looks right at me now, because she wants to know for sure what I think about her.

I don't really suspect her of anything; she's not aggressive. I just feel like there's more going on than she's willing to admit. But she's here and talking now, so I want to keep the dialogue open.

'I don't think that. Let me get my coffee; hold on.'

As I return to the sofa with my drink, she's looking at one of Sofia's fashion magazines.

'Will she be home soon, your girlfriend? I don't want to cause any problems.'

'No, she won't be home for a while.'

Gaynor puts the magazine back on the table and fixes a clip in her hair.

'It's bad enough you thinking I might've let Ellie down – not being there for her. But I couldn't stand you believing I might have been involved in Danny's murder. That's why I looked up your address. I need to convince you that I'm not hiding anything... from you, or anybody else.'

I sense she's more worried about my opinions than anybody else's. I hope that's because she's nipping any suspicions in the bud in case I decide to take them to the police. The only other, rather worrying, alternative is that she really does care deeply what I think of her.

'I'm getting desperate,' I say. 'There's so much about Ellie's suicide that I don't understand. I've been asking everyone uncomfortable questions. Don't take it personally. I always try to get to know my clients. I make a commitment to them at the start of any project. I did the same with Ellie, but it feels so... unresolved.'

She nods, shifting her hips on the sofa to turn my way a bit more. 'My mum died when I was young, too. Cancer, like Ellie's mum. I didn't accept it for the longest time. I couldn't understand how she could just... stop existing?'

'That's a common response. Understandable.'

'But time shifts your perspective; helps you process the truth properly,' she says, and takes my hand in hers.

'That's not what's happening here.' I rub her hand as a friendly gesture and disengage quickly. 'When I know the truth about Ellie's death, I'll let it go.'

'I'm sorry, of course I'm not the only one to have experienced grief... I didn't mean to –'

'You didn't, don't worry about it.'

It's starting to feel wrong, sitting here with another woman. It was strangely pleasant when she took my hand like that.

'Do you not feel it?' I ask her. 'That sense that something's not quite resolved in Ellie's death?'

'I was protective of her when she was alive; I told you. But no, I believe the coroner that she took her own life. I truly feel it's okay to accept that.' She reaches an arm around my neck, and I put my coffee cup down, accepting her hug. She pulls me closer and rocks gently, nestling her head in my chest. The warmth surprises me, and against all better judgement, I allow the contact. A feeling of contentment catches me unawares. The emptiness from my home I'd anticipated, coming up the stairwell, has been filled with an unexpected comfort. I can hear her breathing, feel the pressure of her body against mine with each deep inhale. Her hair lightly brushes against my face.

'I was always the sidekick,' she says, her voice soft against my chest.

'Sorry?'

She giggles. 'In the playground, I mean. When I was small. I would always make sure I wasn't the hero. I liked to have someone to defer to, I guess.'

'Were you shy?'

'Definitely. But I had to play the supporting role. I didn't realise at the time, of course, I just always told whoever I was playing with to be the hero of whatever was on TV at the time.'

'You weren't skipping and playing kiss-chase then?' I chuckle.

'Ha-ha, no. It was always super-heroes for me.'

'And now you fight crime with the police.'

She jabs me in the ribs. 'Shut up, you.'

'Seriously, there must be something in you that's always wanted to help people.'

'I guess there is. But the appeal of the police was becoming part of something. I never had that. It was either me and my dad, or me and Ellie, when she was around. I want to help people as well, of course.'

'I get that.'

She manoeuvres her head out from under my arm and shifts her body. Her eyes lock onto mine. Her face is close, and her expression is neutral, like she's waiting for something. There's a strange tingling across my skin. Time seems to slow.

Suddenly, there's the sound of the gate swinging open. I immediately pull away. I creep to the door and look through the spyhole. If Sofia is there, I've got one hell of a problem. I can't see clearly, but – thank her God – it's not her. I open the door a crack and a delivery guy hands me a package, a parcel for Sofia. I rub my face with both hands, breathing heavily. Gaynor has disappeared. Moments later she emerges from the bathroom.

'I've got some work I need to get to,' I say.

She reaches past me and grabs her handbag, straightening her top as she moves towards the door. 'I could hang around if you want? Meet later for a drink, or something?'

'I don't think that's a good idea.'

'Oh?'

'We probably shouldn't see each other again,' I say, with conviction this time.

She marches out and slams the front door behind her.

I open my laptop and regret not asking Gaynor to look up an address for Andrew Raine. But I quickly decide that would have been wrong. Instead, I bring up Andrew's profile on Facebook and send him a friend request. He accepts it, and a private message appears shortly after: Ian Wren! I'm honoured!

Several messages later, I've established he knows his music and has bought Ellie's charity single. He's also given me his mobile number, and I call it.

'Andrew, thanks for talking to me.'

'Are you kidding?' he says, in a high voice. 'I love your stuff.'

'You said you were in a band with Ellie Beck?'

'Yeah, kind of.'

'I'm trying to learn more about her; can you tell me?'

'I still can't get over what she did. So sad. It wasn't really a band. I met her at an open mic, and we started rehearsing a bit at my place. She stayed for a few days, because she'd only just moved to London and needed a bed.'

'Nothing happened with the band?'

'Nah. She stopped coming after a while.'

'How come?'

'No falling out or anything. I thought maybe her boyfriend didn't like her doing it.'

'Boyfriend? Who was that?'

'Well, I assumed it was her boyfriend because he seemed a bit jealous. Actually, I don't know whether they were together or not. But she stopped coming round after he visited, that's all.'

'D'you remember his name?'

'Jude, I think.'

I wake far too early. The world is still silent and dark. I close my eyes again and try to get back to my dream. It felt like Sofia was with me. We were together again in bed. She held me close, like nothing had gone wrong between us. I must've woken suddenly because I can recall the dream in vivid detail: the feel of her legs clasping the sides of my body, her warm hands on my chest. We were together again, if only for a while in my subconscious. I slow my breathing, because my heart's pounding, and I want to bring back the feeling of the dream. I want to return to her. I resist glancing at the alarm clock on the bedside table. I'm not ready to connect with the real world yet. I let every other thought drift away, focusing on an image of Sofia and the sensation of her against my skin.

The click of a door pulled shut jolts me out of my slumber. Instantly, I'm fully awake, my heart pumping blood around my body. I crash out of the bedroom door and across the flat, flashes of realisation flitting around my brain. Someone has just left. The puzzle pieces are starting to form as my mind awakes. By the time I reach the front door and peer through the spyhole, I can recall last night quite clearly. Gaynor had returned a few hours after she'd left. She'd been drinking. She threw stones at the window. She was in no state to get herself home – predictably – so I brought her up to the flat and gave her some coffee. It was just like the night at the Dublin Castle, but I wasn't prepared to drive her all the way home a second time. I was done with going out of my way for her.

I let her sleep on the couch. When she sobers up, I thought, she can sort herself out. I'd done enough just getting her off the street where she'd have been robbed, or worse.

Now she must've decided she was well enough to get herself home. Probably embarrassed as hell, I'd imagine.

Chapter Twenty-three

Oxford • January 2019

I queue for a table at the café in the covered market. Despite the cold, Oxford is crammed with tourists. The weather is bright, and I've had to fight my way through multiple walking tours, with Americans and Japanese stopping suddenly in front of me to take pictures. I'd expected it to be quiet, with students still away for the Christmas break, but I couldn't have been more wrong. I tuck into my fried eggs, frustrated with my morning's work. Trying to find the de Vries brothers is more difficult than Glen made out. I'd called him first, of course, to get Jon's address, but he's still not picking up. He didn't seem to be in when I went to his house last night either. I tried him again this morning, but nothing. Again, I could have asked Gaynor to look the information up for me, but after yesterday I want to distance myself. Anyway, she said she had a few days off work.

I started at the homeless shelters Glen mentioned, and tried not to appear too desperate. I don't know what approach Glen used, but my people skills aren't working here. I've spent most of the morning trying anyone who looked vaguely medicated, and I've got nowhere at all. Suddenly my phone rings. I don't recognise the number. I hurry to swallow my mouthful of food.

'Hello?'

'Ian, hi, it's Deborah Harvey.'

'Sorry, do I...?' I nod at the family looking expectantly at my table and step outside. 'Sorry about that. Who did you say was calling?'

'Deborah Harvey. You spoke to my colleague at St Peter's.'

'Oh, Deborah, I'm sorry, I wasn't given a name. To be honest I didn't expect anyone to call me back. But I was coming to Oxford and called on the off-chance. I didn't expect anyone to be around in the holidays.'

'I live nearby. Where are you?'

'On the High Street, by the covered market. I'd really appreciate your time, Deborah. I was Ellie's friend.'

'I know who you are. I could meet you in Christ Church Meadow. Half an hour, by the front gate?'

'Perfect, thank you.'

Around the corner, I stare vacantly at what I think is the Radcliffe Camera building. I'm both pleased and perplexed that anyone from the university can be bothered to meet me. Behind, I hear a young couple wondering why a library is called a 'camera', and another voice calls out, 'It's Latin for "room".' I turn my head and the couple mutter a quick thank you before disappearing. They don't want to engage with the homeless girl sat in a doorway.

I smile, moving towards her.

'How many times have I heard that conversation?' she says, flashing a crooked smile. 'They should just change the bloody name.' Her face is round, with long, matted hair stuck to it in places. She has a northern accent.

'How are you?'

'It's a sunny day... makes a difference.'

I pat my pockets. 'I'm afraid I don't have any change.' It all went on the morning's fruitless bribes.

'No bother,' says the girl, and stretches out her legs. The soles of her heavy boots are well-worn, like the rest of her kit. 'I'm Nix.'

'Ian. Where do you… stay?'

'Wherever I can pitch this and be gone before daylight,' she says, tapping a fabric bundle beside her. 'I tried hostels, but I can't be around some of the folk there.'

'Actually, I may have something.' I remember a ten-pound note in my back pocket and press it into her little hand.

A beer-bellied bloke passes by with, 'Yeah, well done, mate,' and claps me slowly.

Nix stands and clinches me in a bearhug. 'Sorry… bit smelly.'

'It's fine. What keeps you going, Nix?' I realise that's clumsy as soon as it leaves my mouth.

'You what?'

I'm wondering if the discomfort of living like she does outweighs any flash of pleasure. 'Oh, just wondering how generous people are here.'

'It's not great,' she says and coughs loudly into a balled fist.

I turn my head away, a bit embarrassed, but then we chat for a while about the unkindness of strangers. She tells me how she's been attacked, more than once.

'I was never injured or anything, but it's frightening. You don't know who they are or what they're capable of. Wouldn't take much to, you know…'

'Terrible.' I empathise with her, and then gently use the violence and drugs link to steer the conversation towards the de Vries brothers. Nix doesn't look like a user, but she admits to knowing who they are.

'I need to talk to them. Do you know where they live?'

'Pleased to say I don't.'

'Oh, okay. Well, I need to get going. Nice talking to you, Nix.'

'Yeah, thanks so much for the cash.'

'Don't mention it. Look after yourself.'

'Be careful,' she calls, as I walk away.

It looks like Deborah Harvey has beaten me to the gates. A tall woman, elegant but with the air of a kindly aunt about her, appears to be waiting for someone. She smiles expectantly as I make eye-contact. I introduce myself and she shakes my hand, smiling broadly.

'Let's walk,' she says. Her earrings dance about her face as she turns. Christ Church Meadow is as busy as the streets, with small, animated groups walking and talking, drinking take-away coffee, or admiring the impressive architecture of Christ Church itself.

'I'm surprised you made the time to meet with me.'

'You knew Danny and Ellie – of course I'm happy to meet you. I haven't stopped thinking about them, you know?'

I like that she uses 'you know' like the rest of us, despite her posh accent.

'I only knew Ellie. I was working with her when she died.'

'Of course. I bought the recording you put out. I'm so glad she carried on with music. I was told you had some questions you wanted to ask?'

'Well... I'm a bit embarrassed taking up your time because there's nothing specific –'

'It's fine,' she says, bumping my arm with her elbow, as we walk. I like her even more for that. She tells me the wide path we're on is called the Broad Walk.

'You were their teacher... lecturer?'

'They used to come to my tutorial groups together. They were lovely. Danny was always so positive.' She pauses, smiling at the memory. 'He found the work difficult at first, but he kept on smiling, kept on going. He had enough natural talent to get through the things he didn't find so easy.'

'Ellie helped him?'

'Oh yes. She was exceptionally bright. But timid, and shy.'

'Did you know they were together?'

'Of course! Ellie tried to disguise it, but I could tell. I like tutorials – you really get to know your students; not like lectures, which I could truly do without.'

'They both had so much to deal with.'

'I can still see them both sitting there. Demure little Ellie with the patience of a saint; Danny's leg starting to twitch whenever he had to sit still for longer than a minute. It's no wonder they got along so well, like... complementary personalities, you know?'

We take a path beside a narrow part of the river, and, after a short while, Deborah stops, raising both hands to her face. 'This is where he was found,' she says, softly.

Even though the area is busy, this spot seems secluded, with bends in the footpath and encroaching trees. And Danny was killed in the evening. I try to make out any scuff marks around the tree, left by the chain, but I don't want to ask Deborah about that side of things.

'He was found in the morning by a homeless person. Poor thing.'

I wonder whether she means Danny or the poor soul who made the gruesome discovery.

This time it's me who gestures for us to walk, and we carry on until we reach a bench, where we sit for a while.

I say, 'Did you ever see any disagreements between them and anyone else?'

'Not at all. I thought hard about it at the time because I

couldn't believe anyone could do this. Danny was too adorable to upset anyone, and Ellie would've walked away from the first hint of any argument.'

'There was no-one hassling either of them, bugging them or anything?'

'No. I'm convinced it was a random attack. There's no way anyone would target Danny if they knew him. Not with everything he was going through with his health. He was a superstar.' She looks away, catching her emotions.

'It's lovely that you knew them so well. I always imagined university to be just sitting up in the gallery listening to a musty old professor rattling on.'

She laughs. 'We still have those as well.'

'I was talking to a friend of Ellie's – her best friend, actually – and she was telling me how she saw one of her old schoolteachers years later in the street. Just bumped into her. This teacher had a huge impact on Gaynor – that's Ellie's friend – recognised a spark of talent in her creative writing and took her under his wing.'

'Lovely.'

'Yeah, the first person to even notice her, Gaynor said. She felt like she'd been given permission to pursue English language as her thing, and she did quite well. But when she bumped into this teacher years later, he didn't recognise her at all.'

'Teachers see a lot of faces.'

'I know. She said it kind of undid that little glimmer of validation she'd been given all those years ago.'

'That's a shame. I understand how it might happen, though. But I won't ever forget Danny and Ellie. How could I? We held a concert for Danny when the new term started. I wrote a piece for him as well. It was a shame Ellie couldn't join us, but that didn't surprise me, poor girl.'

'Same. I wrote something for Ellie.'

'You're a musician too?'

'Sure,' I laugh.

Deborah raises her eyebrows.

'It's how most of us get into engineering and then producing. I started out playing guitar in bands at school. I enjoyed song writing more than showing off, so I never got around to learning music in the traditional sense.'

'That's still valid. If music moves you, does it matter if the composer understand why it works, or how to write it down on paper?'

'Not to me.'

'It's unnecessary for your industry. I didn't have a choice. My father had me practising scales at the piano religiously every evening. But it was necessary for everything I went on to do with the orchestra and then teaching.'

'One day, I keep saying, I'll sit down and try to work at it.'

She nods, and we sit quietly as a family passes by on the footpath. They're all laughing as one of the youngsters pretends to push his brother into the water. They probably have no idea what happened down here.

'You asked me if anyone was hassling them, before...' Deborah says.

'Yeah.'

'What made you think that? Anything specific?'

'No, just fishing for a motive. Nobody seems to think they had any enemies; it's frustrating.'

'We see some bullying from time to time here, but there wasn't even any of that with Danny and Ellie. The only aggression was when Danny's brothers kept coming around.'

'I heard they made a nuisance of themselves.'

'Horrible. We called the police several times, but they couldn't do much. Some of the students said they were intimidated for information on Danny's murder, but they still wouldn't pursue it.'

'I hear the de Vries brothers are dangerous. I wouldn't be surprised if they pressed those students harder than they're willing to admit.'

'One poor boy ended up with a shattered jaw. He told police it was the brothers, but – unsurprisingly – they had a solid alibi.'

That detail concerns me enough that I turn away from her.

'It stopped, thank goodness, when they realised nobody knew anything. One was scarier than the other. Jon, I believe.'

'I'd like to talk to them; that's why I came down.'

'Please don't. It's not worth riling them.'

'Don't worry. I spent all morning trying to find them, but it looks like I'll be going home without introducing myself. I'm grateful to you for meeting me. Do you mind if I keep your number in my phone?'

'Of course not. I'll keep promoting your charity single whenever I can. If I think of anything else I can do, I'll be in touch.'

'Appreciate it. Thanks, Deborah.'

We shake hands again and she heads back towards the main gate, as I leave by a different exit, towards the High Street. I'd like to talk to Nix again.

I head down between some buildings. A few steps into the alleyway and something thuds against my legs. They buckle uselessly beneath me, and in a blur of confusion, I notice my senses gradually shutting down.

Chapter Twenty-four

Oxford/Aylesbury • January 2019

I came to in the ambulance, and now I sit with the masses in the waiting room, in line for a full check-over. No major issues expected, apart from a bump on the head and some bruising to my legs, but they want to monitor me. The nurse asked if I should be reporting it, but the last thing I want is police involvement, just as I'm starting to make some headway. I've made out it was an accident – I told the nurse I heard the sound of a bike behind me, just before the impact – and she hasn't pursued it so far.

A skinny bloke with a shaved head appears in the doorway. The type of character that puts the waiting patients on edge, hoping he doesn't take a seat near them. He quickly makes eye contact with me, striding over to where I'm sitting.

'You're looking for us?' he asks. He doesn't maintain the eye contact but carries an intimidating presence anyway.

'Maybe. Depends who you are.'

'Outside,' he barks, and I follow him, the soreness in my legs increasing.

Under the A&E entrance canopy, he leans against a concrete pillar beneath the no-smoking sticker and immediately lights a cigarette.

'Jude?' I ask, as friendly as I can. The movement has jolted my headache into action again.

He nods. 'Jon doesn't know I'm here, so you're lucky. Why have you been asking about us?'

'Who attacked me in the alley?' I try to convey no malice.

He takes a long drag on his cigarette. 'I'm more curious than he is, so tell me what you want.'

'Ellie Beck was a friend of mine. I'm trying to piece together what happened to her, and I heard you visited her in London.'

'So?'

I just shrug and leave some silence.

'We wanted to see if she'd heard any more about Danny's murder. If you know anything you better tell me now.' I sense a reluctance in him.

'The guy she was staying with thought you were her boyfriend.'

His eyes bulge, and he puts his pale face right up to mine. 'Danny was her boyfriend.'

'Right. She left where she was staying after that. Do you know where she went?'

'No. I didn't see her again.'

'It was just the one time?'

'Yeah – I told you. Why?'

'No reason. Just trying to piece it together.'

'She was good for Danny, innit?' he says, and backs off a bit. 'I thought we owed her for her loyalty, but she said she had to distance herself from everything – I never saw her again.'

'Jon never visited Ellie in London?'

'Jon's a bastard. But she'd talk to me.'

I'm starting to understand the dynamics between the brothers and wonder if Jude is as intimidated by Jon as everyone else seems to be.

Jude suddenly says, 'Danny was fire for her too. It wasn't just one-sided. She was all shy and that. Danny got her involved.'

'And they had the music,' I add.

'Danny had it, man – a natural.'

'How did he become ill?' I ask.

Jude stares again. He's been fidgeting since we started talking, shifting his feet, his hands going in and out of his pockets.

I quickly change the subject, insinuating my question was as nonchalant as the waffle I'm now spilling. He joins in a little but seems more cautious.

'So, what? All you wanted was to find out about Ellie? Don't lie to me.'

'Yes.'

A calm voice interrupts our conversation. 'You can't smoke here.'

It's a doctor, in white coat and NHS lanyard. But he's exuding another level of authority. Jude stubs out his cigarette. The doctor moves away, like the confrontation is nothing more than another ordinary moment in the day. I didn't expect Jude to comply so easily.

A woman shouts at us from the door. 'Ian Wren? They're calling for you.'

I signal I'm on my way, and as I turn back, Jude has gone.

The taxi drops me at Milton House Nursing Home. I slept a little in the hospital waiting room and a little more on the journey to Aylesbury, but I'm still tired. My legs take a minute to free up as I walk to the door and ring the bell. No answer. I thought that might be the case this late in the evening. Movement catches my eye through the glass, and the door swings open, a friendly lady holding it for me as she leaves. I smile back and move inside as casually as I can. But the lack of security shocks me. I suppose they're more concerned with vulnerable patients escaping than anyone getting in.

On the second floor I try the door code they used last time I visited David Beck, but it's been changed. A gaggle of female voices echoes down from the end of the corridor, like they're playing a game. There's no bell on the door and I won't be able to get their attention. Just then a voice from behind says, 'Visiting hours are over, Sir, sorry.' I turn, and it's the Asian carer from before.

'Oh, hello again,' he smiles.

'Hey. Nice to see you...?' I didn't catch his name before.

'Jamie.' He shakes my hand.

'I'm Ian,' I say, but he seems to have remembered.

'I bought the single, even though I still play David the copy you left every day. Love the artwork. I showed it to David.'

'What did he think?' I ask.

He gives a thin smile, shaking his head slowly. 'I don't think he knew what it was.'

'I thought I'd call in and see how he was. I've been in Oxford today.'

'Are you okay?' Jamie asks, as I change my posture uncomfortably.

'Had a bit of a fall earlier, but I'll be fine.'

'Come and have a seat,' he says and keys in the door code.

There are a couple of chairs and a small coffee table outside David Beck's room. His name is on the door plate, and beside it is a display cabinet, where personal items can be placed. I had noticed trophies, trinkets, and cuddly toys displayed by some of the other rooms we passed, but David's is empty.

Jamie pulls out a chair for me, as he pops his head around David's door. 'He's asleep,' he says, 'I'll put the kettle on.'

'Great, thanks.'

After a few minutes he returns with two mugs of tea and takes a seat, perching on the edge quite effeminately.

'Last time I was here I started asking about David's poem and I'd hoped to show him a photograph I took on my phone. It's a sketch his wife did.'

He looks at me sympathetically. 'David's gone downhill quite a lot since you were here last. I still talk to him like I always have, and do the same things for him, but he can't talk to me anymore.'

'Is that expected?'

'Sure. To be honest, David's been with us longer than we anticipated when he was brought in. Often, our residents are only with us for eighteen months or so.'

I've seen Jamie with David, and I admire the humanity and dignity he shows him. It must be especially hard to have his patient's estimated decline in the back of his mind that whole time.

'They still don't know what causes Parkinson's, do they?'

'A mix of genes and environmental factors, like exposure to toxins? But no one knows for sure yet. The nerve cells just die and can't produce enough dopamine.'

'Cruel, isn't it, the slow decline? The brain's so fragile.' My mind wanders to my own weaknesses. 'Something weird happened to me the other night. I was lying in bed and felt like the ground gave way. Like I fell a few feet. It's left me a bit unsteady to be honest.'

Jamie listens with his head cocked to the side, and I'm surprised at my openness. But it feels good to say it out loud. It's easy to talk to Jamie.

'Have you been under a lot of pressure?' he says.

'You could say that.' I chuckle, to hide my worry. 'Since it happened, I've had a few moments where I've felt a bit out of control. Like I'm going to drop what I'm holding or something. Not quite right...'

'Sounds like a bit of anxiety,' he says. 'Look up some breathing techniques, or meditation. Give yourself some time to relax.'

That's what I wanted to hear. Maybe I'll get some rest when this is all over. I like Jamie. I saw his eyes moisten when he was talking about David. The way he listened to me just now leads me to believe I can trust him.

'Does David have any visitors, other than Emma?'

'No.'

'Did he ever?'

'Only Ellie. And after everything happened, she used to Skype him sometimes. I'd set up the laptop for them.'

'Did David ever worry about Ellie being away?'

Jamie raises his eyebrows.

'Did he ever say anything like that?'

He's silent for a moment. 'Honestly, by the time someone comes to us, they're not capable of thinking like that.'

David was a meticulous planner. He looked after Ellie for so long by himself, wrote about having to have 'the force of two' in his poem. Is it a stretch to think he set something up a long time before he became ill? I begin to wonder if I'm trying to convince myself of the protector theory, making the pieces fit whether they belong or not.

A woman calls from the other end of the corridor, and Jamie heads down to see her. I push open the door to David Beck's room, curious to see inside. He is asleep in bed, his thin fingers grasping the clean white duvet pulled up under his chin. I scan the room. There are a few photo frames containing pictures of Ellie and her mother, but otherwise it could be a hotel room. A fidget from the bed, and I turn to see David staring with saucer eyes, keeping a firm grasp on the duvet.

'Sorry,' I mouth gently.

He holds my gaze, his face soon relaxing into a neutral expression, his nose wrinkling like he's woken without a care in the world.

'Hello. We met before; I'm Ellie's friend.'

He doesn't seem to connect, so I search my phone for the picture of the fantasy drawing and hold it up. His eyes close from the glare and I hold the phone further back. He looks at it but doesn't seem to register any significance. It was worth a shot. I tap his hand gently as a goodbye gesture, but he grasps it, and smiles deeply at me. It's a tight grip and all I can do is return the warm smile and wait to be dismissed by my parade-ground sergeant major. I'm sure it isn't as long as it feels, but eventually his eyes close and he falls back asleep. With some uncomfortable manoeuvring, I'm able to prise my hand away and slip outside, closing the door gently behind me.

Chapter Twenty-five

Marlon • London • January 2019

'So, which is it?' Steve Lewis asks. 'Are you a "tool person", or a "partner person"?'

Man, that could be taken in so many ways. I'd be laughing my head off at the rude way if he hadn't been telling me the story. A guitar was nicked at the gig last night. The first time I get to work with him, and something gets robbed. I'm glad no-one pointed the finger at me. It was some little pub in Dalston, but the band had called in a professional guitar player to cover for their usual guy who was sick. I missed the whole theft thing, but Steve's filling me in. It was a Guild Starfire, a red one. It was worth loads, but Steve says it's not about the money.

'I've never owned a guitar,' I say, with a shrug.

'Doesn't matter.' He starts to roll a cigarette, and takes so long with it, I start watching what's happening behind him. Steve told the café owner we wanted a table on the pavement, and there's a few sus kids around, spitting and dissing each other. We're getting a few looks, and I try to watch them without making it obvious.

'Doesn't matter whether you've owned a guitar or not,' he starts again, with his cigarette rolled and lit. 'It's your character. Some people see things as tools, others see them as partners in what they're trying to achieve. Take my old man, for example

– he was a motocross rider, good one in his day. Used to spend all his time in the garage tuning his bike, cleaning it, spending everything he had on parts. One time he set up in the kitchen because the light was better for working on the carburettor. My mum wasn't having any of that. Threw him straight out.'

Steve laughs and takes a long drag on his cigarette, and I keep watching the kids behind him jostle each other closer to us.

'When he stopped racing, he just chucked the bike in the garage. Don't think he even looked at it after that, it just sat there rusting away. It was a tool, see? When he was using the tool, he'd spend every hour available with it, but when he didn't need it anymore, it meant nothing to him.'

'That guitarist, he was a 'partner' person, then?'

'Sure was. He was in bits! Literally in tears that he'd lost his guitar. He said he'd been given it by someone and there was a bit of a story... Jim Mullens, you know? Jim was producing something he was working on and gifted him the guitar because he'd connected with it.'

'It looked nice on stage.'

'A beauty, for sure, but more important was his relationship with it. He said Jim Mullens noticed how differently it made him play. It stopped him playing in a regular way, somehow.'

'Nice one.'

'Have you heard Jim's bands?'

'I don't really know him.'

'He loves it when guitarists don't play the obvious stuff. He'd have felt obliged to hand over the guitar when he saw the difference it made.'

'What's the guy gonna do?'

'Put the word out. But honestly, unless it ends up in the hands of someone famous and gets seen in a magazine, it's

151

probably gone forever. Some doper probably pawned it for a tenner somewhere.'

One of the kids is watching us now. He can't be more than ten or eleven, the only white face in the gang, the youngest too. Nice trainers.

Steve says, 'You got anything you treasure?'

'Um, a dictionary my mum gave me?'

'Do you use it? Would you feel emotional if it got stolen?'

'Definitely. I can't spell.'

'If you suddenly became Susie Dent, would you still keep the dictionary?'

'Who is that?'

'Your mobile phone can tell you how to spell something, but you still refer to the dictionary at home?'

'Yeah, I've had it since I was small.'

Steve bangs the table in triumph, catching his glass just in time. 'There you go, you're a partner person!' He looks kinda relieved. He's smiling at me and shaking his head like it was all worth it. 'I need to point Percy, back in a minute,' he says and goes into the café.

The white kid watches Steve disappear and runs straight towards me. I start to back off, but he stops across the table from me. He's puffing and can't get his words out quick enough. He looks scared.

'If your mate wants to know what really happened with that girl, he needs to be in Maccy D's at one.'

'Oi! Wait!' I shout as he legs it. 'Oi! Which one?!'

'Down the road!' as he disappears.

Chapter Twenty-six

Ian • London • January 2019

Robert Warrister is sitting in the window of McDonald's at one of the long tables. In front of him are three empty Big Mac boxes and a large milkshake. I sit on a high stool, leaving an empty one between us. Even though it's January, he's in his black t-shirt; hopefully, that makes concealing a weapon difficult, but I'll keep my distance anyway. I can't believe he's risking being seen with me. He smirks and says, 'Stop bricking it, man, what'm I gonna do with all these people about?'

'You sent a kid?'

He gazes out at the street. 'Sent a kid where?'

'To Marlon... with your message.'

'Of course.'

'You drag some ten-year-old kid into your business?'

'Hey now, I didn't pay him, what's with you?'

'Didn't pay him? Why else would he run around for you?'

'He knows me, you feel?'

'Bet he does.'

'Well, you came, so you're interested, yeah?'

'Tell me what you know.'

'I'd be a fool to come knocking on your door wouldn't I – with my conditions.'

'Maybe Hannan's waiting for you outside.'

He laughs, throwing his head back. I flinch at the sudden movement.

'I'd be a fool to talk to you without a peace offering,' he says.

'That's what this is, a peace offering?'

'To settle the dust.'

'From ripping me off over the work, or for kicking Marlon's head in?'

'Both, if you want. Look, I tell you what I know about your girl, and you do me a favour.'

'What could you possibly know about Ellie?'

'And yet you're here.'

'Maybe I want you seen breaching your bail conditions.'

'Maybe you're curious.' He takes a long slurp of milkshake and takes off the lid, stirring up the shake with his straw. 'You know who I am. You think I don't know when things happen?'

'What things?'

'The things mans don't hear about, regular people I mean. I hear a lot of things mans like you wouldn't wanna hear about, you get me?'

'Aren't you getting a bit old for all this, Robert?'

He laughs again, still working on the dregs of his shake with his straw. 'Sometimes you hear gold, boy. Like the story of how a nice young girl gets to become dead in some cheap-arse recording studio.'

'So, tell me the story.'

'The favour first.'

'Go on then.'

'Retract your statements, you and Marlon Williams.'

'Forget it.'

'You don't want to know what happened to her?'

'Come on, you're desperate.'

'I got things hanging over me. This assault is the least of them, but if it went away, it'd help me out a bit.'

'Why didn't you give it to Hannan, the story? He could put in a good word in court if you're helpful.'

'You think I'd give the pigs anything?' He turns and stares deep into my eyes. I resist the urge to break the connection.

'I think you'd do anything to save yourself.'

'I am never talking to the pigs. But you I will tell... if you withdraw those bullshit statements.'

'The statements are the truth.'

'But they don't have to be. Not if you want to know for sure what happened with your girl.'

'Stop calling her that. And why shouldn't I tell Hannan right now that you know what happened to Ellie?'

'Because it was nothing to do with me, I told you. I just heard.'

'What if it's crap?'

'What if it's not? What have you lost? I'm still going to jail.'

'But without the assault, you'd be better off.'

'Like I said, you'd be doing me a favour, but it's worth more to you, I bet. It's eating you up, not knowing how and why she died, isn't it? I saw all your press, Mr Media Star, ha-ha-ha!'

'There's no CCTV at the studio, no witnesses; just our statements.'

'Correct.'

'You realise it'd be a clear case of witness intimidation? They're not idiots, Robert.'

'No evidence, is there? I just defended myself when your boy tried to choke me. Remember, he grabbed me first.'

'Are you serious?!'

'You were scared, boy. You thought you saw me draw a weapon, but I didn't, did I?'

'We do this, and you tell me everything you think you know about Ellie's death?'

'Uh-huh. But you need to be quick.' He slides his tray of rubbish towards a girl wiping down the table further along. 'And another consideration... if you do anything other than the favour, you'll be paid a visit, you feel me?' He stands and leaves. The lingering threat jumps into battle in the pit of my stomach with the excitement that I might finally be getting somewhere.

'So...?' Marlon's back is straight, his hands together on the table, trying to dominate me.

'It's not a snap decision, something like this,' I say. But we do have to decide quickly. I need to create some space to think clearly. The bustle of the coffee shop is not helping.

'Nothin' to think about. What we got to lose?'

'Marlon, what if Warrister's lying? And there's a bloody good chance he is.'

'I don't care what happened to me. If we can find out about Ellie, we've gotta do it.'

'Obstructing a police investigation. Letting down everyone else Warrister has messed with. It's not that simple, mate.'

'It's simple to me. What's your problem? You don't want the truth no more?' He's staring me out.

I lean back in my chair and sip my espresso. 'Tell me again about Steve's missus.'

'What? Why?'

'You said she's boring.'

'God's sake... I just said she goes on a bit, moaning about people all the time. I don't want all that negativity. I wouldn't lay all that on someone else, it's bad vibes, man.'

'And yet you told me all about it, word for word, remember?'

His eyes drift for a moment, and he says, 'Screw you! That's not the same.'

'Nothing is "simple", that's all.'

Marlon folds his arms, gazes across the coffee shop. I push my cup away and close my eyes. Whatever I do will be wrong, of that I can be sure.

Chapter Twenty-seven

Marlon • London • January 2019

Steve's in his element up there. He's just saying a few words, introducing the night, but he's got everyone's attention. He's the business, like drippin'. The hipsters, the old blokes, the girls: everyone loves Steve. He bigs up the first band, an indie-folk five-piece, and nods at the sound guy. It's some dude called Tim tonight. I was watching him earlier, but he was giving off hostile vibes, so I gave him some space.

'Alright?' Steve winks at me as he passes.

I follow him outside, where he lights a joint and welcomes some new arrivals, then guides them towards his missus, who handles the entry fees.

'Man, you have this way with a crowd,' I say.

Steve turns away to exhale his smoke. 'I've been at it a while now. Everything gets easier if you stick at it.'

'Nah, you're a natural. Must've always had it.'

He shakes his head and kicks at the dust on the pavement. 'Do you remember anything I said up there?'

'Yeah, you thanked everyone, set up how the night was gonna run –'

'Exactly, I didn't say anything clever. You can't quote me.'

'Hahaha!' I'm clueless how he does it.

'Have you ever been abroad, Marlon?'

'Not yet.'

'I got taken around Germany a lot as a kid when my dad was racing. We stayed with this family once in Bavaria, right out in the sticks. It was one of those traditional houses, with the big wooden roofs and balconies. You know, flowerpots all along the front and that.' He gestures with his arms to paint the scene. 'We're so deep in the countryside, the family there don't speak any English at all. They've got a bed-and-breakfast thing going, so we're in the TV room one evening with a couple of other German families. They're all watching this sitcom on telly. Me and my dad sit there, clueless as to what the hell is going on with this programme. And suddenly, the punchline must've come, because the room erupts! They're all crying with laughter and slapping each other on the back. The scene on the screen continues, and me and my dad are... I dunno how to explain it, but we're cracking up ourselves! No idea what's going on, but we're totally pulled into this new world with these people. They're slapping us on the back now too. We're all in this thing together, it doesn't matter what it is. We're just glad to be in each other's company and having a good old laugh, you know?'

'Sure.'

'So, what I say up there isn't important. It's about creating a nice feeling, bringing everyone together. Easy.' He laughs and I find myself laughing too. He's right.

'Yeah, my mum encouraged my showing off, I reckon. Bless her, she could see I wasn't an academic, so she let me clown about all the time.' He drops his joint and stubs it out with his foot. 'What's going on between you and Ian then?'

'How'd ya mean?'

'C'mon, I said something about him when we were loading, and it was written all over your face.'

'Nothin' going on.'

'Look at you! Now I know for sure. What is it?'

'Just a disagreement. I want to handle something one way, and I reckon he's gonna ruin it all by doing it different.'

Steve's face says it all. How could I possibly be right?

'Marlon, Ian's been around a long time, you know. Have you discussed it properly with him? Got your point across? He's a good listener.'

'A hundred percent. We met and talked about it.'

'There you go. Whatever it is, he'll have given it a lot of thought. Something to do with the studio?'

'Nah, it's more than that.'

'You're happy working for me, right?'

'Yeah, 'course! It's something else.'

'It's not Yannis, is it? Look, if he comes round giving you grief, just let me know. Ian told me what he had you doing.'

'I can't really talk about it.'

'Okay. But seriously, Yannis is nothing. I toured with some edgy bands, all round the world, I've seen it all. If you get any trouble, I'll look after you, right? We're a team here.'

'Appreciate it.'

'Do you want me to talk to Ian?'

'No. He'll have done what he needs to do by now. He wanted to do it alone, and he hasn't answered my calls, so I guess he ignored my thoughts.'

'Wait until you've heard from him. No point winding yourself up until you know for sure. Imagine if you spend your life fretting over everything that might happen? You'd be a quivering wreck' – he ruffles my hair – 'wouldn't ya?'

We go back into the venue and stand by the doors. The band is alright; not amazing. I feel like this indie-folk thing has been done and done and done. My mouth does the equivalent of a shoulder shrug and Steve laughs.

'Sorry,' I shout into his ear. 'Not really my thing.'

'Nor mine but look at the crowd.'

The people seem to be loving it. At least some of them must be friends of the band, but even so, everybody's paying attention.

Steve shouts into my ear, 'This isn't sport, there's no winner. Art is all about taste. I gotta cater for everybody.'

'Sound quality is great,' I say, looking for a positive.

'Wouldn't have it any other way. Tim's amazing.'

'Yeah. I wanted to ask him a few things, but he's a bit…you know.'

Steve cracks up at that; says, 'Tim just likes to focus on the job. If you're interested in the engineering, Ed would be a better guy to talk to. I'll introduce you next time I use him. But when the show's over, I'll introduce Tim properly. Honestly, he's a gentleman when he's not focusing on the mix, just probably not as patient as some of the others. But like I said, we're a team. If you've got any worries, you gotta tell me. It'll be fine.'

Chapter Twenty-eight

Ian • London • January 2019

The bruising on my legs has turned blue and purple. It looks even worse when I use a mirror. Still hurts like hell, but I'm trying to rest up properly. That's not like me at all, but something Jamie said on Wednesday made me think I should probably look after myself a bit better. After seeing Scott Hannan, I spent the next day indoors, trying to unwind.

I put the mirror down and go to the kitchen to put some coffee on. It's still a bit of a struggle, but I can disguise the limp if I need to, like I did with Hannan. The trouble is, it's easy to fall into a trap. If I spend too much time holed up trying out these breathing exercises and meditation apps, is that going to become my focus? Will I become too worried to even leave the flat? I've always used work to get through any stress or worry. Is that wrong? Saturday night with my YouTube relax videos – how's that going to work? The only face I've seen is a workman from a flat across the way. I felt myself go a few times yesterday. Everything kind of dropped away for a moment, like it did before; I wasn't in control.

I take the coffee over to the sofa, and put my legs up on the beanbag. That was Sofia's choice, must've been. Not something I'd have chosen, but it's doing the job now. I automatically start noticing my breathing again. Funny how quickly your habits change. It does seem to relax me for a bit, though. It stops me thinking about everything that's been going on, although it took a bit of practice to be able to let the thoughts drift away when they appeared. When you keep getting threatened by people you shouldn't really be messing with, it tends to keep your brain busy. I bring Sofia to mind again, picturing her next to me on the sofa, snuggled up with her frothy coffee. She's been gone six days. I pull my phone out of my pocket, wince at the movement in my leg, and call Simone.

It rings for an eternity before I hear her say, 'Ian.'

'Look, I know she wants some space, but I need to tell her something.'

'She really wants to try this out, just let her have some time without you, yeah?'

'Look, I agree she should be away from the flat for a while. I just want to talk to her.'

'Shocker! Actually paying attention to what Sofia wants. Progress!'

'Can you put her on?'

'You'll undo it all if I do. No, let her see this through, yeah?'

'Well, at least tell her there's a package arrived for her.'

'Hold on...' After a few moments, 'She said open it, it's for you.'

'Yeah?'

'She ordered it ages ago, but it was out of stock. Right, I need to go now, bye, Ian.'

The line goes dead before I can speak.

I play with the package, a smallish square box, turning it over in my hands. Something's stopping me opening it. Like I prefer the not-knowing. Don't want to kill the warm feeling I'm getting from remembering her. I close my eyes, drifting away for a few moments. A gentle tapping noise catches my attention, and I sit up. It's difficult to place, coming from somewhere behind me. Over by the front door now, but the noise has stopped. I lift the blind and notice the window by the door is open a crack. The wind must've been rattling the blind. But I never open that window. I take a moment. There's a lurch in my stomach because I don't say that lightly: I mean I *never* open that window. It's too close to the catch on the front door. I slam the window shut and lock it. Then I take the key out and put it on the kitchen worktop, far away from the window. What's happening here?

I massage my face with my palms. A bloke knocked earlier, said he was a decorator working across the way and needed some water because it was off. I let him in. I didn't question it at the time. I don't remember what he said, exactly. I didn't get any bad vibes from him. He called me a lifesaver, thanked me. I said he could come back for a refill if he needed it, but he said one bucket was plenty. This is crazy! He was just a decorator. So, has that window been open since Sofia left? No chance. She would never open it anyway. I take my coffee over to the sink and chuck it down the plughole. The china handle breaks off in my hand, and I let the mug fall into the sink.

I go into the bedroom and curl up on the bed. Maybe Marlon was right, and we should have retracted our witness statements. No, I couldn't allow that, even for a vague chance that Robert Warrister might know something. I made the right choice. Hannan will have picked him up by now. But Warrister promised me a visit if I didn't do him this favour, and I'm starting to think that leaving that window ajar would be an economical way of opening my front door. I take a deep breath and exhale slowly, like I've been reading about, as if through a straw. Then I dial Marlon's number.

'Hold on,' he says. 'Let me go outside.'

'Where are you?'

'I've been trying to get you for ages!'

'Mate, I didn't go for it.'

There's silence for a few moments; then he says, 'Dickhead! Why would you do that?'

'The first thing we need to do is make sure we stay safe, okay?'

'Are you kidding me?'

'It was only me he threatened, okay? But just... keep an eye out, yeah? Is Steve driving you home?'

'Yeah. I'm not scared.'

'Marlon, that doesn't matter. People like that don't care what you think, don't do anything stupid, just carry on as normal but be aware... and stay close to Steve.'

There's a change in his tone when he asks, 'Are you okay?'

'Actually, yeah I'm alright.' It's the truth as well. I'm looking out for Marlon, resorting to my natural instincts, taking a bit of control again, and I have to say it feels good.

'What shall I tell Steve? He was asking.'

'Not everything...' I take a moment to think. 'You can tell him about the threats and about Warrister encouraging us to change our statements. Don't mention him claiming he knows what happened with Ellie.'

'Okay.'

'As far as Steve knows, this is all connected to the feud over Warrister's recordings, and you backing me up when he went for me.'

'I don't want to lie to him.'

'Just keep back the details. You're not lying. How's it going tonight?'

'Fun.'

'Are you keeping an eye on the engineer?'

'Trying to. He's a bit of a dick.'

'Ha! Take him a drink. Tell him you heard a couple of blokes in the toilet saying how great everything sounds tonight.'

'God's sake!'

'Ha-ha! Talk to you soon, mate.'

I feel better. The dread that filled me before I spoke to Marlon has cleared a little and I find myself thinking logically. I wouldn't have let just anyone into the flat to fill up a bucket of water. That guy was genuine. I didn't let him out of my sight for a second, anyway, so there's no way he could've opened that window. Gaynor was here that time; it's more likely that she opened it for some reason, and I just missed it, being so wrapped up in everything. She'll get an earful from me if I see her again.

I feel like going for a walk. There'll be enough people around still, and I won't go far. But I will recce the building to see if any of the flats are having decorating work done.

Chapter Twenty-nine

London • January 2019

It feels good out here, rather than wallowing at home. I stop at Islington Green for a rest, and without much idea where else to head for. The drunks are settled on the bench opposite mine. They must be grateful for the warmer nights this year. As I left the building, I found a couple of flats that looked like they were having work done and it convinced me the decorator was genuine. Now I just need to speak to Gaynor and confirm she was responsible for the open window. Her phone has been going straight to voicemail. It pains me to have to chase after her, but what choice do I have? I seem to remember her saying she'd be going onto a set of night shifts after her days off. I pull out my phone but hide it when a couple of youths pass, and glance at it. They say something to the drunks and kick over a couple of their cans. One of the drunks chases them a few steps, and they laugh at him, easily slipping away. I try again, googling a non-emergency number for Thames Valley Police.

I speak to an operator, giving her my name and contact number, explaining how Gaynor Kinderman had asked me to call her back. Then I watch the drunks for a while. I feel a little pang of jealousy. I can't imagine the hardships they have to deal with, but right now the Tennent's Super is keeping this gang of four happy enough. I could do with numbing my own worries. A nice-looking woman in an expensive dress passes by and does a double take. No, I'm not with them, I'm just enjoying their vibe. But she makes me think of Sofia again, and of the package I still can't bring myself to open. I wonder if she ordered it after the episode with Ellie's note. I want to imagine her ordering a present for me from a place of love and guilt. I think I'll hang on to that feeling. I won't open the package until Sofia comes back to me. Like a kid with a birthday present, I'll inspect it and rattle it right up until the big day. That's what I need to do – keep thinking about her return and stop dwelling on the fact that she's not here now.

I people-watch for a few more minutes, until my phone rings.

'Gaynor?'

'Hello.'

A few moments of silence.

'I'm on a break, I can't be long.'

'I need to ask you about something.'

'I… I'm sorry. Surely we don't need to get into it?'

'It's not about coming back drunk, it's something else,' I say.

'I know what it is. You don't need to remind me. Yes, I did. You know I did.'

Her reaction is odd. She's making it sound like leaving the window open was intentional, and she's guilty about it.

'Say something then,' she says.

'Why did you?'

'I don't know.'

'You must have had a reason.'

'You know why. You're an idiot if you don't.'

Silence again, as my mind races. Gaynor is breathing heavily. If she wasn't at work, I'd suspect she'd been drinking again.

'I don't –'

'Yes! I came into your room to… see you.'

I pull the phone away from my ear. The drunks have started heckling me. They love a good domestic.

I walk away, dodging between other pedestrians. Trying to piece it all together. When Gaynor woke me, letting herself out of the flat, I was in the middle of that dream with Sofia. She was on top of me. I remember it vividly; it seemed so real. I slap the phone back to my ear.

'What did you do!?'

'I told you. I wanted to see you.'

'That's it? You came into my bedroom while I was asleep just to see me? Why?'

'Because I've never been into a man's room before, and I wanted to see if you were still awake.' Her tone is edgier, like she's the victim here.

'And...?'

'And what...?'

'What happened?'

'You were asleep.' Sarcastic now.

People everywhere, in my way, as I stride up Essex Road. 'I know I was asleep! Tell me what happened.'

'Well... I wanted to take my clothes off and lie next to you.' Her breath is heavy again.

'What!?'

Every molecule in my head is buzzing. I feel sick in the pit of my stomach. A passing car honks, and I step out of the road.

'Relax,' she whispers. 'I'm teasing you.'

'Come on!'

'I didn't do anything.'

'You just said you wanted to.'

'I did want to. But I would never take advantage of you. Take it easy, nothing happened.'

'Then why come in?'

'To say goodbye if you were awake, and to apologise for my behaviour, mainly.'

'Mainly?'

'Yes. And partly because I wanted to look at you in bed.'

'Did you open a window?'

'What?'

'The window next to my front door; did you open it?'

'Yes, I think so.'

'You think so?!'

'I did open it. It was stuffy in your flat, so I let some air in. Did I forget to close it?'

'Yeah, you bloody well did! Now, promise me you didn't do anything stupid while I was asleep.'

'I watched you sleeping, that's it. You looked happy. I watched you longer than I probably should have. Then I left.'

'You promise that's all?'

'They're calling me, something's come in. Bye.'

The line goes dead.

I've come to the studio. It's all I can do to straighten myself out. There's relief about the window, but Gaynor, what the hell? I need to forget all about her and her stupid little games. I'm done with her. At least here I can do something productive, whatever the time is; I've no idea. I take a semi-acoustic down from the wall and plug in. A few jazz chords, mellow. A couple of bars have something about them, and I loop them, opening up some plugins and finding some drum samples I like, sequencing them into a lazy beat. And then nothing.

I was expecting to hear some melodies, but nothing comes to mind. But I mustn't think too hard. I have this feeling about creativity: if you push it too much, if you try to dissect it, it'll disappear. There's so much gear here. I remember when I was young, having all these ideas, and thinking if I could just record them, layer them all up, it would be easy. I could take those stones from the garden and create something percussive from them. I'd be infinitely creative. Then I got my first cassette four-track and realised it's not that simple. But look at me now… surrounded by ridiculously expensive equipment, and I can't find a way to complete this stupid jazzy beat.

Maybe Warrister was all bluster. When I saw Hannan, he said Warrister would've known he didn't stand a chance. He's in too deep. I'm hoping it's deep enough for him to forget about me and Marlon. Hannan thought there'd be no more trouble, but said to let him know the minute anything happened. He started telling me a story about when he was on traffic for a while, before he joined CID. He was still quite new in and stopped a guy who gave him the name David Holland. Hannan let him go when the checks came back clear, but when he got back to the nick his mate told him the guy was wanted. Holland was his first name. He'd given it to the PNC operator the wrong way around and they hadn't been switched on enough to dig any deeper. The guy wouldn't have believed his luck. Hannan said he sat up on Holland David's house every shift for two weeks until he saw him again. It was the stick he got from his teammates that got to him most. It's taken him this long to be able to laugh about it, he said. I guess he was being friendly because I was so worried about Warrister. But I think he was also telling me that ever since that early cock-up he hasn't left a stone unturned. I didn't tell him about the attack in Oxford. I can't prove anything, and I don't want to keep wasting police time.

Chapter Thirty

London • January 2019

I don't know what time I fell asleep at the studio, thinking of Ellie. Wondering what might have been going through her head on those nights leading up to her death. Walking home now, feeling the winter sun on the back of my neck, I almost fall over a mother pulling stuff out of her son's rucksack. The boy is in his Arsenal football kit and neither of them remembers seeing his shin pads. She pulls him to the side and empties the rest of the contents onto the pavement. The pads aren't there. She says she'll walk him to football and run back for them. He's one of the lucky ones, I guess. Makes me wonder if Sofia and I will ever have kids. What the hell would I be like as a father? I'm obsessed with helping my friends, and in some ways, I need that. I'd imagine it's a whole new level with your own flesh and blood, though. I can't think of many things I wouldn't do to save my children if they got into trouble.

I think that's what keeps niggling away about David Beck. I know it all sounded a bit far-fetched when Marlon recounted Ellie's story about the protector, but, when I strip it right back, it starts with a single-parent loving his daughter. The blood's not on David's hands, it's on the hands of whoever he asked to keep an eye on Ellie. Granted, he made a terrible choice there, but he was desperate? There I go again, getting sucked into theories. But I get it. I can see myself in David's position. If I could feel

172

myself getting weaker, unable to protect the daughter I'd spent so long safeguarding, I'd sure as hell at least think about some alternatives. David had raised Ellie single-handedly since she was seven. He did a good job. It must have been difficult to let go.

I go into the Starbuck's where the community café used to be and order a black coffee. It's faceless, this kind of service. The couple that used to run the café really cared about their bakery, cared about the service they gave, made sure you got the best coffee they could prepare. They used to put bands on at the weekends too. That's how I came to know about the place. Ellie would've totally loved it; she'd have fitted right in. It was well before her time, of course. Where were they from? Slovenia? God, my memory! Somewhere around there. They were trying to replicate something they'd seen in Paris before they settled in London. The money they spent on the stage and gear was ridiculous in comparison to their takings from the café. But it was the lifestyle they wanted. Of course, they were eventually driven out by the landlords, like idealists always are. But while they were here, it was an incredible little scene.

I look up, and the woman at the counter is Simone. When she's got her skinny latte, I call over to her, and she rolls her eyes.

'What are you doing here?' she says.

'Join me?'

'She wouldn't want me talking to you right now.'

'I know, but I was just walking back from the studio.'

'Ian, you know bloody well when I come here.'

'Sofia might've mentioned it. How's your book coming on?'

'Good, thank you. You look like crap.'

I laugh and ruffle my hair. 'How's she doing?'

'She's doing okay, but you don't deserve to know.' She can't hold back a little smile, even though her tone is fierce. She brings her cup to her lips to disguise it. I like Simone; she's protective. To be honest, I wouldn't mess with her. She looks like a model, but her eyes can be menacing. 'Ian, you know she loves you.'

'I used to know.'

'You know she does. This is just some cooling off she needs to do. You can be difficult, you know that.'

I just raise my eyebrows, which makes her laugh.

'We met some friends the other night and Sofia spent ages telling them about the single you did for that girl. Really pushing it for you. Do not tell her I told you that! So just wait, yes? She'll be back.'

'I thought all that business was part of the reason she left?'

'A girl can change her mind.'

'Who were these friends you met?'

'Ian!'

'I'm only kidding. Are you still with Zach?'

'John.'

'His name was John?'

'No, John is who I'm with now... sort of.'

'But you might go back to Zach?'

'I may go back to Zach, or I may move on to Ron.'

'Nice.'

'Shut up. Like I said, a girl can change her mind.'

She pulls out her laptop and sets up the table methodically.

'I'll let you get on with your best-seller. Just tell her I'm thinking of her, okay?'

'I'll tell her nothing. It's between you two.'

Simone. She can have any guy she wants.

I've showered and changed and I'm feeling a bit more human again. I was thinking about Marlon. I meant to try and meet his sister but haven't had a chance yet. It must be a worry, being responsible for her little brother, knowing the areas he's out and about in. Despite his energy, I have to remember he's quite vulnerable. He decided not to mention Warrister's attack to her, but things are different now. No matter how hard I try to convince myself, there's still a high chance of Robert Warrister sending people after us. Would it help if Cassie knew about that? There's a good chance she'd hole him up at home, and that might keep him safe, but would put him right back where he started. He'd lose the job working for Steve and probably end up with Yannis again, or worse. Nobody ever wants to take a chance on kids like Marlon. I've got to try and shield him from all this without getting in the way of his progress. But, deep down, I feel like his sister should know. I sit and procrastinate.

I flip open the laptop and log in. The streams are looking great for *Under the Tree*. Maybe there is a good enough audience to create some merch now. In another few days I'll draw some more revenue from the CD and vinyl sales and transfer it across to the charities. Ellie's story has really captured people's imaginations. There are some sick comments from faceless trolls, but I scroll quickly past them. Won't give the cowards the attention they want. What I really need to see is something to point me towards the truth of the whole thing. Just someone to approach us with new information that will get us closer. I realise it is wishful thinking, but I'll be checking regularly anyway. If nothing else, we're keeping Ellie alive in the digital domain and doing some good for the charities.

I'm still impressed with Glen's video work, but he doesn't seem to have added any new posts, wherever he is. I understand if he wants to ignore my calls for a while, it's been a rough ride. He probably needs some space. Story of my life, people needing to distance themselves from me. I start typing out a quick hello in the messaging section of the app but, after a moment, backspace it out. He couldn't have Ellie. He knew he didn't stand a chance of being with her, but couldn't hold it in. Well, I can relate to that kind of heartache now too. Whatever Simone says, there's no guarantee things are going to get back to the way they were. I grab the package off the side and turn it over in my hands again, wondering what it could be and enjoying not knowing. I'll keep on wondering for as long as it takes Sofia to come home. At least I know she's safe.

The phone rings. Angus. I've worked with him plenty of times, but I've not heard from him in a while.

'I bet you've forgotten all about the rapper you mixed for us, haven't you?'

'Haha! Took a moment, but yeah, I remember. Fun times.'

'Thought you might like to know it's just been released,' he laughs.

'Mate, when was that? Five years ago?'

'I think so. Sounds fresh, though.'

'Course it does! I'll have to give it another listen.'

'Also... are you busy?'

'Funny you should ask. No, why?'

'I need a live mix doing real quick, like tomorrow. They wanted Flood or Alan to do it, but they passed.'

'Who is it?'

'Not saying, until you say yes,' he laughs. 'They need a track from one of the recent shows, but quickly.'

'From five years to one day, eh?'

'You know how it goes.'

'Send me the files, and I'll have it done, end of tomorrow.'

'Legend!'

I take my laptop over to the sofa and plug in my headphones. This is great; I can really use the work. But first I want to hear the track I did five years ago that's just been released. I've had that happen a few times. People still can't believe that sort of delay is possible today, when everything seems to run at lightspeed, but that's the way the music biz goes. It doesn't matter if it's independent or major label, it's weirder than most people realise. I press Play with a little apprehension. Five years is a long time and I know I'll hear things I could have done better. I know I'll miss not hearing the gear I've since acquired and become attached to. But as the track starts, I like it immediately. It's a different thing, listening after time has elapsed. I can listen as anyone else would. When you're so involved with the minutiae of the recording, you can't see the wood for the trees. But I find myself enjoying the track, like a fan. I'll give myself until at least the last chorus before I allow the perfectionist in me to start listing the tweaks I should've made. But honestly, kicking back and enjoying something you've been heavily involved in is nice.

Chapter Thirty-one

Marlon • London • February 2019

Something different tonight. Photography exhibition at a place called Proud Galleries and Steve's pulled together a few mates to form a scratch band. They're playing songs from a '70s album I haven't heard of, but it sounds good. Best bit is I get to sit up with Tim.

He suddenly remembers I'm here. 'See that?'

I peer round at what he's doing.

'Guitarist went to a dirty sound. Where did it go?! Totally dropped out.' He's shaking his head, working the faders. 'Dunno why I bother sound checking them, they're just gonna go stomp on some pedal they never told me about.'

Steve introduced us properly and hooked me up to sit at the mixer. I'm trying to match up what Tim's doing with what Ian showed me, but I don't wanna invade his space too much. Could be a winner if it goes well, coz the exhibition's running for a few weeks. So, I'm trying not to balls it up on the first night.

I spotted Yannis as soon as he came in, halfway through the evening. Kept my head down and checked where he was before I went to the toilets. It's a bit tight squeezing past the bar, and I didn't want to end up getting trapped. Now it's over, there's only a few people milling around but he's still here, talking to some girls.

'Hello, mate,' he says, as I try to duck behind him.

'I don't want any trouble.'

'I see you've found a new job,' he says. The girls look happy for the excuse to leave. 'I was only looking out for you, you know. I didn't need you. What you doing here then?'

'We do all different venues.'

'Oh yeah? What do you contribute?'

'Bit of everything. Trying to work up to running sound someday.'

He laughs. 'Come on, like Steve Lewis is gonna let you do that! How'd you get in with him? Through the photographer?'

'No.'

'What did you want with him, then?'

'Who?'

'That photographer guy, Glen Crane.'

My mind races. I can feel my expression giving it all away, but I can't pull it back.

'You asked me where he lived,' he says. 'What was that all about if you weren't looking for a new job?'

'I said: a friend wanted some shots done… for her band. She needed some flyers.'

'Nothing to do with Ian, then? You've been cosying up a bit lately, haven't you?'

'He's a mate.' I love that I can even say that.

'You might think that, young man, but you wanna watch your back with him. What happened with Robert Warrister? Attacked him, didn't you?' He finds that hilarious for some reason.

He runs a hand through his hair and leans against the wall with his pint. He's not leaving anytime soon.

I ask before I can stop myself, 'You know Warrister?'

'Who do you think put him in touch with Ian for those

recordings they did? Well, the junior did the work, didn't he? I told you Ian can't be trusted. You want to stay away from him.'

'I just want a proper job, don't want any trouble.' I put my hands up, surrendering, and Steve must've been watching, because his voice, loud from behind, says, 'Marlon, everything alright?'

Yannis smiles and raises a hand, but I can tell from his face that Steve has blanked him.

'Give us a hand,' Steve says.

I don't need asking twice and follow him through the doors to a storeroom at the back. Flight cases and boxes are crammed into the small space. Steve motions for me to follow his lead, wrapping the tangle of audio cables at our feet.

'Any bother there?' He expertly coils his cable around his arm as I wrestle with mine.

'Nah, it's fine.'

'It's not about you, you know.'

'Huh?'

'Dickheads like that.'

I grin at the face he pulls. I've learned to spot when a story's coming.

'My old dear was a teaching assistant back in the day,' he says. 'For a special school. There was this book they used to use. Had the term 'status quo' in it, right? The teacher, every time she got to that bit, she'd pause and look around the class. Know why?'

I shake my head.

'Because it was the name of a massive rock band back then. So, this teacher would look up and try to spot any boys laughing and playing air guitars at each other. She'd holler at the kids, make a right song and dance about how immature they were and all that. Until, eventually, the kids stopped picking up on it because the band weren't on Top of the Pops anymore. And my old dear noticed her, the teacher. She'd still stop at the same place, just to see if she could catch anyone out. You know why?'

I shake my head again.

'Because it was never about kids being disruptive. It was because she wanted to be seen as culturally aware. That's it. When the schtick dried up, so did she. The band dropped off, so did she. Remember that when someone's being a dick. It's not about you.'

I can't stop grinning. 'Yeah, I like it.' And I like my new boss. He jumps in when I need him. And I'd do the same for him.

When I'm done, I look for Yannis again. I find him outside, smoking on the pavement, like he's waiting for someone.

'How well d'you know Warrister?' I ask him.

He stubs out his cigarette with his boot. 'A little bit,' he says.

'Did Ellie know him?'

'Now, why would you ask me that?'

'You managed her, didn't you? Wouldn't she have come across him?'

'Not that I know of. But it's a small scene around here. Maybe they met, I dunno.'

'You didn't know her at all, did you?' I turn away from him.

'That's what happens when people sneak around behind my back. Like your best mate, Ian! Whispering with her and keeping secrets from me. Look what good it did her in the end.'

I spin straight back around and stare him down. He's backing off, and it gives me time to calm it a bit. 'Look, I just wanna know if it's worth talking to Warrister about what happened to Ellie.'

'What would he know about it?'

'You tell me.'

He thinks that's funny. 'I'll book you an appointment with him if you want.' He rolls his shoulders and turns his back on me. When he's a few steps down the road, he shouts, 'I could've stopped her. Ian will have to live with that.'

Chapter Thirty-two

Ian • London • February 2019

This feels great. Maybe I didn't appreciate how much work does for me until I became too wrapped up in the rest of life. Here at the mixing desk is where I'm at peace, alone and perfectly focused. The files I received via Angus are of excellent quality. There are lots of them: several mic options from the amps, DI feeds and FX sends. The vocals sound good and clean. It amuses me that Angus is still referring in whispers to the 'stadium act' even though I now know who the super-famous band is. The singer has done well, and whoever engineered the gig made good choices. They've captured his nasal tone perfectly, retaining a super-clean signal: challenging at a large arena gig. I was gutted when I discovered that the live albums I listened to as a kid were mostly tweaked and fixed in a studio. Sometimes a whole 'live' album was produced entirely in the recording studio, with the crowd noise added later, along with fake firework sounds in some cases, to round off the trickery. I'm glad that's not what we're doing here. I like things to be real. The band want crowd noise, but it's the real deal I'll be mixing in, from some nicely placed ambient mics the engineer set up around the venue.

I put on some coffee. Now I've got the folders how I want them and loaded in everything I need, this should be a fairly straightforward project. I haven't worked with this band before, but their people obviously know me. If I can hit the mark with this track, I might be able to secure future work with them. It's about time I started thinking about myself again. The revenue streams have been slowly drying up. I'll run the finished mix by my mate Gareth before I submit it to the label. He's produced this band before and is on good terms with them. He's looking after a new baby right now, so I guess that's why he's not picking this one up. I was at his studio once, and he had a huge oil painting of Mother Teresa on the wall behind the mixing desk. He said it was a present from the band, which surprised me. But he smiled and flipped a switch, and Mother Teresa's eyes blinked on with demonic red LED lights. He appreciated the gift.

Sipping my coffee at the kitchenette, I talk to Ellie. Just a few words of reassurance. Daft, I know, but I want her to know I haven't closed the sessions we did to start anew on something else. I tell her I'm still working on her project, still working on the promise I made her when she sat here with tears in her eyes. When we were connected as perfectly as I'd ever experienced with any artist before. I know she'd get it. She was an inspiration.

Back at the mixing desk, I work on the kick drum track. 60hz boost, 350hz cut, a bit of 10k on channel one, like I've done a million times before. It's just housekeeping to me now, getting the basics in order before digging into the more creative side of mixing. Younger engineers ask about getting those classic kick drum sounds, and I guess it's because they've come up with digital workstations. They can manipulate any frequencies they choose too easily. I tell them that those classic sounds they know were created on a desk, like a Neve with fixed EQ points. The options were more limited, but they were all that was needed to sculpt those perfect drum tones. I smile. It's like coming home. It's a different frame of mind for mixing like this. I wasn't involved in any of the mic placement decisions; I didn't even see the performance. All I have are the audio files and a long list of notes from the record company, which I haven't looked at. And don't intend to until the mix is done. I can't allow myself to be influenced by anyone else until I've had a first pass. If I trust my ears and experience, I'll be happy with the result. Only then will I peek at the notes to see what the label had in mind. If I've missed anything important, then I'll humbly make the changes. Maybe. We'll see.

Chapter Thirty-three

London • February 2019

Everything's new this morning. Camden seems to be smiling with me. The mix is with the record company and they're happy. I wasn't overly confident because when I did check their notes yesterday, I found them contradictory and, in some parts, completely baffling. It was clearly a document written by several people who all had some vague artistic vision of their own, and they hadn't come together. Still, I know it's a great mix; it was easy. Too easy, maybe, but it's what I needed. I'll always prefer working with new artists than seasoned pros, but I need to pay the bills as well. With Ellie, for example, I could develop her, focus on technique and routines she wouldn't know about yet to help pull her natural talent to the surface. It was teamwork; each of us was learning from the other every day we were in the studio. I like to try and create that ethos with the established acts as well, but of course it can be difficult. Save for a few humble pros who understand that they're fallible humans and see the worth in a true collaboration, it's often a case of having to speak loudly to be heard when producing established acts. But let's not look a gift horse in the mouth.

The front of Glen's house is dead. I knock. No answer. But it's time I tried a bit harder, so I walk around the back, trying to push out the memories of last time I was here. I haven't heard anything from him since then. It's been over a month, and I've been a coward for too long. At the back door, things are still quiet. I turn the handle and find the door unlocked.

'Hello?' I'm in two minds.

'In here,' comes a reply, and it's a relief. Partly because he's okay, and partly because he sounds unthreatening.

In the small living room, Glen is sitting upright. No TV, no book, nothing. He looks like his spirit has deserted him. He hasn't shaved since I last saw him, his beard or his head, and I now know that what remains of his hair is ginger, with lots of grey in it.

'Are you okay, mate?'

'What do you want?'

'Come to see how you are.'

'Who cares?'

His body odour hits me as I perch on the arm of the sofa.

'Naff all on TV then?'

Not even a hint of a smile.

'Marlon knows he was wrong. It was good of you to let it go.'

He doesn't say anything. His lips are rubbing against each other, scrunching his face into strange contortions. I can't tell what he's thinking. It's like he's tuned out.

'Can I see your arm?'

He stays silent and makes no effort to show me what's under his sweatshirt.

'You've been alright, changing the dressings?'

He turns his head painfully slowly and says, 'Tell me why I should bother.'

I find myself spurting out a kind of uncomfortable half-laugh. After a moment to compose myself, I say, 'Well, if it falls off, you'll struggle with your camera.'

'I'm not doing that anymore.'

'Taking pictures?'

'Any of it,' he says, turning his head away from me again to stare at the window.

'Mate, I know what it's like. I had the same, all the distractions. But getting back into work helps. I've only just got back into the studio, a quick turnaround job came in, just what I needed. The longer we sit around, the harder it is.'

'You heard what he said, right?'

'Who?'

'That Marlon kid.'

'Forget all that. I told you he knows he was wrong. He feels terrible about it, just terrified you were gonna report him to the police.'

'Not all that. I mean what he said.'

'Remind me.'

'I was too old for Ellie. I was too close to her. There's something wrong with me. That's what he said.'

'Marlon's got problems of his own.'

'No, he was right.'

'Which part?'

'All of it. I've heard people whispering about me. Maybe there is something wrong with me.'

'Why? Because you help people who don't have the means to drive themselves around to gigs? Who can't afford professional shots for their press-packs? That sounds pretty bloody admirable to me.'

He shakes his head. 'I don't know why I do it.'

'Because you care, I'd say. And because when you've got a skill, it's an obligation to use it. You hear about writers that suffer for their art but have to write because they need to get it out –

like they don't have a choice. That's what it's like for people like us, what we do.'

'What did you think when I told you I was in love with Ellie?'

'Doesn't matter what I think.'

'Matters to me.'

'Well, what do you mean by love?'

His eyes open wide. 'See? You're wondering if I tried anything.'

'Did you?'

The life has disappeared from his eyes again. He says, 'I've always helped younger artists. I've heard people saying things behind my back. Sometimes the kids I've been helping have told me.'

'Which was what?'

'You know what. Ellie was the first person I ever fell in love with.'

'You knew there was a massive age-gap. You realised it was a fantasy?'

'God, that sounds disgusting! I wasn't looking at her like that.'

'You can't help who you're attracted to. You only spoke to her about it, right?'

'Of course. Stupid bloody thing to do.'

'Surely better than holding it all inside. What good would that've done you both?'

'I wondered for ages if I'd tipped her over the edge. If I'd added to whatever issues she was struggling with. Worried that I'd killed her.'

He's crying softly. No effort to disguise it.

'Maybe we'll find out what happened. Maybe we won't. But I don't think it was you.'

'Neither do I now, deep down.'

'So, come on then, ease up on yourself.'

'I can't do it anymore, the work.'

'Why not?'

'Because I don't know why I was doing it.'

I let that sink in. I can't think of anything to say that will help. The silence passes slowly.

'I'll make some tea.'

In the kitchen, I find tea bags and rinse a couple of mugs out. There's no milk in the fridge. In fact, there's nothing in there except some ketchup and a smell of mould. When the kettle boils, I find a jar of coffee and use that instead. I can feel some anger building inside me about Glen. How could he approach Ellie like that? Why didn't he see her as a friend? He could've been a father figure, for God's sake. I don't like the feeling that's welling up. I haven't faced up to it before, but I can't ignore it now. Stirring the coffee, I try to balance out the facts. I haven't seen anything in Glen that suggests anything perverted. In the short time I've known him there's never been a roving eye or a comment that could've flagged up some suspicion. I can't judge him without any evidence. If I had to tick a box, I'd go for 'asexual' over anything else. Maybe I should give him the benefit of the doubt that he genuinely fell in love with Ellie for who she was. Not what she was.

'Here you go. You're out of milk.'

He ignores the mug. It's not the sort of coffee I'd usually tolerate, but I sip it anyway.

'Did you know Jude de Vries?' I ask.

He looks up quickly. 'No, why?'

'I found out he visited Ellie, while she was in London.'

'Jon never told me that.'

'He didn't sound like the helpful sort, did he?' My instinct is to keep the attack on me in Oxford to myself. I still don't know for sure it was Jon de Vries, though any other theory seems pathetically inadequate.

'Did Jude do anything?'

'No, I asked him about it. He said he just wanted to know if she'd heard anything new about his brother's death.'

'You talked to him? When?'

'He's not a problem. He was friendly with Ellie, liked her.'

'How can you know that?'

'Do you know Andrew Raine? Tried to get something going with Ellie at one point.'

'She mentioned him. Wasn't going anywhere, she said.'

'That's where Jude came to see her, at Andrew's. He assumed Jude was her boyfriend.'

Glen's deep in thought, and I wonder if I've said too much.

'I can get you some stuff from the shops if you want,' I say, to change the subject. 'Anything you need?'

Chapter Thirty-four

Ellie's Diary • Valentine's Day 2016

Rough day today. The worst. Okay, maybe not the worst, but fucking bad. I hate seeing Dad in that place. I want to know how much he understands when he only sees me on the screen now. He can't know the truth, of course. He's better off without me. But Jamie's great. I'm glad Dad has him.

I've been reading up on music production, to see if I can record some of my songs, get them out online. Might be my way back into the world. A way to dip my toes without having to leave the house. Thank God for my guitar, it lifts me a bit, but I keep coming back to Danny. They say time is a great healer, but how long is grief supposed to last? I can't stop crying. And thank God Gaynor's on nights this week and out of my hair. She keeps on at me to get out and active again. Makes me mad because she's just as bad herself. If she didn't have this new job, she'd be the same as me. Except she'd be doing the puzzle pages instead of the music.

Then Dennis came in and flung a red envelope onto the bed with a stupid grin on his face. Tells me he thinks I've got an admirer.

No stamp. Probably from Dennis himself, trying to cheer me up, I thought. There are some stupid hearts drawn on the back. Just my name on the front in a childish scrawl. Some kind of sick joke? I should just have just binned it. But curiosity got the better of me. Inside the card was a typed message printed on a sticky label. It didn't make sense at first, until suddenly I understood it and it made me sick. Like literally.

Banged my elbow on the toilet door. Vomit all in my hair. The room was spinning, and I couldn't stop throwing up. All I could smell was the bleach my dad used to put in the bucket when I was sick as a child.

Dennis tried to help, bless him, but I couldn't stand him being there, I pushed him off me, slamming the door with my foot. He wanted to help but I couldn't bear it. I told him it was just a troll. Someone's idea of a joke. Now I can't stop crying. Shivering. I can hardly bear to write the next bit.

Underneath Philippa's tree is what he signed off with. You'll always be safe underneath Philippa's tree. How would anybody else know about that? He must be telling the truth. He killed Danny. He killed Danny... for me.

And then, when I went to check the envelope again, Dennis had burnt it!! Put it straight in the fire. It was like all life had drained from my body. I couldn't even speak, I just pushed him away and closed the door.

Now I'm sitting here, craning my neck to look at Mum's drawing. You wouldn't have known, Daddy, would you? Did you get us into something bad? Who is this monster? Help me, Daddy, help me understand.

Gaynor was furious. She kept asking who it was, who could have been so mean. I told her it could be any sicko anywhere. Just some troll trying to amuse himself. She was raging but holding it in for my benefit. Her mouth did that funny twitch she does when she's angry. She smothered me in a big hug on the bed. She thinks we need to tell the police. I just want to forget it. I need to get out of this place.

If there's someone out there watching, someone who could do something so horrific to Danny, then nobody's safe.

I begged Jamie to set up another Skype call. Once I plucked up the courage to speak to Dad, I couldn't wait until tomorrow. Dad was in his pyjamas, looked like he'd just been showered. His hair was damp but neatly combed. I touched my screen where his face is, like I always do, but this time for longer because I was summoning all my inner strength.

I told him this was important. I said Did you ask someone to look out for me? Keep me safe?

But he couldn't follow me. All he could say was he loved me.

I tried again. I asked him Daddy, do you have a friend? Someone to help me if I need anything? Is there someone like that?

Ellie, he said. Like we were playing a game. He looked so proud. It made me cry.

I tried to get his attention. Can't remember exactly what I said. Something like Daddy, something terrible happened, and I need you to try and think back. Can you do that for me, please?

It was useless. The thing is, I've been losing him for so long. Every time I see him there's another wide gulf to cross before we can reconnect. It makes me so angry. I never resented him when I was caring for him at home. When I cleaned him up after accidents, did everything for him, never once did I feel anger. But now, with so much at stake, I am raging with frustration.

What did you do, Dad? I asked him again. No reaction. He got distracted by an itch on his neck.

I will never know the truth. But I must protect him – he protected me for so long. It scares me. I can't process the fear properly, but it's eating me up slowly and slyly from the inside.

I reached out to touch his face through the screen again. Everything's okay, I said, and then I repeated it because I really wanted him to believe it. You don't have to worry about anything, I said.

Maybe he understood, but impossible to tell for sure. Moments later, his expression was neutral again.

Now what?

Chapter Thirty-five

Ian • London • February 2019

I'm thinking about going to bed when the phone rings. I slide over to reach my mobile from the coffee table. Simone. It's gone eleven o'clock. My gut turns over.

'What's happened?'

'Ian... look... I need to speak to you.'

'Is she okay?'

Silence, but I can hear the sound of a busy street in the background.

'What's happened, Simone?!'

'It's my fault... I shouldn't have...'

'Where are you?'

Nothing for a moment, then she says, 'Are you sober?'

'It's Wednesday night, yes, I'm sober. You're not though, are you? What's happened.'

'It's Sofia.'

'Right. Where is she?'

'She...erm... she wants to come home.'

The clip-clopping of heels, like they're staggering about in the road.

'Because she's pissed?'

'Don't blame her. She's had a crap day, and I took her for a couple of drinks on Kingsland Road.'

'A couple?'

'Cocktails... at Jaguar Shoes... they kept buying 'em.'

'Why am I talking to you and not Sofia? Put her on.'

'But she wants to come home, Ian.'

'Are you still on Kingsland Road?'

'Eh?'

'Are you still there? I'll get a cab.'

'No... no... she can't come home until...'

'Go on. Until what?'

'Something happened, alright. It wasn't her fault, she can hardly stand. Blame me if you need to blame somebody.'

'Oh, for God's sake.'

'They kept bringing us cocktails. She knew straight away she'd made a mistake, told him to go. C'mon, she wants to come home, but she's scared now.'

I hold my breath, count to ten, and then hang up the phone.

All I can see is a huge dark chasm waiting for me. Nothing else computes, no understanding. After a moment, my eyes start to refocus, and settle on the package on the table. My talisman for Sofia's return. All my presumptions about it have shattered. If I got it wrong about her, how can I trust my own mind? All the beautiful times we had together, my memories; I can't even trust them anymore. Were they illusions? Too many thoughts now, and they explode into chaos. I fall into the sofa and gaze into the distance. As I shut my eyes, the universe closes around me, and I drop a few feet into the depths. I shake my head in my hands to bring myself back around, grab onto the arm of the sofa and try to recall those breathing techniques. I exhale as slowly as I can. I start to feel some balance return. I look at Sofia's package again. Its meaning has vanished along with everything else, so I go over and take the little box in my hand. I fling open the front door, stomp onto the walkway and without any need to turn the box over in my hands, launch it out into the dark night. I'm back inside before it even hits the road. One of the gears in the mechanism of my life has slipped; the teeth have burred, and it'll slip forever.

I sit for a long time. Eventually, I head back out. I can't see the box down there now. That's London for you. I trusted Sofia because I had to. If I hadn't, she'd have been like the rest of the world out there – terrifyingly complicated. Because I trusted her, I believed I understood her. But it was fragile all along; I see that now. Memories of her getting emotional keep swimming around my brain. Why those memories? I'm not remembering her laughter, or mundane evenings in front of the TV. There's nothing everyday about these memories. Instead, I'm watching her crying, because she's hidden the letter from me, and on her knees praying for forgiveness. She looks different to me now. I thought I understood her; I thought I knew her as well as anyone can know somebody else. Even when she surprised me, I thought I knew her. Now, I don't even know where I am myself. My safe little home has collapsed.

I pick up my phone and hit Simone's number.

'Tell her not to come home.'

'Let her speak to you,' she says, and I can hear Sofia wailing in the background. No street noise anymore. Helpful strangers have taken them in? Put a blanket around their shoulders? Poor downtrodden girls.

'I don't want to. Just tell her that's it.'

'Ian... It's her home... you can't just kick her out.'

'Yeah, I thought it was her home, as well. I thought a lot of things about her, and that's all in the past. Do you know? – I thought the past was always safe. That stuff's already happened, so it's fixed, isn't it?' – Simone's crying herself now, they're sobbing gibberish to each other; I can't tell if she replies – 'But nothing's fixed. Everything that happened with Sofia and me has just been changed. And I don't recognise any of it. You can tell her that if you're not too mangled.'

There's no reply. It sounds like the phone's being passed between them, like they're school children trying to duck the teacher's question. It's pathetic.

'She wants to know if you opened the package,' Simone says.

'Her stuff will be boxed and ready next week. I need some time before I can face it.'

'Ian, the package. Did you open it?'

'It's gone... and so is she.' I cut the call.

I pour myself a large glass of neat Johnnie Walker and gulp it at the kitchen counter. But it makes me as stupid as her, so I flick the glass and what's left of the whiskey into the sink. I look at the mess of it for a moment. Then I grab a steel colander and smash the glass to smithereens.

I don't know how long I've been lying on the bed. Gaynor popped into my head some time ago. Automatic. When my first proper girlfriend finished with me at school, I scoured the estate on my bike for another girl who I'd heard liked me. Sad, really. I was more fixated on saving face with my mates than I was about the dead relationship. Maybe that's why I suddenly started thinking about Gaynor – has that desire to save face ingrained itself into my character? I certainly don't want anything to do with her. With any of them.

But there's been a little worm of doubt slipping around my mind since Gaynor confessed to coming into my room. She said nothing happened, and I believed her because I needed to. But how would I know? For sure? She could've done anything while I was asleep, and I'd never know. I mean, what if I'd responded? People sleep-walk, don't they? What's the difference here? My dream of making love to Sofia was vivid. But what if Gaynor arrived at that moment, and switched places with Sofia? I'd know, surely?

Suddenly I'm questioning everything that's ever happened, just because the chair's been kicked out from under me. God, why am I being so bloody stupid? I've got to keep my mind in check before the whole world starts to look alien. But I'm thinking back to the moment of comfort I felt when Gaynor moved close to me on the sofa. When the empty flat was starting to feel cold. I shake the thought away quickly, but it introduces a new doubt: how can I judge Sofia so readily when I recognise moments of weakness in myself?

I open my laptop at the table and dig into the social media accounts for Ellie's single. I fumble with my headphones and play *Under the Tree* in the background, as I read some of the new comments. Music – the same piece can invoke so many moods depending on where you are with your life. It can never be judged. It's beyond that. I can no longer hear the skeleton of the music – the nuts and bolts of the architecture that I spent so long setting up and re-arranging – only the emotion. I stop reading for a moment and allow Ellie's voice to carry me away.

It works, but only for a while. Now I'm jogging down the steps, with my bike over my shoulder. A cursory glance, as I start off – still no sign of the package I chucked. I cross the main road and hit the darkened streets towards Kingsland Road. If they're walking, I know which route they'll take. They've almost certainly called an Uber, but something has brought me out here against my will. Call it instinct. There's plenty of time to analyse it, but right now I don't know whether I'm worried about the girls' safety, or whether I want to see who they're with.

There's no sign of Sofia and Simone. I scour the area right down to Kingsland Road. This feeling is strange. Whatever it is, I'm somehow a low-resolution version of myself, like my body's taken over and left me behind. That tunnel vision again, but different this time. I can't feel the weakness in my bruised legs anymore, even though they're pumping the pedals. I don't feel like I care.

A guy astride a bike flags me down. The blonde with him looks scared.

'Don't go down there, mate,' he says. Australian accent. 'Gang's pulling people off their bikes.'

'Thanks. You guys okay?'

'We're good. Had time to turn around, but a load of 'em jumped some guy further up the road.'

I give them time to get on their way and then continue along the same route. Am I worried about the girls, or does some part of me need a release for this anger that's engulfing me? Do I actually want to be jumped tonight? I feel a buzzing in my head as I race further down the road, keeping to the middle, and keeping my periphery as wide as possible. All senses heightened.

I catch movement up ahead on the right. Two guys in hoods waiting on the pavement. They're on edge. Poised and ready. I pump the pedals harder, and my body starts to respond on impulse. The bike steers towards them and I stand up on the pedals, throwing the bike side-to-side, generating all the speed I can. They're responding too late. They can't decide which way to move. I connect with them hard. Scrambling to get my bearings. It's a pile of crumpled bodies and metal. I wrestle an arm free and wrap it around the neck of someone beneath me. I squeeze it as hard as I can. My legs kick about in defence, but I can't make out where everyone is. It's raw. I'm vulnerable, and my body is somehow handling it.

I can feel nothing. I squeeze harder, no idea if it's working, then I feel hands grabbing onto my forearm. He's choking, scratching my skin. I pull hard, rolling the attacker over, while keeping a firm grip on his neck. And I see the back of one of the attackers running away. Why's he running? The struggling gets weaker, and I slowly release my grip on the neck. Letting go of him completely, I push away from the body on the ground. He's coming back to his senses, a vacant stare in his eyes. There's no one else around. Where's the rest of them? He mumbles something incoherent and scrambles to his feet. He looks different now. I've made a mistake. These two weren't part of the gang. I'm the only attacker here. I try to apologise and go to assist him, but he's got his arms out in front, backing away. Sprinting away now. I call after him, but it's too late.

Chapter Thirty-six

Kent • February 2019

Anthony's uniform looks like he hasn't taken it off since we last met. He shakes my hand and leads me through the main building. It hadn't taken much to persuade him to let me come down to the farm park. There's only two of them on duty tonight; he's telling his mate all about me and Sofia, and they're both loving getting one over on the boss.

'That bloke...' says his mate, an overweight bloke with a big black beard, 'is a complete arse. Do you know what he had us do last summer?'

I shrug.

'He'd ordered this bloody Punch and Judy set-up, right? For the man-made beach he's got over the other side there. Got the red-and-white striped tent, the puppets, props, the lot.'

'But didn't think about who was gonna operate it,' chimes in Anthony, puffing on his vape.

'He had a brilliant idea,' his mate continues. 'Who do you think he thought would be good at that sort of thing?'

I grin at them. 'You two?'

He's holding his arms out at his sides, indicating the sheer size of his torso, before going over to Anthony and tracing the girth of his belly in a similar way.

'The two biggest blokes in the place, squeezing into this tiny little puppet tent. Amazing idea, wasn't it?'

Anthony takes up the story. 'I asked him if there was a script. Hadn't thought of that either, had he?'

His mate interrupts, 'So, I says to him, "Tell you what, McKelvey, lose the puppets and tent, you stand there in front of the mummies and the kids, and I'll batter you with Mr Punch's bat."' They both laugh.

'So, you got out of it,' I say, trying to end the story, because we're coming up on Mum and Dad's spot.

'No, because he's a complete tit,' says Anthony. 'He was quite happy for us to squeeze into this stupid little tent, two biggest blokes here, and make up some stupid little story as we went along.'

'I'm sure you did amazing,' I say. Need these two to go now, please.

'No,' Anthony says, big grin on his face. 'Nobody turned up for the show. Know why?'

His mate sounds like he's delivered his line a thousand times. 'Because it was a shit idea!'

They both crack up.

'That's it, by the oak tree, isn't it?' says Anthony, pointing with his torch beam. He takes a small Maglite out of his pocket and hands it to me.

'Thanks.'

As they make their way back, I push through the tall grass, towards the spot where I finally laid Mum and Dad to rest. I speak quietly, the torch beam fixed on the ground where I'd scattered the ashes.

'I hope you like it here. I know you do; it's where we were happiest, isn't it? Thank you for those times with the caravan. I still come back to the memories when things are tough. Mum, do you remember one of the last things you said to me? You said, 'look after Sofia'. Remember that? I made some dumb joke about her being more likely to look after me. That made you laugh, but you probably knew it was true, didn't you? Mum, I've screwed everything up. Everything's gone wrong.'

I kneel down in the clearing, grabbing some of the tall grass behind me and breaking it up in my hands. The smell of the grass I remember clearly, and it's still the same. The trickle from the stream is not there. Either it's not flowing as well as it did back then, or, more likely, my hearing isn't what it used to be. But I can close my eyes and remember everything I need. I'll never lose that, whatever happens to my ageing body. I try to feel the presence of my parents, picturing them as they were when we holidayed here, willing them to join me. I remember watching Sofia when we'd scattered the ashes. She had her eyes closed too, whispering a prayer.

I stand and push through further into the foliage, aiming my torch beam beyond the oak tree. The feel of the leaves brushing my skin. The branches and thorns catching me. It's all familiar. Back when I was a child, I didn't care if my t-shirt ripped, or I got my trainers muddy. Those things didn't matter then, and, in this moment, they don't matter either. I come to where the stream always was. Where I cooled my hands and face when it got too hot. Where Dad used to pretend to push me in, before grabbing my shoulders and pulling me back. Where I launched the tiny balsa-wood ship we built together under the light of the caravan's gas-lamp. I train my torch beam on the spot, and it's no longer there. It's dried up. Lifeless.

Back out in the clearing, I straighten my clothing.

'Everything comes to an end, doesn't it? But I've got it all up here,' I tell Mum and Dad, tapping my temple with my forefinger.

'And it's not going anywhere. I love you lots. It's been nice talking to you, I'll come back again soon.'

I blow a kiss, because I don't know what else to do, and it feels right. Then I head back towards the main building, hoping I can sneak away quietly.

The phone rings, and I reject the call, don't recognise the number. It rings again almost straight away, so I accept it this time.

'Is this Ian Wren?'

'Yeah.'

'Ian, this is the fire service. You're listed as a keyholder for Wren Studio?'

'Yes. What's happened?'

'Sir, I'm afraid there's been a report of a fire at the premises. We're en route… if you could meet our units on scene, please?'

The shock sends electricity pulsing under my skin. I fumble for the car keys as I race back up the track.

The journey takes forever, and as I pull into the yard, my heart pounds. I saw the black smoke rising as soon as I hit Holloway Road. Four fire engines are here, and at least twenty firemen. Hoses are trained on the roof of the studio, trailing in loops back to the vehicles. The acrid odour stings my nasal passages.

'Stay back, please, Sir.' A police sergeant raises his hands.

'This is my unit.'

He ushers me back behind the appliances. 'They've got it contained now, but you need to keep well back, okay? Can you confirm there should be nobody in the premises?'

'Yes. I work by myself. How did it start?'

'We don't know yet. There'll be an investigation, but the commander's first thought was arson. The front door had been smashed in and windows were open when they arrived.'

I rub my eyes with my palms.

'A passer-by called it in,' the sergeant says. 'Been going for a couple of hours at least. I'll need to take some details from you.'

He goes over to his car, and I take a seat on the same wall where Hannan first spoke to me. Is there a curse on this place? My second home, my livelihood: gone. The shell of the building looks reasonably intact, but the roof's fallen in and whatever's left of what's inside will have been completely destroyed by fire and water. Insurance money won't help, either. My gear's been a journey of collection and gathering for decades. Every single piece of kit in the studio has been selected for a specific use. Building it back up will be impossible. Whoever did this to me couldn't have chosen a more precise hit. An image of Ellie with the guitar I loaned her plays in my mind. And then a smiling Robert Warrister, telling me how he's not paying for the work, because my engineer was too junior.

The sergeant returns with a clipboard and wrestles with the sheets of paper he's folding over the top.

Chapter Thirty-seven

Ellie's Diary • Halloween 2016

I don't know how I feel about the dark. It's a handy excuse for not being outside. It's acceptable to be holed up in your room on Halloween, isn't it? But at the same time the dark evenings amplify the terror that somebody's out there. I keep telling myself that you can hide easily in the dark. Right?

Gaynor bustled off, expecting a busy night in the control room. Hooligans ruin the whole thing for the kids, she said. She laminated some poster she got from work and taped it to the front door. A warning from Thames Valley Police that we weren't participating in trick or treat. Like the troublemakers are going to pay any attention to that. It annoyed Dennis because he'd bought a load of sweets to hand out. I switched off the doorbell power supply as well, but he hasn't noticed yet. He's got a new dog to keep him occupied though.

I don't hate that there's a big German Shepherd around now. So long as it stays on the other side of the house. My whole life seems like one big love/hate relationship – the dark, the bloody dog. I appreciate the extra level of security, but I can't be around big dogs. When I was ten years old, I was flattened by one in the park. The owner didn't even have a lead for it, just opened the door of his car and let it run across the football pitches. Me and Dad were trying to get a kite up, with nowhere near enough wind, when the dog charged me, knocked me clean off my feet and ran off again. I was in shock, but it was the look on Dad's face that really freaked me out. I started crying. He carried me back to the car and checked me over, asking me where it hurt and whether I'd banged my head. I hadn't. Tbh it didn't hurt physically at all, but I've never forgotten it.

Dad pulled my sketch pad and pencils out of his rucksack and asked me to draw him something nice while he went to use the public toilets. I knew where he was really going, though, and watched him out of the back window. The dog owner was leaning against his car smoking. He must've seen what had happened and started squaring up to Dad as he approached. Dad was smaller, and I'd never have put money on him in a fight. But I'd seen something in his eyes that changed all that. I watched from the car as the man threw a punch at Dad's face. But Dad stood his ground and traded blows with him. It was awful. I turned back around and slid down in my seat. It didn't take long. Dad came back, checked on me again, and we pulled out of the carpark. I peeped out of the window and saw the man doubled over against his car, spitting blood on the ground. We never spoke about it.

The whole German Shepherd thing was really odd. Gaynor appeared with it in the hallway and gave Dennis a glance like they'd already arranged everything. I suspect I caught them before they had a chance to butter me up. She said I didn't have to do any of the feeding or anything, but I could take him for walks if I wanted. A way of getting me back out into the world, I suppose, but then they don't know everything, do they? Of course, they gradually fed in how he might help me feel more secure and protect me if anything did happen. It was no big deal, they said, while making it feel like the most important thing in the world. Gaynor remembered about the dog that knocked me over when I jogged her memory. She felt terrible and immediately ordered Dennis to take the German Shepherd outside.

Turned out he came from Emma. One of her kids was getting the sniffles from the dog's shedding fur, and she had to rehome him quickly. Gaynor probably jumped at the chance when she found out – a quick fix for her fragile little bestie. Took me ages to get to the bottom of how it came about. Gaynor knows Emma doesn't like me and so she didn't want to admit that's where the dog came from. But I don't have anything against Emma. She resents me for some reason, but I have no idea why. And I struggle enough with normal people – difficult characters are entirely out of reach.

I'm getting the hang of recording on my laptop now. Some of my songs are starting to take shape, the layers of instrumentation suggesting new melodies, as the inspiration builds. It's the one place I can be free. Where I can be safe for a while, even on Halloween. Let them celebrate the dark and mysterious. It's easy to hide in the dark.

Chapter Thirty-eight

Marlon • London • February 2019

These boys need to count their lucky stars they don't have a sister like mine. She'd be giving 'em the biggest slap right now. He's in the centre of it, the white boy with the trainers he shouldn't be able to afford. It took some waiting around to find him again, hanging by the café where he gave me Warrister's message. He's taken a flat cap right off of an old guy's head and his mates are throwing it to each other like a frisbee. Not bothered by all the people around. All the locals looking down and pretending they haven't seen the old man flailing about, trying to grab it back. The boys are teasing him, big group of them. Bullies. They want shooting. The old man's swearing his head off, slowing down with each attempt to reach his hat. They're laughing at him.

I pull my hood off and step out into the middle of the pavement. Some of the black kids see me first and ask me what I'm gonna do about it, and if I've got a problem. They've lost interest in the cap for now. The white kid's still goading the guy, but when he turns to see what else is happening and spots me, his face drops. He pulls his hood up and takes off. I sprint after him, glancing over my shoulder, but his gang of cowards aren't joining the chase. He's bent forward, quicker than I expected. But that's okay. Must be those hot sneaks he's wearing. He's gained some distance on me now. Glad to see he didn't jump on the back of the bus that pulled out. Around the corner now, as a big guy steps out of the off licence, nearly taking my legs away. I keep the boy in view as the guy shouts abuse at me.

A woman is screaming at me now too, telling me to leave the poor little kid alone. I keep on his tail, close but not too close. He's heading for the market. I'll lose him in there, for sure. The green-and-white covered stalls are crammed into the tight street, people packed in like sardines. Long strides to try and make up some ground. I catch sight of him slipping down the side of a vegetable stall and see his back as he legs it. I reach the end of the stalls and find him waiting in a shop doorway. He's grinning at me because next to him stands a right menace. Could be his dad, or a much older brother. There's a strong resemblance. Except, this monster has a look in his eyes that tells me he's good at this sort of stuff. Neck ink. Ripped. He's grinning at me too. He rubs his buzzed head with his hand, then grabs me by the arm, practically dragging me back behind the last stall. My legs give out under me, and I can't get anyone's attention before we drop out of sight behind the green plastic sheets.

He stands over me.

'Giving my fam some bother, are ya?'

I try to say something to calm him down, but he hits me hard across the face. It stings like hell. He pulls back his arm for another shot, but he's grabbed from behind.

Steve Lewis has his arm in some sort of lock. Steve's out of breath, but he kept his word and got to me in time. I'm the one doing the grinning now, as Steve puts the nutcase on the ground. In seconds, Steve is sitting behind him with a choke hold on his neck, his legs wrapped around his thick waist. The bloke can't move. He tries to reach back, but Steve squeezes his neck a little and describes in detail what'll happen if he's forced to apply more pressure. The boy starts kicking at Steve's legs, but I grab his arms and pin him against a lamppost.

'You're hurting me,' he shouts.

'That's for the old man,' I say.

I get now why Steve's so quietly confident – the guy's a superman. He speaks calmly to the bloke whose limbs are all tied up and useless.

'Tell me if it was you.'

'What was me?'

'Somebody doing a favour for Robert Warrister gives Marlon here a message. But he does not look to me like he's capable of setting a precise, deliberate ignition – no offence, kid – and when we follow him, he runs straight to you.'

'Dunno what you're on about,' the hulk stammers.

'I mean, you're not particularly clever either, are you?'

The bloke thrashes around a bit at that, but Steve squeezes his choke hold tighter and he gives up again. 'But you might be able to handle a break-in and arson with help,' Steve continues. 'If it wasn't you, I want to know who it was... please.'

'I don't know anything about all that.'

The boy's head drops. He's not struggling any more.

'Kenny's got nothin' to do with it,' he says.

'So, who should I be asking?' Steve says.

'I dunno.'

Steve tightens his grip on his prisoner. 'Are you sure?'

Colour all gone from the boy's face. He's never seen his hero Kenny manipulated so effortlessly before. He says, 'I don't know nothin' about no arson, but I can give you the name of Warrister's soldier, just let him go.'

Steve laughs, 'I didn't realise we were at war, did you, Marlon? What's his *soldier's* name?'

'Dexter Wilson. You didn't hear it from me, alright? Let me go now, yeah?'

Steve keeps the hooks in. 'Where does Dexter Wilson live?'

'I dunno, he's not from the estate.' The boy is even more panicky now.

Steve releases Kenny carefully, like he's done this a million times, asking him if he's gonna behave.

Kenny nods and Steve demands a verbal answer. Then he releases the arm lock he used to stand up and backs off slowly.

'Thank you, gentlemen,' he says, pulling me with him as we merge back into the market foot-traffic.

'That's good enough for now,' Steve says.

I just look at him, as we walk quickly back towards the tube station. 'Can you teach me some of that?'

'I've been training a long time, mate.'

'Just give me one technique I can use.'

'Knowing a little is more dangerous than knowing nothing,' he says.

I'm wondering how that can be, when he changes the subject. 'Ian's a partner person, isn't he?'

'Definitely.' I feel so sorry for the guy, even though a part of me always knew it would come to this. What did he expect, ignoring Warrister's threats like that?

'Crowd funding's not gonna help him, is it?'

I shake my head. 'Man, the love he had for his microphone collection... he was telling me how they all have their own character. He'd have the shop line them all up so he could shoot test them. He knew that gear inside and out. Won't be able to replace it.'

'He told me everything yesterday, you know.'

'What did he say?'

'All about the theory of Ellie's nutcase protector.'

I'm stunned. 'I thought that was private. He was just gonna tell you about Warrister trying to get us to drop our statements.'

Steve wraps an arm around me as we walk. 'He's worried about you. The fire freaked him out. You stay close to me until we can sort this out, alright?'

'What are we gonna do about this Dexter bloke?'

'Give his name to the police to investigate.'

'That's it?'

'Of course. What else could we do?'

'Dunno. Find him ourselves?'

He laughs loudly at that. 'We get back to my car, I drive you home. You stay there until I come pick you up for the show tomorrow.'

'You're worried about me too.'

He slaps me hard on the back as we turn down into the subway steps.

'You're just gonna give this Dexter Wilson name to the police?'

'That's all I'm gonna do,' he says.

Chapter Thirty-nine

Ian • London • February 2019

Sofia suggested the park in Highgate. She'll be waiting at the bench. I know exactly where she means. She's already there, dressed simply in a long coat and jeans. As I get closer and she smiles, I notice she's wearing no makeup either. That's new. She's humbling herself. For me or for Jesus?

She doesn't say anything, smiling through a scrunched-up puppy-dog face that says, 'I'm sorry, I can't change what happened, but here we are.' It feels sincere, but I have no words either, so I hug her as if she is an aunt I haven't seen for years. It's strange what being apart can do. All the intimacy you've built up kind of resets a little. We're the same, but not.

'Can I try and explain?' she says softly.

'Before you do, let me tell you what's at stake now.'

I tell her what I kept from her, and what is completely new to her. I tell her all about Gaynor, although I don't include my absurd paranoia around what she could've done while I was asleep.

She listens, and when I'm done, says, 'Feelings are fluid aren't they, but they can fool us.'

She's talking about how I felt when Gaynor seemed to fill the gap of the empty flat. But she could be describing herself as well.

'You felt the same?'

'If you mean what happened on Wednesday, with that man,

then no. That was because I was angry with you.'

'And because of the cocktails?'

'That too. But if I wasn't angry at you, it wouldn't have happened. I let him kiss me by the way.'

'That's it?'

'The fact that I let him is the big thing here, not what happened or didn't happen.' She looks away.

'I wanted to kill him,' I say, then pull a face that suggests only cartoon violence.

She turns back to me, shaking her head. Her dark ponytail dances enticingly across her shoulders. She says, 'I wouldn't recognise him if I saw him again.' She sneaks her fingers around mine, but I don't squeeze hers like I used to. We sit holding hands and looking across the clearing, like uncertain teenagers.

'I tried to see you as soon as I heard about the fire,' she says.

'They kept me forever. Statements, forms, interrogation.'

'They thought you were involved?'

'Ruling me out, they said. Just a formality. Luckily, I had Punch and Judy to back me up.'

She laughs but she can't know what the hell I'm on about.

'Shall we head for one of the forest trails, get some shelter?' I suggest.

She nods.

'I went to see Mum and Dad again,' I say.

'I wish I could've come with you.'

'Well, I was talking to them out loud, so it's probably good nobody else was there,' I laugh.

'Your mum and I had the best chats.'

'One of the last things she told me was to look after you.'

'We look after each other,' she says and pumps my hand in hers a couple of times.

'Funny, I said something similar to her... well, sort of.' I drift for a while, memories of my parents appearing again.

Sofia says, 'What'll you do? You have the setup at home – is that enough for now?'

'For certain things.' I rub my hand across my eyes. 'But I don't know.'

'Don't know what?'

'If that's what I want to do.'

She's shocked. 'Music is your life. It'd be a mistake to drop it.'

I can see how absurd that must sound to her, my work having been a major contributor to our falling out.

'Mistakes can be opportunities,' I say, almost to myself.

She smiles, and says, 'Miles Davis's guy.'

'Huh?'

'You told me about that musician that played with Miles Davis. He played the wrong chord, but Miles Davis used the mistake to create a new melody on the spot. You don't remember?'

''Course I do. The guy applied that idea of mistakes bringing new opportunities to the rest of his life.'

'Why so confused then?'

'Because you remembered it,' I say. 'I talk a lot. I assumed you weren't always listening.'

She playfully swipes at the back of my head. 'Women can multi-task – I am always listening.'

My brain immediately lists the hundreds of instances I've multi-tasked while engineering a session. 'Yeah, I've heard you girls are good at that.'

She's off in her own world for a while, then says, 'You did that talk once at the university.'

'Yeah, I remember.' It was a guest spot on microphones at London Met.

'You came back buzzing.'

'It was fun. I got a real kick out of their enthusiasm.'

She nudges me with her shoulder. 'You could help a lot more people doing something like that.'

'Lecturing?'

'Sure, why not?'

It's an interesting thought, and melds with something else I've had my mind on since working the social media platforms for Ellie's release.

'There are ways to reach so many people now. Something to think about,' I say.

'You can only help so many people in the studio. Many more in the university.'

'Even more online.'

She smiles, and finally reaches an arm around my back. I allow her to pull in close, but don't commit to a full hug.

Ellie does feel like a full stop in my artist development work. Nobody else could compete. Some form of teaching would also help me build a solid relationship back up with Sofia. I lost my parents, Ellie, my livelihood. I'm trying not to lose Sofia as well.

'Do you think they'll be able to prove it was Robert Warrister behind the fire?'

'It's obvious he put it together, but we need proof.'

'Forensics can do that, surely?'

'We'll see. Most of the evidence will be burned to a crisp. I'm holding out for something they can find in the witness statements. Or some CCTV somewhere that nobody knew about.'

'Will they try anything else, Warrister's people?'

'That's what I wanted to talk to you about. I think he'll feel like he's won now, but who knows? Maybe it's better if you stay with Simone.'

She pulls my face towards hers, clasping it with two hands, and kisses me deeply. 'I'm coming home,' she says. The fiery Italian passion I fell for when we first met: still there. 'But I still can't believe you threw my present.'

She goes to speak, and I'm afraid she'll tell me what was in the package.

'Don't say anything else!' I say quickly. 'I was keeping the package until you came home. Just something that kept a little spark going for me.'

'So sweet.' She kisses me again. 'I can show you a lot of things you missed out on,' she whispers.

She leads me by the hand down the path. The dappled light of the weak winter sun has thrown down a disruptive pattern on the forest floor, like a camouflage smock: patches where she can warm her face, patches where I can hide.

Chapter Forty

Ellie's Diary • June 2018

I took the first step towards a brand-new world today. I called Gaynor. Made me sad even before she answered. I could only whisper hello.

She was nice, even though she said 'I thought you'd forgotten about us,' which was a bit pointed. But it had to be this way. She'll thank me when she finds out why. I told her I missed her, thanked her for the comments she posted about my videos, which obviously she thought I hadn't seen, so then I had to apologise for not answering them.

I wanted to tell her that I was going to the police about the Valentine's card, the one Dennis threw in the fire. I'd hardly mentioned it – I've got news, I said – when she went really quiet. Turns out she'd had one too, a few days after mine. Exactly the same – hearts on the envelope, childish handwriting, a message typed on a sticky label. Except hers was about how she should keep her distance from me, what I might have caught from Danny, that sort of thing. Just regular abuse. I've heard worse, but even so – all this time, and she's never told me. Oh, she says it's because I was petrified about the murderer never being found. How could she have burdened me with it on top of everything else? Jesus, does nobody think I'm capable of looking after myself? I thought my heart would burst out of my chest.

Then, for a moment, I was excited, I'd have something to show the police, but – of course – she doesn't have the card, she threw it away. I told her I didn't believe her. She'd wanted me to report mine, but she said I was adamant I wouldn't, and she'd always do what I wanted, and we'd always be together in this. In the end, I tell her she did the right thing.

I know exactly why she received the card. Suddenly everything has changed. I've been working up to this day since I came to London. Getting out here, away from home, away from the past, starting fresh. Part of the new me was encouraging the bravery, to finally talk to the police about the protector's message. I was ready to face him head on, flush him out like the coward he is. To get justice for Danny after all this time. From my viewpoint in the city, he seemed like a big fish in a small pond. I've swum in deeper waters now, and I was ready to take him on. But the card Gaynor received has changed everything. He wanted me to know that she is a target. I can run wherever I want, but my friends and family will always be there to pay for my actions. It's clear: I talk, she dies. Thank God, she told me in time.

Once I've reassured her that I'm not cross, she asks me what the news was and what it had to do with the Valentine's card. My mind races for a response, so I tell her I've found a manager, and he's got me in to record some demos with a top producer, and he's great though the manager's a creep, but he's got contacts and he says he'll take the demos around all the labels, all of which is true – and that I've moved on from the Valentine's card thing, and I'm over all that now. Which is so not true.

She tells me she loves me, and I tell her the same. Lovely hearing each other's voices. Yadda yadda yadda.

My direction has shifted 180 degrees. All the bravery, all the determination I'd worked up has corroded. But at the same time, a huge weight feels like it's been lifted from my shoulders. I can't talk to Gaynor again. I've been protecting her – all of them – and it turns out I was right to be so paranoid. There's only one option left as far as I can see, and I find myself so easily resigned to it. I'm running my fingertips over the leather couch. I wouldn't have noticed its knobbly texture before, but the world seems simple now, like it never has before. I can't change what's already happened, but I can fix everything in the future by simply removing the cause. I wonder what Jude would think if he knew I still have the pills they gave me three years ago. It freaked me out, having him appear so suddenly so soon after I got here. Somewhere, in the back of my mind, I always knew I might need them.

Chapter Forty-one

Marlon • London • March 2019

Steve's quiet this morning. He says it's because he hates Mondays, but I think it's something else.

'Give us a hand with this?' he says, rocking a big speaker cabinet out from the corner of the room. It's a lock-up he uses in Bethnal Green to store the extra equipment he hires out. He's been telling me about his side-hustle, providing PA and lighting for corporate events. He keeps the best stuff back for our gigs, but there's plenty of decent kit here too, by the look of it.

I take one end of the cabinet and we shuffle over to the roll-up door with it.

'Just here,' he says. 'I'll come back for it in the van later.'

A train rumbles overhead, rattling a loose strip-light on the ceiling. There's a recording studio further down the road, in another railway arch unit, and I can't understand how that's even possible with the amount of noise I'm hearing. I ask Steve about it, but he doesn't hear me.

'I've gotta pop down the road for a bit,' he says. 'Bookshop might want a small PA for some signing event.'

'Need me to come?'

'Nah, won't take long. Can you dust off some of the cabs at the back, and anything else that needs a bit of a spruce-up.' He throws me a duster. 'There's some polish in the cupboard there.'

When he's gone, I grab the padlock and key and leave, rolling down the metal door behind me. Unit secured, I sprint up to the main road. Steve is some way ahead, and I need to keep him in view. He's been weird since Saturday when we got the name of Dexter Wilson. He said he was gonna tell the police, but I know he's got something else in mind. I was asking him about his fighting skills, and he told me he goes to an MMA gym in Tottenham. Started doing Taekwondo when he was little and moved on to some other martial arts I hadn't even heard of. I need to get him to show me some stuff.

When Steve reaches the steps leading down into the tube station, I race to catch up. I skip down the steps but his distinctive blond hair has disappeared. I check the eastbound platform first, poking my head round the corner. It's not busy so I quickly see he's not there. I sprint over to platform one. He's at the far end, waiting up by the yellow line, keen. He's so after Dexter Wilson, I know it. Westbound. Where could he be heading, and how does he even know where Dexter is? As the train pulls in, I track along the wall, no closer than I need to be to see where Steve gets on. Then I get on two carriages along. As we rumble out of the station, I pull my hood up. The wait begins.

He doesn't get off at Liverpool Street or Bank, as far as I can tell, as I duck down behind a couple of tall blokes and scan the platform. I relax a little. Those stations have too many options and it would've been tough to keep track of him. When we stop at Holborn, Steve strides off down the platform and I follow him to the Piccadilly line. He boards a northbound, and I just squeeze on before the doors close. Arsenal? Holloway Road? Where are you going, Steve? An old lady in the seat opposite pulls her bag closer to her body. She's just looked at me and clearly doesn't like what she sees. I'm not surprised, I'm buzzing with energy now, and more than a little scared of what this might turn out to be. But Steve's been there for me, and I'm not gonna let him do this on his own, whether he wants me there or not.

He doesn't get off at King's Cross, thank God, but at Caledonian Road I think I see him. A small group heads for the exit and I'm nearly positive he's in there. I take a chance and slide out of the carriage as the doors are closing. I catch up with the group, and Steve is way ahead. I'm soon at the exit. Steve's gone right out of the station and has crossed the road. I stay on the opposite side, keeping well back. He's walking fast. At a zebra crossing he stops and looks right, but I get lucky and pull back just in time. He doesn't spot me. Carries on up the road, past the church. A woman in a hijab gives me a funny look. I'm not good at this, I know. I'm half wondering whether to catch up with Steve and ask him what's going on. I think he'd appreciate my loyalty. But I don't want him to call it off. He's made it clear he's gonna protect me; even lied to me to keep me back at the lock-up. I can't ruin it for him. But if he needs me, I'll be right there, ready to help.

After a few minutes, he turns off. I can't believe it. I think that's Pentonville. I duck behind a big tree, until he's out of sight, then run across the road and look in. I watch him carry on down and turn into the prison's main gate. If Dexter Wilson did the arson, he's not going to be in there. Who is Steve going to see? He lied to me; said he was going to see someone from the bookshop. If he hadn't done that, I'd assume he had a mate inside or something. But he lied. That sucks. I thought I could trust him, man. He was one of the good guys. I cross back over the road and lean against one of the trees. If he comes back out, I don't want him to see me. But he must be visiting an inmate. How long do those things last? Fifteen minutes? First of all, he's not gonna need my help with anything in there. Also, why the hell should I help him if he can't even be honest with me?

After five minutes, I lose patience, and call Ian.

'Marlon, how are you?'

'Alright. Anything new on the fire?'

'Nothing we couldn't have guessed. Steve with you?'

'I'm getting a drink from the shop. He's gone to see a client.'

'Okay, cool. Keep an eye out, won't you? I think Warrister knows it's all down to me, but I don't want you hanging about on your own, alright?'

'They found any decent evidence?'

'Multiple seats of fire, all in the main studio. Right where the expensive gear was. All the windows were left open. No signs of any electrical fault. It was deliberate ignition.'

'But hard to prove it was Warrister.'

'Probably impossible. I'd imagine every single one of his associates are criminals, so where would they start?'

'Cops still got him?'

'He's on remand, apparently. When I spoke to Hannan, our witness intimidation thing was the icing on the cake. He's got a lot hanging over him now.'

'Where's he on remand? In prison?'

'I don't know. Most probably.'

'That'd be Pentonville, wouldn't it? For this area?'

'Guess so. Why?'

'Dunno, just worried about where he is, I suppose.'

'Look, as long as you don't go hanging around in the wrong places, you'll be okay. Like I said, I reckon it's over now anyway.'

'Cool. I just can't believe you've lost everything.'

'We're both alright, that's the important thing,' he says. But he's only saying that for me.

'What you up to today?'

'Sofia's moving back in. We're changing the flat round a bit.'

'That's amazing. So pleased for you guys.' I cross over and check there's still no sign of Steve. 'Right, I've got massive speaker cabinets to dust, see ya later.'

'Take care, mate. See you soon.'

Well, at least Ian's not lying to me as well. I'd be able to tell. He sounds a bit brighter now he's got his girl back. I head back on the tube. I'll grab a sandwich in Bethnal Green, go back to the lock-up, dust off some of the equipment, and wait nicely for Steve to get back. I won't even ask him where's he's been. If he tells me he had to change his plans and visit a mate in prison, I'll pretend none of this ever happened. But if he tells me he had a successful meeting with the bookshop guy, I'll just walk away and never speak to him again.

Chapter Forty-two

Ellie • London • August 2018

Dear Ian,

I'm glad I found you. You understand me, like few people ever have. I'm sorry to be writing this to you, but I wanted you to understand. I wasn't being paranoid; there really is someone out there, someone dangerous. 'You'll be safe underneath Philippa's tree' he wrote to me – only my dad knows about that. It's how I know Dad made a terrible mistake. The calm that came over me when all the other options were stripped away is still here, but I can't help thinking about what will be lost. My memories and experiences will vanish with me. Only the music will remain. At first, I was going to use Dad's poem simply to let the monster that's supposedly protecting me know that it's over. But I decided I'd use the whole poem to set some of those memories in stone. Like making a digital back-up of my life before I close down.

Everything was still set up from today's session. You've been generous in sharing your knowledge and process with me. Listen to what I made. I didn't need anything fancy for this. I know I'd only need one take, and if there are flaws, well then, it'll be a true expression of my life.

But it had to be a good quality recording. It's going to capture my life forever. I want you to know, Ian, that when I sing, a floating feeling comes over my body, and everything feels easy. When I sing this song, I see my mother's tree, with my dad and me underneath it; my mother's spirit hovering beside us, strengthening Dad, channelling her love through him.

I've listened back and I think the vocal is perfect. Not perfect in the usual sense, but what could ever be truly perfect? But it is entirely what I wished for it to be. I hope you like it. I can rely on you to do the rest, I know I can. I've struggled to write this. It's hard to express everything you meant to me. I guess the constant stress has been pulling me down this whole time. This may well be the end, but to me it feels like something fresh. Like falling asleep excited on Christmas Eve.

I've got what I needed. I was surprised when I read how many pills it would take. Danny's family gave me enough to help me through my grief. I told them I didn't think I'd ever sleep again. But I didn't want to cheat Danny. If my mind wanted me to stay awake keeping his memory alive, then I would get through it for him. And maybe fate wanted me to have enough pills for the final push. In the end, it'll be easy. I've worked hard to keep my friends apart. Anything I can do to make my supposed protector's job difficult.

Just so you know everything, there's a boy, Marlon, who lives near. I made friends with him. I hope he makes contact with you. Look after him, Ian – he's a great kid.

I've finished my housekeeping. It's time for the journey. I've picked out my spot, on the floor behind the sofa. I don't know why. If anything, the area is a bit tatty. Don't be cross with me for saying that. But there's nothing grandiose about this. If nothing else, I should be humble. A promise I made to myself is to not back out. I won't potter around the studio waiting for something to happen. I'll lay down on the floor, close my eyes, and accept whatever happens to me. I will block out everything I've read on the internet and simply allow the changes in my body to happen. I've done all I can, and I'm content. I'm glad you sprayed the perfume, by the way – in the vocal booth. It's something to think about. Something nice.

I'm sorry I lied about the new direction. But Yannis would've ruined the music, wouldn't he?

Thank you for everything, and don't feel bad. Take care of yourself.

Chapter Forty-three

Marlon • London • March 2019

It's nearly three o'clock when Steve appears back at the lock-up. All smiles and innocence, wiping a couple of speaker cabinets with his palm and inspecting for dust.

'Sorry, mate, I got stuck talking. Looks like you did a good job here,' he says.

I'm trying to keep it together. 'You've been gone ages.'

'I know, but we've got the thing at the bookshop. Good, eh?'

I know how confused my face looks right now. I can't even speak.

'Turns out it's today. They need us down there by four. You had lunch yet?'

'I got a sandwich.'

'Good, I might grab something on the way. Thought we could walk the gear down there. We'll only need a few bits and it's a nice day.'

'Right.'

He fishes around in one of the old wardrobes he uses as cupboards. Pulls out a plastic case and opens it up.

'These'll do nicely,' he says, turning a couple of microphones over in his hands. They don't look as good as the ones we normally use.

'Bit short notice, wasn't it?'

'Yeah. The company they normally use let them down this morning.'

He packs the microphones back into the case and goes over to the back of the unit. Now, he's asking me about PA choices. He knows I wouldn't have a clue. He's gotta be covering up for something.

'What d'ya reckon?' He's holding up an amp with the mixer built in.

'Well... what did you promise them?'

'I didn't. They don't know anything about sound gear.'

'What were you talking to them about then? You were gone hours.'

He puts the amp down and turns, hands on his hips. 'What's going on, mate?'

'Nothin'.'

'There's something on your mind, I can see it all over your face. Look, I know cleaning's no fun, but it's important. It's a small rig today; I can show you a bit more about how it all works, yeah?'

'Sure.'

He picks up a small speaker and carries it towards the door. 'Grab the other one, will you?'

'These gonna be big enough?' It's light as a feather.

'These things, right – it's a bloke sat on a stool talking to a small group of people in a tiny space. They don't need any amplification.'

'Why have we got the job then?'

He grins at me. 'Because they want the guest speaker to feel important, and it makes the event seem a bit more professional.'

He pulls a long canvas bag out from under some boxes and opens it up. Speaker stands. He takes a few audio cables and throws them into the bag, zipping it back up. 'I'll take the amp and the speaker stands if you can manage the two speakers.'

''Course I can manage them, they're super-light.' Is he taking the mick? How dare he talk to me like that. Liar and an idiot.

We're shown to the back of the bookshop, where there are some chairs set out. Steve was right; it is tiny. He pulls the speaker stands out of the bag and hands me one. I watch how he does it and put the other one together. The manager comes in to shake our hands.

'Excellent,' he says. Then, to the young girl who showed us in, 'Could we have two stools over here, please?'

The guy is exactly how I would imagine a small bookshop manager to look and sound like. I can't imagine him and Steve having much at all to talk about. They're chatting now, and I'd say it confirms what I'm thinking.

Steve shows me how he connects the speakers and amp, which he puts on a table off to the side. Then we plug in the two microphones and rest each one on a stool.

'Give us a one-two,' he says, walking over to the amp.

I hate doing that, even when there's only four of us in the room. Then he asks me to read a bit from one of the books on the shelf behind me. I pick up a kids' book, just in case, and read a few lines. Sounds alright to me.

'Come over and have a look.' He shows me the EQ settings and levels he's using, then gets me to duplicate it for the second mic. He goes over and does a quick line check on it. All is good.

He says to the manager, 'All ready. Just switch on the microphones when you want to start.'

'Will you monitor, for the talk? We've had problems with feedback in the past.'

'You won't have any problems with feedback,' Steve says, and I recognise the look he has when he's cracking up below the surface.

He says to me, 'Going outside for a smoke,' and I follow him out the back door into the carpark. He rolls one, lights it and rests against the wall.

'I went down to that studio down near us,' I say.

'Oh yeah?'

'Yeah. I wanted to ask him about the noise from the train tracks.'

'What did he say?'

'Quite a lot. I didn't understand any of it. Something about the science of acoustics, but I stopped listening after the first few words. Basically, he called in a specialist.'

'Haha! Absorption coefficients of the materials and other absorbing facts. Good fun.'

'Yeah, he did say something like that. Oh, he said he recommended you. The bookshop guy came to the studio to ask him about the PA.'

'That's right, he did.'

'He said he gave you a phone number for the bookshop days ago.'

'Yeah. What the hell is going on, Marlon? Why are you so suddenly interested in how I get our contracts?'

I pause, unsure where to go next.

He says, 'Are you looking to undercut me, now you know what you're doing?' and playfully goes to slap my head.

'No,' I say. 'It's just that I followed you to Pentonville.'

His face hardens. He throws his smoke down.

'What did you say?'

'What were you doing there? Why did you lie to me?'

'Now, hold on a minute, I –'

'Come on, Steve. Why couldn't you say you decided to visit a mate in prison? Why lie to me about going to the bookshop?'

'Why follow me when you're supposed to be working? Sounds like it's you that's got the issues, not me.'

'I knew there was something up. I thought you were going to look for Dexter Wilson.'

Something changes in his face, and he drops his shoulders a little.

'Marlon, look… I don't want you involved in this, alright? I'm trying to keep you out of any more trouble.'

'Dexter Wilson is in prison?'

'No. Robert Warrister is on remand at Pentonville. I wanted to talk to him.'

'About what happened to Ellie?'

'No. I needed to know if he was done with you and Ian.'

'And?'

He puts a hand on my shoulder. 'It's over. He's got other things on his mind now.'

'He admitted to the fire?'

''Course not. But it was one hundred percent his call.'

'You gonna tell the police?'

'Tell them what? That I spoke to Warrister and I think he did it? No, mate. I just wanted to hear him say that you and Ian are off his hit-list.'

He looks at me in a way that brings me back down.

'Appreciate that,' I say, finally.

He steps over and grabs me in a massive man-hug. He's a strong dude. 'Just trust me, will you?'

We go back in, and people have started arriving for the event. The author is sitting on his stool, shaking a few hands.

Neither of us recognise his face or name, but some of the women seem in awe of him. The manager has set up a table at the back for a book signing session afterwards. Now he slips onto the other stool and shakes hands with the author. More people have arrived. It's underway. The manager puts his glasses on and starts introducing the author from a card he's holding. He's very clear, but after a few words, he taps on the mic.

'Can everybody hear me okay?'

Steve has an enormous grin on his face. 'Turn it on!' he shouts from the back, cupping his mouth with his hands.

Chapter Forty-four

Ian • London • March 2019

Sofia has put the kettle on. I stretch out my stiff shoulders. I'm exhausted, but changing the rooms around is good for both of us. It gives me a chance to get away from form-filling and having to think about the fire. Everything gone so quickly. You don't imagine how swift the smite of devastation can be until you experience it first-hand. And all because of some personal disagreement. There are some twisted people out there. Sofia hands me a mug of tea and curls up beside me on the sofa. I shift along a bit to give her some room.

'Do you believe what Steve said?' she says, raising her mug to her lips.

'I don't think he'd lie to me.'

'No, I mean, do you believe what Robert Warrister told him about leaving you alone now?'

'Yes,' I say.

'That sounded forced, baby.'

'Sorry, how should I say it?'

She rubs my arm gently. 'It didn't sound like you really believed it, but you're trying to.'

'Maybe. I mean, who knows whether he's done with me or not? But I need to move on. If I walk around looking over my shoulder all the time, I'll never get anything done.'

She's gripping my arm now, and says, 'I can feel pulsing.' She shifts position, observing my body.

'It's nothing, my nerves or something.'

'You've noticed it before?'

'Sort of, feels like something's a bit... off... sometimes. Weird.'

'Tell me more about it.' She sits up properly, like it's no longer a casual conversation.

'I don't know how to describe it better than that.'

'Any changes in your body, apart from the pulsing?'

Man, I could share this stuff with Jamie at the nursing home, but not with Sofia? First, I don't confront the guy who tried to steal her from me and now I'm pointing out all my weaknesses. I massage my temples.

'Couple of times I felt like I'd fallen through the bed.' I laugh, like it's the most ridiculous thing anyone could imagine.

She doesn't laugh. Says, 'Feeling a bit off balance, tunnel vision, palpitations?'

'I guess so.'

'I'll make you an appointment.'

'Don't, please. Everything that's happened... it's just being on high alert all the time. I keep meaning to do those breathing exercises, but it seems pointless until I've dealt with the arson thing.'

'Ian, it's not pointless. It's the reason you must start doing exercises now, especially if you won't see the doctor. The earlier they see you, the more they can do.'

'They'll just hear about what's been happening and attribute it to that. What's the point?'

'Then, we'll do some exercises on our own, together.'

She takes her phone and pulls up an app. I watch her while she's concentrating on the screen.

'I didn't know you did these.'

'Always. I pick up my work emails first thing, have breakfast and then give myself ten minutes for well-being.'

She sets some audio file running and lays the phone on the table.

'Close your eyes,' she says.

Deep breaths, followed by a focus on the steady breath as it flows in and out. Then the gentle voice guides us through a scan down the body, relaxing each part, and then back to the breath. I do feel more relaxed. The same worries keep crossing over each other in my mind, but I feel slightly more at ease dealing with them.

'Notice the thoughts that pop up,' Sofia says. 'See if you can experience them from a distance. Don't apply your emotion to them.'

She's telling me now not to think, but only to notice what's there. But, in this state, the standout item looming large in my mind is the thought of Ellie's protector. I don't know why that in particular, with the fire and threats from Warrister being my most recent focus. But all I see is the image of a murderous protector, a formless shadow casting its suffocating power over Ellie and her friends. Released, unwittingly, by David Beck in a misguided attempt to continue guarding his little girl.

'Remember to detach emotionally,' Sofia says.

I try to envisage myself looking down on the images, like they're happening in a world far beneath mine, where I can sit and watch impassively. I feel relaxed and weightless, as I see the journey of the protector unfold. I see David Beck, following his diagnosis of Parkinson's Disease, feeling his control ebbing slowly away. I watch him struggling with simple tasks, like writing a shopping list. Walking differently. Becoming confused suddenly in the middle of a conversation or thought. Who is with him? His daughter, Ellie, is tending to his everyday needs, and his personal needs too. It's hard for her. She's seeing more of her father than she's ever needed to before. She can't do everything. She'll be getting help from agencies, surely. I can't know who they are. Any friends? Yes, Gaynor would be with her some of the time, covering when Ellie needs to run an errand, maybe. I see Dennis too, an encouraging older male voice. Yes, Dennis would certainly have been there some of the time. Somewhere in there is the seed of what would eventually spawn a murderous Beelzebub.

'How do you feel now?' Sofia is stroking my arm again, surreptitiously checking for the nervous tremors, I guess.

I open my eyes, and squint from the sunlight bursting into the flat. 'Better.'

'The app finished a while ago, but I could see you were deep,' she says. 'Ten minutes is good, but longer is even more beneficial. You need to do this every day. I'll do it with you to make sure you don't forget. Prevention is better than cure.'

Sofia straddles me on the sofa, starts unbuttoning my shirt. The relaxed state adds a new level of sensitivity. I've felt her restraint since we reconnected. We haven't talked about it; it just seemed apparent to both of us, instinctively. But there have been moments where she's tested the waters. Now she's letting go and my mind is overruled by an urgency of passion that's quickening my pulse. She continues to the last button of my shirt, and I don't stop her.

My phone is vibrating on the coffee table. I don't know how much time has passed.

'Let me check this.'

It's a text from Glen Crane. Doesn't make sense to me at first glance.

Decries knows protector th

Does he mean de Vries?

Of course, he must, and he hasn't noticed that predictive text has kicked in... because he had no time, the message was cut-off. De Vries knows about the protector? Protector thing, protector theory?

My nerves twitch under my skin, my focus kicking wildly against the relaxed state I'm suddenly jerked out of.

'What is it?' Sofia says.

'Later! Just let me think.'

Which de Vries brother, and how the hell did he find out? I try to call Glen but it's just ringing. I try again and again, each time getting voicemail. Why would he not answer after dropping a bombshell like that? I leave a message to call me urgently. Then I reply to his text, saying the same thing. One immediate thought sits right in the eye of the oncoming storm: David Beck is now in danger. The de Vries brothers will want his blood for Danny's murder.

Chapter Forty-five

London/Aylesbury • March 2019

I dump the Mini at the back of Glen's house and bang on his door. No reply. The curtains are open and there's no sign of movement inside. I hammer on the door a few more times.

'He's not in!' At the upstairs window next door, a grey-haired woman is glaring at me.

'You know where he's gone?'

''Course I don't. That's enough banging though. He's not there.'

'Are you sure? He might need help.'

As she's closing the window, she says, 'He will do. Woke me up leaving this morning. I've been waiting for a word in his ear.'

Hannan returns my call.

'What have you got for me?' he says.

'This isn't about the fire. It's Glen Crane. He sent me a text that says de Vries knows about the protector.'

'The brothers? What exactly do they know about that?'

'I don't know. Glen's text was cut off.'

'Have you tried calling him?'

'Won't pick up. I'm at his house now, but he's been out since early this morning, according to the neighbour.'

'And when did you receive the text message?'

'About… twenty minutes ago. I came straight to his house. I'm worried.'

'You think he went to see the de Vries brothers?'

'Must have. Can't think how else they'd have found out about the protector thing.'

'We can only guess what they heard, but it's possible they think David Beck put it together.'

'Exactly. I'm worried about both David and Glen.'

'I'll tell Thames Valley. But you're making a lot of assumptions here.'

'Can they trace Glen's phone? They'll need to send officers to the nursing home.'

'I'll talk to them, and we'll assess it from there, okay? Leave it with me. It'll be quicker if you give me Glen Crane's mobile now.'

I read off the number and Hannan says, 'Try not to worry. And leave it to us. I'll call you when we know more.'

I pace on the grass, then sit down against the house, waiting. I could check Glen's social media, see if he's posted anything today. Fingers crossed for even a quick comment somewhere. It's bright and I cup my hand over the phone but can't see any activity. My body is trembling. It's engaged and wants to get going, but I feel useless. If I stay here, Glen might return and I can find out what's happened. I sit picturing David Beck's face. His vulnerability, his frailty. His potential innocence. He's a sitting duck. I can't shake the memory of going to the nursing home. The lady that held the door open for me with a smile. The de Vries brothers could walk right into that place any time they chose.

When I can wait no more, I check my watch. I've been here an hour. I look for the Milton House telephone number online and dial it, asking for Jamie.

'Ian.' His tone is serious.

'Are the police there with you?'

'No. But they called to talk to management. We've got to ring them if those guys turn up.'

'That's it? They're not sending anyone?'

'No resources available, but they'll redeploy if something happens. Why would these men be after David?'

I phrase my answer carefully. 'They may have heard some false rumours. It's precautionary, but can you stay with David, can you take him somewhere secure?'

'Not just like that, no.'

'Right. Don't take him into any of the open areas then.'

'How serious is this?'

'Jamie, I honestly don't know.'

It's taken me two hours to get to the outskirts of Aylesbury. Jamie called back while I was stuck in traffic to say everything's still quiet there. They had a neighbourhood van come by and a couple of officers tried to reassure them. Gave them advice and reiterated to call 999 if necessary. There's an incident log they should quote, and officers will attend immediately. I can't believe the police aren't taking this more seriously. I texted Gaynor. She'll call me back as soon as she can. I try to put myself into the mind of the brothers. Would they come in the daytime when more is happening, and they might slip past reception? Or at night when staff numbers would be lower?

The phone's ringing again.

'It was nice to hear from you,' Gaynor says.

'What's going on with the nursing home?'

'Pardon?'

'You must have seen it; police went to David Beck's nursing home. And went away again.'

'What for? I'm not covering Aylesbury. What's happened?'

'Have a look at your system. Basically, your lot aren't worried that an old man is about to be attacked by the de Vries brothers.'

'What? I can't check – I came outside to call you. Why would they be after David?'

I bang the steering wheel hard with the palm of my hand.

'Ian? Where are you?'

'I'm in Aylesbury. They heard something about David, and they probably think he had something to do with Danny's murder.'

'What the hell? What have they heard?'

I blow out a long breath of air. 'It's a long story. Ellie said her dad asked somebody to look out for her when he got sick. This guy, whoever he is, killed Danny de Vries because of his HIV. Protecting Ellie.'

Silence. 'Gaynor, are you there?'

Nothing. 'Gaynor?'

'That's ridiculous,' she says. Her tone has changed. She's scared. 'Ellie didn't tell me any of this.'

'It seems she tried to keep it from all of us.'

'The police need to talk to de Vries and sort this out.'

'I assume they're trying to. But you'd know more than me.'

'I'll go back in and see what I can do. Would they really attack a vulnerable old man over a rumour? It doesn't even sound plausible. I don't think David would do that.'

'I only know a bit about them, but Jon is, by all accounts, a complete nutter. And he's waited three years for this first bit of information to come to him. That's a long time to stew.'

'But he hasn't turned up there yet?'

'No. Your lot basically left a calling card with the home.'

It bothers me that Jon has restrained himself. He's had hours at least to get his revenge. Everything I've heard about him has smacked of volatility. But there's no sign of him. Maybe the police are right not to assume?

Gaynor interrupts my thoughts. 'Wouldn't he try and qualify the intel first?'

'How?'

'I don't know. He could take revenge on David, but he wouldn't get any answers, would he?'

'Maybe he's Neanderthal enough to just see red and then worry about the answers later. Where would he get answers from, anyway?'

My thoughts turn immediately to Glen. Somehow, I know my visit the other day got to him. He re-energized when I let slip that Jude had visited Ellie in London. Like he had something new to follow up on; a way to prove to himself that his advances didn't cause Ellie's suicide. Did he go to see the brothers in Oxford? Did he get talking to them and give away the protector theory?

'If they heard it was Ellie's family who started all this, they'd want someone they could force the details out of, wouldn't they?'

'Emma,' I say. 'Emma would be a much better option.'

'Oh my God!'

'Can you get me her home address?'

'Yes. She works at Lloyds Bank in town. I'll tell my sergeant I've got personal knowledge and get him onto it.'

'Text me the home address.'

'Wait for the police, Ian.'

'Just send me the address. I'll check the bank in the meantime. Where is it?'

'Corner of Market Square and Kingsbury. Be careful.'

The bank is closed, but maybe she's still there. I leave the car on double-yellows and try to look through the windows. Too many reflections and advertising posters. At least if she's inside, she's safe. A traffic warden is walking around the Mini.

'Hey, I'm just leaving.'

He says something, but it doesn't register. I'm starting the engine and moving off.

Gaynor's text comes through. It directs me to a large, detached brick house in Stone, just off the main drag through the small village. I pull up outside, out of view from the house, behind some trees. Emma's family seem well off. There's only one car on the large driveway, a black Merc. I text Gaynor again to ask what Emma drives. A few cars pass, but no sign of any trouble. My phone pings a few minutes later: Silver Audi A6. I scan the area again. There's no sign of it.

I get out of the car and stroll casually past the house. People are home. I can see the reflections of a TV show in the window. Probably Emma's husband and kids. Does she come home via the supermarket? Call in on friends? I carry on to the end of the road, trying to fit in with the different pace of a small village. I could ring the doorbell and talk to the husband, but I can't think of anything acceptable to say. It's got to be better to stay sitting up on the house. Besides, if Gaynor's sergeant is competent, he'll have units dealing with the threat already. I have to try and believe that. I go back to the car to wait.

My phone pings. Scott Hannan. Good news, hopefully.

'Ian, I need you to come to the police station. Now, please.'

'I'm out of London. Have you found the de Vries brothers?'

'Where are you?' His tone is stern.

'I can come later. I'm busy sorting out some insurance stuff. Any news on Glen Crane?'

'Ian, the body of a white male has been found. You need to

come to the police station, please, so I can speak to you properly.'

'Uh? Is it... Glen?'

'We don't know for sure, but there's a chance. I'm sorry. Can you make your way here, or shall I send officers for you?'

My limbs are trembling and I'm struggling to keep the phone to my ear. 'I'll... be there soon,' I say.

My world has collapsed in on itself. Then my phone rings again, and I scramble to accept Gaynor's call.

'A body was found in a park in Aylesbury. Is this... anything to do with it?'

'Are you at your desk?'

'In one of the training rooms, so I can speak. I've got the log in front of me. White male, late fifties, early sixties, balding. Oh my God!'

'What? That sounds like Glen, Glen Crane, friend of mine, friend of Ellie's.'

'That's the name they've got here. Ian, the limbs were mutilated.'

'What?'

'I... can't... Ian...'

'Are police on their way to Emma's?'

'No.'

'No? What the hell is going on? I've just had a call from a DI in London who wants me to come to the station.'

'Hold on.'

She's tapping at her keyboard. I can barely focus. Glen is dead? Tortured?

She takes a deep breath. 'Intel received that a Marlon Williams was asking for the deceased's home address. The deceased was seen with injuries later that day.'

My brain is throbbing.

'Ian?'

'Look, they've got it all wrong. Marlon is a good lad, he's nothing to do with this.'

'Oh my God!'

'What have you told your sergeant? Tell him they can look into Marlon as much as they want later, but they need to protect Ellie's family. Get a watch out on Emma Tate's car!'

I can tell she's pulled the phone away from her ear. Tears.

'Gaynor, talk to them.'

'I... I will,' she says.

'Good, do it now.'

'But I'll tell you first,' she says, tightly, as if she's struggling to breathe.

'Tell me what? Gaynor, a good friend of mine is dead. Another innocent woman could be mutilated, if you don't act now!'

'I made it up.'

'Made what up?'

Fits of sobbing now.

'Made what up?' I repeat.

'The protector. The one who killed Danny. I invented the protector. I wanted Ellie to feel safe again.'

I can't speak.

'I was looking after her. I always looked after her.'

My mind is turning over on itself, suppressing the anarchy running wild around it.

'Say something.' She sounds like she's the victim.

'Why?'

'She wouldn't leave the house. She was terrified whoever killed Danny was coming for her too.'

'So, you made up a story about her father hiring a protector. And Ellie believed you?'

'David was always over-protective. And I knew more than she realised... because I loved her... I knew everything. What else could I have done?'

'You could have admitted what you did sooner! That's what you could have done!' I slam the phone into the dashboard. It bounces off into the footwell.

I bury my face in my hands. The loss and despair have crippled my useless, weak body. But one thought summons an edge from somewhere deep within. I grab the phone off the floor.

'Gaynor? There's still a murderer out there. Go to your sergeant and tell him absolutely everything, now. If you don't ring me back in fifteen minutes and tell me you've done this, I will phone in and tell him myself.'

'I will. Ian, I never meant for any of this to –'

'You've known all along why Ellie killed herself.'

'We don't know that. I... always told myself it was something else. She was always so... sad, Ian.'

I end the call and punch the window.

Chapter Forty-six

Marlon • London • March 2019

'Cassie, this is well good.' The sauce smells like heaven, and I cram a forkful of meatball into my mouth.

'Watch your table manners,' she says. Her eyes bulge and her head tilts to the side.

I laugh.

'What's so funny?' she says.

'That face. It cracks me up, but I like it coz it means you're not real angry at me.'

'Marlon, I'm super-angry at you right now.'

She stares, until we both break into hysterics at the same time.

'What did Steve have you doing today?'

I smile because I like being able to tell her the truth. 'A bookshop. They had a guest speaker and wanted a PA set up.'

'Ah, that's something different. Did you brush up on your English Literature while you were there?'

'Actually, I did a reading over the microphone.'

She puts her knife and fork down against her plate. 'You did?'

'Sure. I did good.'

'What did you read?'

'Oh, I can't remember. It was just something they gave me.' Struggling to contain my laughing now.

'Marlon, I'm so proud of you. Did you come over well?'

'Yeah, man. Steve said I should keep on doing the mic checks coz I was so good at it.'

'You little...' She reaches across the table and slaps my hand, giving me the bulging eyes again.

'Hey, now. Watch your table manners,' I say.

She slaps me again.

I run the plate under the hot tap to rinse the sauce stains off. Then I plunge it into the warm, soapy water. Washing up is a different thing when the water's clean. I kind of enjoy it, even. I started filling the bowl before Cassie even had time to ask me. She couldn't believe it. She says there's been a change in me since I've been working with Steve. I think Ian would be more her thing, though.

'I'll come dry in a minute,' she calls from the sofa. 'Just want to watch a bit of this.'

'You watch your programme. I got this. You did all the cooking.'

My back is to her, but she goes quiet, and I can feel those wide eyes on me.

'You should invite Steve over for dinner sometime soon.'

'Sure.'

'He should bring his wife, too.'

'Nah... no need for that.'

'Why not?'

'She's well boring.'

'Marlon! Don't you speak about people like that.'

'Sorry. I mean, she goes on about people all the time.'

'Like a gossip?'

'Yeah, a gossip.'

'Well, I don't like that either. But I will give her the benefit of the doubt until I meet her myself. Invite them over this weekend, if that's convenient.'

'Oh, it's not really. I've got some things on.'

'I meant if it's convenient for them, Marlon...not you.'

She goes back to her telly, and I finish the washing up, looking out over Hackney and grinning.

The bell rings. Cassie gets up to answer it. I hear voices, and something about showing ID, and then Cassie invites them in. It's the woman detective that took my statement, and another guy I don't know.

'Marlon, what's this about?' Cassie's tone has changed.

I shrug, but I feel bare jitters.

The woman speaks first. 'We're dealing with a serious incident, and we'd like you to accompany us to the police station, Marlon.'

'Is he under arrest?' says Cassie.

'No, he's not under arrest. But it would be in his interests to help us with our enquiries.'

'Can't you talk to him here?'

'We'd like to do this at the station, Ms Williams. It's regarding a Mr Glen Crane. I believe you've had dealings with him, Marlon?'

The air is sucked right out of me. 'I know him,' I gasp. 'Yeah.'

The man detective says, 'Get your shoes on, then. Sooner we get going, the sooner we can clear all this up.' He's not like Hannan. This guy just wants to knock off for the night. But I'm trembling and my jaw is going.

'Marlon?' Cassie is saying to them. 'He wouldn't have anything to do with any trouble, he's a good boy.'

The guy says, 'He's shaking like a leaf.'

His colleague taps his arm and glances at him.

Cassie says, 'Of course he's shaking, he doesn't get police come round taking him away every day of the week. At least tell us what's going on.'

'A body was found in Aylesbury. It's not been formally identified but matches the description of Mr Glen Crane. There are suspicious circumstances. We need to rule Marlon out of any involvement, Ms Williams.' The officer's expression is friendly in a professional way, but it doesn't help my nerves.

'Oh, my goodness! But he's not under arrest?'

'No.'

'Then let me bring him down to the station. I don't want the neighbours seeing him taken out in handcuffs or any of that.'

'We won't be restraining him,' the guy says, and looks directly at me.

Glen is dead? That hits me like a sledgehammer. Do they know about the knife thing? Is that why they're here? How would they know about any of that? Glen must have told them at the hospital. Or Yannis said something? He was hassling me about why I'd needed the address.

'It's okay, Cassie. I know him through the music scene. Nothing to worry about. I'll go with them and clear it all up. Something's messed up here.'

But inside, I know I can't go with them. Whatever happened is bound to get pinned on me. Cassie always said I was an easy target.

I can't believe he's dead.

Cassie hands me my smart shoes.

'Not those, Cass.'

I go to the door and slide my trainers on.

'You'll need a coat for later. I'll come and get you,' Cassie says. I can see the worry in her eyes.

'I'll be alright.'

'Thank you, Ms Williams. Hopefully we can clear this up quickly,' the woman officer says.

We take the lift down, one of them either side of me. As the door opens, the man detective grips my upper arm. That's enough to seal the deal.

I look over my shoulder and my sister is up at the window. She raises her hand gently and disappears.

As we approach their unmarked car, I let my arm go limp, and then explode away from his grip. Before they can react, I'm gone.

I feel light as air. Numb, but charged.

They'll have regrouped by now and be on my tail, but they don't know the streets like I do. And that guy will not be quick as me. I can hear them shouting into their radios.

I bomb through an alley between a housing block, then double back, sending them the wrong way. I head for Victoria Park. I'll take my chances there.

Chapter Forty-seven

Ian • Aylesbury • March 2019

My phone pings on the dashboard. I ignore it. I focus on my mirrors for any sign of Emma's silver car.

Moments later, I read a text from Gaynor: Jon de Vries now wanted. Seen in car with Glen Crane. ANPR image from a traffic unit. I'm sorry, about to go in –

Another message pings while I'm reading. She gives me the reg of Jon de Vries' car. A white Golf.

I bow my head for Glen. Of course, it would be Jon. He would've battered anyone to get to the truth about Danny. Anger fills the void left by the sadness. Deep down, I reject any notion that it was my fault Glen went to see Jon. I only told the truth about what Andrew Raine had said. Glen must've wanted to find out why Jude visited Ellie in London. It's not my fault. Which is more than I can say for Gaynor. She betrayed her best friend, Danny's memory, justice, everyone.

A car is approaching from behind. It's silver in my rear-view mirror and I spin round in my seat. An A6. Emma's home. Thank God. There's a blue Ford Transit behind her, so I stay where I am for now. I've been playing my approach over in my mind since I got here. I want to deliver the news appropriately; I don't want her freaking out and putting herself in danger.

The silver Audi slows to pull into the driveway. As I turn back around to avoid suspicion, I catch sight of the Transit behind her coming to a stop too.

The driver jumps out and runs towards the house.

I fumble with the car door, pulling myself out and racing up the path.

Emma is being dragged back to the van. Jon de Vries is exactly as Glen described. Wiry and strong. He has Emma scooped up, manhandling her. She kicks out violently with her heels. She's freed an arm, pulling at his jet-black hair.

I try to keep out of his line of sight.

He has her at the back doors of the van. I'm there. I smash the back of Jon's head with my fist, putting everything into it. He drops Emma, turns to face me. I've only aggravated him.

Emma runs to the house. I throw the same strike again, and he easily parries it. There's commotion from the driveway. Emma's husband is shouting at the children to get back inside, pulling Emma to him.

Jon's eyes are burning, but his expression is controlled.

I see it at the last minute. A flash of metal, and then a sudden sensation. I've failed.

Chapter Forty-eight

Marlon • London • March 2019

Sirens and dogs, but no helicopter yet. What was I thinking? My brain took over when I got to the park, and I nearly gave myself up, but it's too late. I'm already guilty. I just hope Steve will come through for me.

I keep moving down the street. I told Steve to run the length of it and I'll flag him down. I think I've got far enough away from the park now. The noise died down, but I'm taking no chances.

There he is.

I jump into the road and wave my arms. Steve hits the brakes of his Escort van and signals for me to jump in the back. I pull the doors open and climb inside.

He takes off, saying, 'Right, what the hell is this?'

'Where we going?'

'I'll take you back to the lock-up. I was there when you called. Go on...'

I lean on the back of his headrest, steadying myself as he takes a corner. 'They want me for something, but it wasn't me.'

'Well, bloody well tell them that, then,' he says.

'It's complicated.'

'Isn't everything? Get your head down and you can explain yourself when we get there.'

I curl up with a sheet in the back of the van. Through my fear,

Steve provides a little relief. He's angry with me but gives off a vibe that he's into this. I reckon he likes the drama of it.

The van slows to a stop.

'Stay in the back. I'll open the door, make sure no one's about.'

I hear him working the padlock and the grind of the metal roller-door going up. Then footsteps. People coming. I pull the sheet over my head and get down low. They've found me already.

'Good evening, Steven.' A fake posh accent.

'Alright? Do I know you?'

Another voice says, 'Nah, you don't know us.' A deep voice, black.

'Well, you know me. What do you want?'

I strain to hear them. I think they're moving further into the lock-up.

Steve says, 'Put it down, yeah?'

I crawl up the van on my belly and try to see through the windscreen but the angle's all wrong.

'Put it down,' Steve says again. He's calm.

The white guy has dropped the posh accent now. 'He's not looking very scared, Dex.'

'Does he look like a problem?' the black one says.

'No problem.'

Steve says, 'Dexter? You're blind?'

'I can hear perfectly well,' Dexter says. 'When my boy here starts working on you, I'm gonna visualise every grimace of agony on your little face.'

Steve says, 'Dexter, I went to see Robert today. Pentonville postage is slow. It's over.'

'Oh, it's over?' Dexter says. 'We can go then, can we?'

'That would be a good start,' Steve says.

My hands are trembling, but I manage to crawl into a better

position. Their voices are raised now, and I take a chance, peering over the front seats.

'It was over,' Dexter says. 'But my man doesn't just let people come and see him without an invitation – doesn't let people start disrespecting him.'

Dexter's tall and wide. All in black sports gear. He's behind the white bloke who could reach Steve quickly from where he is. He's shorter, t-shirt bulging.

'Right, okay,' Steve says. 'Send him my apologies. I didn't mean to disrespect him. I thought we'd had a civil conversation.'

'Nah, Steven. Too late. I need to make sure you properly understand.'

Dexter takes a few steps back and his mate raises up a sword, swings at Steve's head. Misses. Steve backs away.

I throw myself forward and bang on the van's horn. They both turn in surprise and the sword raises up again.

Steve is quick. A flick of his arm and the white guy falls face first to the ground. Limp.

'Alan,' Dexter says.

Steve picks up the samurai sword.

'Alan?'

'He can't hear you,' Steve says.

'Is he dead?'

'Dunno.'

'Check, will ya?' Dexter says, his voice higher now.

I climb out of the van and feel for a pulse. My fingers are trembling. 'I think he's alive.'

Steve hands me the sword and threads his arms easily through Dexter's, putting his thick arm in a lock. 'He was out when his face smashed into the concrete. You're on your own now, big boy.'

Dexter cries out as he struggles.

'Are you gonna go quietly?' Steve whispers in his ear.

'Yeah, yeah...'

'Hold on,' I say. 'What do you lot know about Ellie Beck's death?'

'Killed herself, innit?'

Steve squeezes, and Dexter cries out in pain.

'Tell us what Warrister knew about it,' I say.

'Or we're calling the police to come and collect Samurai Alan and his sword,' Steve adds. 'You can tell them all about the arson while they're here.'

'Was Alan the guy looking out for Ellie?' I say.

'The hell you talkin' about?'

'Was he the protector?'

That doesn't seem to mean anything to him. Steve squeezes his arm again.

'What makes you think I know anything about it?' Dexter says.

'Maybe we should just give him to Jon de Vries,' I say. 'He'd be interested as well.'

Dexter laughs.

'You know him, do you? What about his little brother?' I ask.

He laughs again. 'De Vries still doesn't know, does he? So funny. Makes no difference to me. Relax and I'll tell you.'

Steve keeps his arm locked up.

'My guide's out of action, where'm I gonna go?'

Steve releases Dexter and walks over to Alan, who's starting to twitch. Steve wraps his arms around his neck and, after a few moments, lays his head gently back down.

'He be alright?' Dexter says.

Steve steps between Dexter and the door. 'He'll be fine.'

'Go on then,' I say. 'What do you know?'

'Then we're good?' he says.

I shoot Steve a look and he says, 'Then we're good.'

'Jon and Jude de Vries distribute for the top-tier in London. It's no secret down here. They did something foolish. They got penalised.'

'That's it?' Steve says.

'That's how it goes.' Dexter shrugs his shoulders.

Not what I was expecting. 'Danny was killed because of something his *brothers* did? So, why are they running around trying to figure out what happened? It's bullshit!'

'That's what's so funny,' Dexter says.

'Give us the name of Danny's killer,' Steve says. 'There's nothing funny about it.'

Dexter scrunches up his fat face.

'We can still give you and Alan here to the police,' Steve says.

I wish he wouldn't keep mentioning police. It gives me the jitters.

Dexter raises his arms in surrender. 'I heard it was Mitchell Henry.'

'You heard?' Steve says.

'It's not exactly public domain, this stuff, is it. It would've been him; I believe it. He's the top-tier's boy.'

I turn away, raising my face to the ceiling. If anything, I'm even more in the dark. What happened, Ellie? Why did you do this?

Steve's dragging Alan outside by the legs.

'Out you come, big boy,' he says to Dexter.

Alan looks like he's coming round again.

Steve pulls the door down and locks up. 'Let's find somewhere else,' he says.

I brace myself in the back of the van. Steve's obviously keeping off the main roads. Every corner catches me off guard.

'How we gonna get that Mitchell Henry name to the police?' I say. 'Crimestoppers? That's anonymous, isn't it?'

'I'm calling Ian. Better coming from him.'

He puts the phone on speaker, but it goes straight to voicemail.

He slows to a stop at the side of the road. 'Right, why were you running?'

He's looking over the seats with that same look Cassie gives me.

'Ian tell you about Glen Crane?'

'The photographer guy?'

'Yeah. I went to his house. I thought he was this protector Ellie told me about.'

Steve puffs out air, puts his head in his hands.

'And it all got weird. I ended up having to threaten him with a knife.'

His eyes are saucers now.

'His arm got cut. Ian smoothed it all over.'

'But the police come to your door.'

'I reckon Yannis told them. I asked him for Glen's address.'

'That twat's at the bottom of everything isn't he? You shouldn't have run, mate. You need to hand yourself in.'

'There's a lot more,' I say. I rub the back of my head to ease the throbbing. 'They told me they found Glen dead. In Aylesbury.'

'No way.'

'It's suspicious, they said.'

'Any idea why?'

I shake my head.

'You better lie low for now.'

Chapter Forty-nine

Ian • Location unknown • March 2019

My head is pounding. Fear and adrenaline must be keeping the worst of the pain at bay, but still my body feels like a slab of pounded meat. I came round in the back of the van. I was kicking the sides and trying to open the back doors. De Vries stopped and must've knocked me out again. I can't remember exactly. I'll wait this time; I don't have the strength to fight him again, and I'm praying Emma's husband called the police.

The van slows. I've no idea how long we've been on the road. We come to a stop, and Jon slams his door. The back doors creak open. He shows me a black handgun. Heavy in his hand.

'This will be in your back.' It's his eyes that terrify me. Otherwise, he seems remarkably calm. His hood is up.

'And this' – he shows me a large chef's knife – 'will be in your side.'

He gives me a moment to appreciate both weapons.

'Get out. Slowly.'

I struggle to slide across the van floor, then swing my legs out the back. It takes a moment to find my balance, but he's already pushing hard into my back.

'Keep your head down and walk.'

The prod in my back pushes me over a patch of grass from the carpark to a block of flats. I won't antagonise him by lifting my head up, but I try to gather as much information in my periphery as I can. Shabby, but not the worst flats I've ever seen. When we reach the entrance doors, he shoves me hard in my back, but I catch a glance of the sign with the name of the building. I commit it to memory, repeating it over again as he shoves me into the lift. He's particularly careful in the confined space and pushes my head down further with the butt of the pistol. I can't see which floor we exit on. We shuffle along an outside walkway.

He's hammering on a door. It opens. I'm shoved onto a threadbare brown sofa. A woman stares at me with dead eyes. Her dressing gown is open, showing her underwear and pale skin. She's skinny as hell.

'What's this?' she says. Still transfixed on me.

Jon addresses me instead. 'If you move or shout out, I will shoot you in the head, okay?'

I nod carefully. My limbs are trembling, and the room is spinning around me.

'Although, people don't take much notice here, do they, Sharon?' he says.

The woman continues to stare, then shakes her head like a child.

'Don't let us stop you,' he says to her. 'Finish up what you were doing.'

She turns and looks at him.

'Go on, piss off,' he says and slaps her face.

She doesn't react. Just skulks off into another room.

Jon goes to the window and peers through the net curtains. Sharon's housekeeping is a disaster. The whole place smells of her. The only furnishings are a coffee table and dirty mugs. A TV is on in the corner. Horror movie. Jon goes to the front door and locks it, puts the key in his jeans' pocket. He picks up a wooden post and wedges one end under the door handle. Kicks it firmly into the carpet at the other end. Then he stands looking at the TV. I can almost hear the gears crunching in his mind. A picture forms in my head of him savagely beating Glen. The expressionless face and piercing eyes. Was he trying to force information out of him? My head starts to vibrate now, worse than my body. He's considering how best to get me talking. I can't leave that decision to him; I need to take a chance.

'I know you think –'

'Shut up!' He points the gun directly at my face, and I instinctively cover my face with my hands.

I have to try again. If it's left to him, I'll become a workout bag. I speak quickly and clearly. 'The protector was made up.'

He opens his mouth and grunts, like he suddenly stopped himself cursing me. He stares, the gears crunching harder now. 'The bloke that came to see me didn't believe it either.'

I've got him. Got to keep him engaged and talking to me. 'What did Glen tell you.'

'Everything. Had to, didn't he, in the end?'

'Jon, I promise you David Beck had nothing to do with Danny's murder. Nor his family. And obviously not me.'

'I can't know that, now can I? Because you've offered yourself up in that family's place, haven't you?'

'Jon, please. We want the same thing. I've been trying to get to the bottom of all this. I'm not the enemy.'

'You are not family!' He comes over and pushes the barrel of the gun against my nose. 'Which makes you nobody.'

I focus on keeping as still as possible. I've pushed it too far.

'You screwed this up, so I'm not letting you go to waste.'

The thought of what that might mean sends a cold shiver down my back and into my legs.

'They'll have found your mangled mate by now. It's pretty much over for me.' He lifts my chin with the barrel of the gun. 'Isn't it?'

I try to keep my head still but tuck my lips in. A desperate show of empathy.

He goes back to the window.

'There's still a chance to find out why Danny died,' I say. I prepare to deflect an attack, but he stays where he is.

'Why are you so sure the old man didn't hire somebody?'

'It was a rumour, Jon. The police tore that theory apart. There's no way.'

He's lost in his thoughts.

'If you run, I won't call them. Tie me up if you want.'

He stares at me.

'Give yourself time to find answers. You can't learn anything here,' I say.

The trouble is he already knows that. His eyes are blazing.

Sharon appears in the corner of my vision. She's woozy, a stupid smile on her face. She's heading for my sofa but doesn't get that far. Jon cracks her across the face with the back of his hand. She collapses on the floor like a ragdoll. He kicks her in the ribs while she's down, venting his hatred of me.

'Jon, no!' I hold my hands up in surrender.

Sharon grabs onto Jon's leg, dragging herself to him. She looks up at him, blood dripping from her nose. He pulls his leg away and backs off to the window again. She pulls herself up onto the sofa next to me. Uses the end of her dirty dressing gown to stem the bleeding. Her expression seems to imply she's already forgotten what happened.

Jon's over again, jabbing her in the ribs. 'You watch him. If he moves, you shout me, right?'

His stare bores through me. 'I'm only in the next room. I will blow your head off.'

He's gone. Sharon gazes at the TV where absolute carnage is being played out. I can't watch. Instead, I try to focus on my breath. I try to imagine Sofia beside me as the calm voice on the app takes us through the motions of relaxing. But I can't; this is too real, I can't stop the spinning in my brain. Or the buzzing in my nerves. A splitting headache has emerged now from beneath the adrenaline.

'Sharon, is this your flat?' I whisper.

'Shhh!' She puts a finger to her lips.

She doesn't want Jon to hear us. I lean closer. But no, she wants to hear what's happening on TV. She's leaning forward now to catch what's being said. She's rocking gently from side to side.

'Does he force you to help him?'

She scrunches up her face, like the idea is ridiculous. Her eyes never leave the screen.

'I can help you. Do you have a phone?'

'Don't need no help,' she says. She leans back into the sofa now, her dressing gown falling open. She grabs both sides and wraps herself back up in it. Her eyes close and her head lolls.

I take in the small windows, the locked door. I nudge her. 'Sharon, stay awake.'

Her head tilts my way now, and I flick it with my own head. Her eyes open a crack.

'Can you bring me your phone? I'll make him leave you alone.'

I listen carefully. Jon's making himself something to eat in the kitchen.

'He's helping himself to your food, Sharon. You gonna let him just take what's yours?'

269

She's giggling softly now.

'He didn't even ask you. That's no way to treat a lady.'

She opens her mouth to speak, but seems to forget, and chuckles to herself.

'Sharon, you useless bitch,' I say. My heart drops through my ribcage. 'You want another slap?'

She looks at me. Unsure.

'Get me your phone, now.' I grab a bunch of her robe in my fist and pull her face against mine. 'You want your head bashed off that table or what?'

Her eyes widen.

'The phone.'

She stands and wobbles across the room.

'Oi! Sit down!' Jon's through the door, spinning her around. Throws her into the sofa. 'Where you off to?'

'Dunno,' she says.

'Right, get in the bedroom,' he says, pulling her up by the hair.

She screeches at herself and leaves the room.

Jon has finished off his sandwich. He's left the crusts. Takes a long swig from a can of Red Bull.

'You're right, you don't know anything about Danny's murder.'

I shake my head.

'The only reason you're here is to keep me safe. That's it. I don't care what happens to you. I don't need you able to talk. You know what I'm saying?'

I nod. I knew that already.

'Danny was a good boy; he wasn't a soldier.'

'Ellie only had good things to say about him.'

'I'll cut your tongue out! I told you... I don't need you able to talk.'

I drop my head.

'He was doing something with his life. That disease couldn't stop him. He was battling through it. My little brother was better than any of us.'

I don't dare look up.

'He was strong.'

He's emphasising his words like a corporal energising his men.

I keep my posture neutral, avoiding any eye contact. My goal is to keep giving myself another minute of life, one at a time.

I use Ellie's image to tune out Jon's monologue. The smile that once broke out across her entire face. I tried to get that again, but she was too guarded. But I have it stored away, and I'll have it forever. She never suspected her best friend of betraying her. It's so needless. If only they'd have found Danny's killer, things would have eventually been easier. If only she'd talked to her friends. If she'd told me the truth. The sadness in her eyes, her absolute determination to finish her piece of art before she died... that was all honest emotion. But I didn't dig deep enough. I should have read her better than I did. I let her down like all these other friends, who allowed her the space to make a wrong turn. We all failed her. Especially Gaynor. I was looking after her, she said. I don't doubt she believes that too, but underneath there was a vacuum in Gaynor's own life that she needed to fill. She'd spent a lifetime on the outside. She made herself part of something, she said, when she joined the police. I think it gave her a misplaced confidence to try and fix Ellie on her own. How could she have got it so wrong?

Chapter Fifty

Marlon • London • March 2019

I can feel goosebumps on my arms. I wait for the traffic to clear. Steve's dropping me off, and he's still talking.

'Are you sure you want to do this?'

'I have to.'

'You've got this,' he says softly, and I hear the van door click shut. The engine revs as he pulls away and I cross the road.

DI Hannan sits silently across the table. His colleague does all the talking. The woman detective I ran from. She's bolt upright in her chair.

'Why did you run?'

'I was scared. I know it was wrong, but I can't change it now. Can I call my sister?'

'She's on her way here.'

Hannan says, 'You're a man, Marlon. You need to take responsibility yourself.'

'I know. I wanted to give you some information.'

'About what?' the woman asks.

'Ellie Beck's boyfriend, Danny de Vries. I've got a name for his killer.'

'The name...?'

'Mitchell Henry.'

She looks at Hannan, who shakes his head. He doesn't know the name.

'Age? Address?'

'I only got the name. He's London, though.'

'Where did you get his name from?' she says.

I break away from their stares, need time to think.

'Marlon, this is important. Who gave you this name?'

Hannan stands and passes a piece of paper out of the door to somebody.

'I don't want to say, but it's reliable.'

'Think about that, Marlon,' she says. 'Because it might save your friend Ian Wren's life.'

I freeze. 'Ian?'

'He was abducted yesterday evening. We don't know where he's been taken. You need to tell us everything you know. Now.'

'Abducted? Who by?'

'Talk to us first,' Hannan says.

'Dexter Wilson, friend of Robert Warrister's, told me. He said it didn't matter to him, he thought it was funny that Jon de Vries still didn't know why his brother had died. He said Mitchell Henry killed him to penalise the de Vries brothers for something.'

'Something like what?'

'I dunno. That's all he said. I think he was telling the truth. He didn't care, no skin off his nose.'

They both look at me, silent.

'What can I do to help Ian? I'll do anything.'

'Why were you looking for Glen Crane?'

'I thought he was Ellie's protector.'

The woman thinks it's pathetic and huffs. I look over at Hannan. He's waiting for more.

'I broke in and he caught me. There was a knife. I tried to

protect myself. It was all so quick. He got a cut to his arm, and I held him until Ian came.'

'Ian was there too?'

'I promise you, we had nothing to do with Glen being attacked in Aylesbury.'

'We know that. But you've made a right cock-up of everything, haven't you?'

I bow my head and raise my eyes to apologise. 'Did the de Vries brothers do it?'

'Just tell us everything,' Hannan says. 'From the beginning.'

Chapter Fifty-one

Ian • Location unknown • March 2019

I don't want to open my eyes. I was better off asleep. I can fool myself into thinking it was all a nightmare. But that childish thinking's not going to get me out of here. I flick my eyes open and squint against the sun coming through the net curtains. My arms ache. De Vries cable-tied them before I fell asleep on the sofa. My body weight's been on them all night. My legs are tied together too. I shuffle upright into a sitting position, and it eases the pressure. The plastic is cutting tight into my wrists and ankles.

Jon de Vries is asleep, sitting against the front door, next to his makeshift jamb. His head hangs down and he's holding the gun across his lap. I shake my head to clear the mind. Consider what it would take to get the gun from him. But I'm useless, trussed up and impotent.

'Sharon,' I whisper. I can hear rustling from the kitchen.

She's in the same open dressing gown and underwear as last night. Takes a seat next to me on the sofa with a mug of coffee.

'Can I have a sip?'

Her face is more human this morning, some colour.

'He…he wouldn't like it… if I did that.'

'He's asleep, Sharon.'

She hides her face in her mug with a noisy slurp. I'd most

likely heave if she gave me any of her coffee, anyway. More sugar than Brazil in there, probably.

'If you went over and took his gun, it'd all be over.'

She stares at him sleeping.

'No more hammering on your door at all hours. No more having to hide in the back wondering who the hell all those strange men are.'

She's put her mug down, hands laced across her belly.

'No more wondering what they're gonna do to you when they've finished whatever they're doing. You can get your flat back. Get your life back.'

She turns her face towards me. Her brain's done all the thinking it needs by breakfast. 'I need him,' she says.

'No, you don't,' I whisper. 'He only needs you.'

'I need what he gives me,' she says. Her expression is one of resigned hopelessness. She leaves the room, already needing some medicine to get through until lunchtime.

I lean forward to see where her mug is. Then I shuffle over on the sofa, grasping it between my trainers. I twist against the handle. No luck.

Instead, I tip it on its side and smash down on it with my foot. I glance up at Jon, but the noise hasn't woken him. The carpet muffled it just enough. I reach down and grab a shard of broken china.

It's a few minutes before Sharon reappears, looking more like her old self from last night.

'Hey, you knocked your coffee over,' I whisper. 'Better clear it up before he sees it.'

She looks but it takes a moment before she registers any interest. Then she grabs a magazine and pushes the remains of the mug onto it. Rubs at the wet carpet with the sole of her foot.

She looks over at Jon and takes the debris into the kitchen.

I start working the plastic cable-tie against the shard I'm gripping between finger and thumb. It might be impossible, but it's progress. I have to try everything. I finally have the truth about Ellie. As soon as I get free, I'll tell her story: the honest truth about her death. I'll finally rest. Then I'll start to rebuild my relationship with Sofia. There's been too much suffering. The studio gear has slipped somewhere into the recesses of my concerns. It's just stuff. I'm resourceful; I can work with whatever I've got. It might even be time for a change. The thought is uplifting. I rub harder against the shard of china. Jon de Vries starts to look less terrifying. Asleep, he's as harmless as any of us sane people. I visualise the plastic snapping, I visualise taking the gun from him. I can see it clear in my mind. Will I shoot him, or give him a chance to co-operate first? Doesn't matter. I'm becoming instinctive, like a predator. What happens, happens.

Jon is finally stirring. He stretches his arms up and opens his eyes. Squints, takes a moment to remember where he is and what's at stake. I witness the change in his face. The situation makes him what he is.

He looks at me. I can't tell what's behind it. He jumps to his feet and strides over, his gun swinging loosely at his side.

'I'll do you some toast.'

'Thanks.' I slide the shard under my leg.

He returns a few minutes later with a buttered slice. No plate. It's good to get something inside me.

'It's not my fault, any of this,' he says. His back is to me, he's looking out of the window. 'People just need to tell me the truth.'

I take another huge bite, so I have an excuse not to be responding if he turns round.

'I've got theories about hired protectors, all sorts of crap from arty-farty students, nobody telling me any truth.'

I can't miss the opportunity to ask about something. 'I heard you were leaning on Oxford students. Nothing useful?'

'Again, nobody telling me any truth.'

'I heard you shattered someone's jaw.'

He takes that in for moment, then shakes his head, laughing. 'See what I mean? I've done a lot of stuff, man, but I can tell you for a fact I haven't never shattered no jaw. Dickhead probably fell over from the smack… now that probably was my fault.' He laughs again.

'But you attack people from behind,' I say, and my sudden candour surprises me.

He snorts. 'Ah, that was nothing.'

I grin like it hasn't affected me after all. He's joining in and I want to keep it that way.

'You were sniffing around. I can't have it. The thing with this game is you gotta be in charge. People up the chain from me? They think they're in control, but I run my own ship, man. I am the man in charge of this world. People don't give me the truth – they need to expect some damage.'

'Sharon not truthful with you?'

He looks at me and his face breaks out into a grin. 'That's different, innit?'

This time I don't play along. Instead, I subtly work the cable-tie, rocking my hands forward and backwards, a tiny bit at a time.

'Oi, bitch!' he suddenly shouts.

Sharon comes in, head down like a dog who's taken the pie.

'Who do you know got a car I can use?'

'Nobody,' she says without looking up. Flinches as he starts to speak again.

'Useless… dunno why I bother with you.'

'Sorry, Jon,' she says, and backs off.

'Seems pretty safe here,' I say.

He ignores me, and addresses Sharon again. 'Take the keys and move the blue van out there somewhere else.' He throws the keys at her, and they hit her in the face.

'I've never driven a van,' she says.

'I don't care. Move the van, now.'

'Where to?'

'Wherever you want, stupid. And put some clothes on, you look like a crack-whore.'

She goes into the bedroom. Jon looks out of the window. Thinking about his next move has made him jittery again.

Sharon emerges in grey joggers and hoodie, and Jon removes the door jamb. He sends her out with a kick.

I wonder how low he has categorised Sharon. I've already decided to make sure he pays for his treatment of her, as much as for what he did to Glen. The thought of Glen's murder sharpens my focus again. I need to be careful with de Vries. Just because he's talking now, doesn't mean I'm not in danger of getting the same level of violence for an ill-judged comment.

After a while – I've no idea how long – Sharon returns. With her is Jude, his shaved head covered in flaky bits of skin. He spends too long looking at me. Then acts as if he's never seen me. Maybe he never got around to telling Jon he came to the hospital.

'Turned your phone off?' Jon says, locking up and replacing the wooden door jamb.

''Course. Before I left.'

'I couldn't call. All got messed up. Had to bring him with me instead.'

Jude glances my way. 'What we doing with him?'

Jon cocks his head towards the kitchen and his brother follows him out of earshot. Sharon sits on the carpet, hugging her legs.

'Hey, are we in Aylesbury?' I whisper.

She starts to rock her body back and forth.

'What was the name of the road you took the van to?'

She inspects her fingers and picks at the skin around one of her nails.

'I didn't mean what I said to you before. I think you were about to bring me your phone?'

She looks at the kitchen door, then back to me. I'm getting through to her. She slides over to the coffee table and opens a couple of the drawers. Pulls out papers and bits of junk.

'Shhh! Keep it low,' I say. 'Is it there?'

Her head snaps up to the kitchen door again. 'Jon!'

'No! Don't!'

Jon comes crashing through the door, looks straight at me, still tied up on the sofa. 'What?'

'Can I have a little something now?'

The rage turns his face crimson. He grabs her by the hair and slams her face into the wall. Takes her arm and drags her into the bedroom. She's screaming as he slams the door shut. Jude joins him in the living room.

'Easy, man, we need her,' Jude says. But without conviction.

'This place is all I need her for,' Jon says. 'She's too slow at everything else.'

He paces the room, rubbing his palms over his face. 'I need to get out of here. Can you have a look round the carpark?'

'Don't worry, they haven't got a clue where you are. They got no pictures.'

Jon stops dead still. He doesn't turn to his brother. 'The pigs? How would you know that?'

'They pulled me in. Got nothing out of me. I was out after a couple of hours.'

Jon spins towards him, grabs his neck in a tight grip. Jude backs off, stopped by the wall. Jon eases off a little, wants him to talk.

'I didn't tell 'em nothin', bruv.' He's dribbling down his front. Jon releases his grip and Jude slides down the wall.

Jon goes to the window and cranes his head both ways. It hasn't clicked with Jude yet. He's not the full ticket. Jon's kicking the door jamb out and fumbling with the key. He steps outside. When he returns, he's buzzing.

'You absolute prick!'

Jude's open-mouthed, following Jon into the bedroom.

'Where did you take the van?' Jon shouts.

A dull thud, like kicks to a body.

'Where is it?'

'She's out of it, man,' says Jude. 'I saw where she came from, I'll go have a look for it.'

'Too late,' Jon says. He's at the window.

My pulse races.

'What? What's up?' says Jude.

Jon buries his head in his hands. A long, deep breath in. He holds it. Jude edges cautiously over to the window. Peers out. His legs start to tremble in his jogging bottoms. It's almost comical to see.

'How?' he says.

'Did you not wonder why they let you go?' Jon says. It sounds like a calm before one hell of a violent storm. 'The criminal brother of someone wanted for murder...'

Jude is frozen to the spot. He's crunched the numbers and finally caught up with the situation. 'They followed me, didn't they?'

But my eyes are fixed on his brother. If the police are outside, this could go either of two ways. He'll either become extremely desperate, and thus incredibly dangerous. Or he could see his position as completely useless and surrender himself. I know enough now to believe he'll calculate his chances thoughtfully. The thing that worries me most is me and Sharon. We're his only ticket out of here. I try not to guess how far he'll be willing to go.

The shrill ring of a landline breaks my thoughts. Jon's eyes dart around the room, suggesting it's not a phone that usually rings. He finds it on the stand behind the TV and holds the receiver to his ear. He just listens.

'Call me back in five minutes,' he says. I barely make out a tinny voice protesting before he hangs up.

He takes Jude's face in his hands and rests his forehead against his brother's. 'The murder is on me. Get yourself out of here.'

'Sorry... I –'

'There's nothing on you. I need you to keep looking for Danny's killer, yes? When you find them, you pay them back in full. Understood?'

'Jon... what are you going to do?'

He chews on his bottom lip, scanning the room. 'Don't matter. When they call me back, I'm gonna tell them you're coming out unarmed. I want you to co-operate with them. Yes? Then I want you back in business, sorting out our family's problem, got it?'

Jude is hanging by a thread. He's nodding, but I don't believe it.

'I need to take a piss,' he says and leaves the room.

I track Jon as he goes to the window, clock the pistol hanging limp at his side.

I push on my bound legs, softly rising out of the sofa. My limbs are unsteady and ache with every small movement. I pause, check for any sign Jon's turning back. He's still preoccupied with the outside. I move slowly across the carpet, taking tiny steps. Then I cover the remaining couple of metres with a big jump, landing by the door. I grab the wooden jamb as Jon registers the movement. He's raising up the butt of the gun as I swing the solid post. It glances off his head. My grip is poor and the post slips out, splintered wood taking a chunk of flesh with it. Bound and entirely useless, I wait for the punishment.

Jon pushes me to the ground. I fall heavily, but there's no pain. He pushes the cold metal of the gun into my cheek. His head's bleeding, but not enough. I squeeze my eyes closed. That's it, I tried everything. Let's hope it's over quickly.

In the pause, I catch his rotten scent. It reminds me of a schoolboys' changing room.

The gun barrel's pressing my gums into my teeth and all I can hear is his heavy breath. But something's holding him back. I grab the chance.

'Why send Jude to see me at the hospital?'

He pulls the gun away, and I sheepishly open my eyes. He grabs me by the throat. 'What did you fucking say?'

'You didn't know?'

He's chewing his bottom lip again. He doesn't know where to go with this. I've given him just enough to hang in for a bit longer. The police must have a plan. I pray they do.

I guess little red dots suddenly appearing on Jon's head and chest would be too much to wish for. But I need a little faith.

'What's going on?' Jude's voice is shaky.

'Have a seat,' Jon says. He stands and faces his brother. Above him in every way.

'I won't go out there,' Jude stammers.

I stay where I am on the floor. I figure it's the best place to be in the event of a raid anyway.

The landline rings again, and Jon storms over to it.

'Not yet,' he says and slams the receiver down.

He returns to Jude. 'Why do I get the feeling you've not been a hundred percent honest with me, bruv?'

'Jon... I want –'

'Just get out. Go. Now!'

'I'm not leaving. I won't lose another brother, Jon.'

'Consider me already dead. Get out there and get some justice for Danny. Make sure you show them you're not carrying.'

'I know what you're going to do, Jon. You don't have to.'

Jon turns his back on his brother and stands over me instead. He takes the chef's knife from his waistband. 'Let's be absolutely sure you don't know anything,' he says. He grabs the lobe of my right ear, pulls it out as far as it can go. The pain is less than I expected, but the fear is paralysing.

He hovers the blade's edge over my eyeline. Then brings it down towards my outstretched ear. He says, 'My brother will need every fucking detail you know. I don't care how insignificant you think it is, okay?'

I try to shout, but my brain has stopped sending the right signals. I can only squeeze my eyes shut.

'Think carefully,' he says. 'You need your ears, don't you?'

My mind is flashing fractured images of people I've loved.

'You can't be involved in this,' he says to Jude. 'I'll message you anything useful. Go.'

'Don't do this,' Jude says. 'You don't know everything, bruv.'

Jon releases my ear. My eyes flick open.

'And you do?' He snorts and wipes his face with his t-shirt.

'I won't let you give up for no reason, Jon.'

Jon looks over his shoulder, the knife still close to my ear. 'You're the only one who can sort out our little brother's murder, yeah? It's up to you, now. Go and get ready.'

Jude suddenly breaks. His face contorts. 'I did it.'

He collapses like a bunch of rags. Jon is on him in a flash. The tip of the knife now pressed against his brother's forehead.

'Say that again,' he says. His eyes are wide.

Jude's eyes are tightly shut. 'Danny's dead because of me.'

The room goes dead. Jon's breathing is filling the space. He goes to speak, but something stops him. It happens again.

Jude's face carries the strain of his secrets. His jaw is grinding.

What the hell does he mean? How is he to blame? My brain kicks back into gear and skips through every angle. Nothing makes sense.

All life has been sucked from Jon de Vries. The knife is still at his brother's head, but he's not focused. He says, 'Tell me.'

Jude's face quivers violently under the tip of the knife. 'I got a… call, from Merseyside. They wanted to talk to me. And somehow… they found out about it.'

'How did that end up with my LITTLE BROTHER GETTING BATTERED TO DEATH?'

'I met them once. Only… only once.'

'WHY DIDN'T YOU TALK TO ME?!'

'I… I didn't realise what was happening. But they found out.'

'What did they do?'

'They said they needed an apology. Had to be one of us.'

'You gave up our little brother?' Jon's voice has shrunk to a cold whisper.

'There was no way out, Jon.'

Jon stands and pulls back his boot, kicks his brother hard in the legs, then again and again, more wildly each time. He's crying himself now. He gets back in Jude's face.

'WHY?'

'It couldn't be you, Jon. You're head of this family. Danny… he was sick…they made me, bruv.'

'YOU'RE WEAK,' Jon screams. 'It should've been you.'

He raises the pistol up to Jude's face, cocks the hammer.

I push off with my legs and hurl my body weight into them. It knocks Jon off balance. The surprise stuns him for a second, and I bat the gun from his hand with my bound wrists, like a double-handed baseball hit. Jude scrambles to his feet as I throw my arms around Jon's neck and pull the cable-tie deep into his throat. But he's too strong. He elbows me in the face and charges out of the door. His brother is the quarry now.

Cracks of gunfire, and Jude's body slumps on the walkway. Jon's profile surges back past the window, generating warning shouts from armed police below. Then a single shot. Another dull thud, closer this time. I keep my head down until all I can hear are voices and commotion from below. Then I caterpillar across the carpet to the door. Jon's corpse is face down, spread-eagled on the ground.

Sharon appears in the doorway. Her hands are over her ears and her eyes are like saucers.

'It's alright, love,' I say. 'Scissors?'

She pulls her hands away from her ears and I repeat it. All the air rushes out of her, followed by convulsions. Her face bears the weight of more trauma than any human being should carry. I wait and then ask her again. She shuffles towards the kitchen.

Chapter Fifty-two

Marlon • Aylesbury • August 2019

We finally hit the motorway. Ian's driving Sofia's Mini and she's in the passenger seat, looking chilled. It doesn't mean as much to her, seeing where Glen was killed. But she bought some flowers from the garage when we stopped. I want some sounds on, and Ian plays Ellie's song. Even from back here I can tell how emotional it still makes him.

'That part's intense,' I say.

'David was becoming aware of his responsibilities,' Ian says. 'Double the authority being a single parent. All the discipline had to come from him.'

'Bet he was strict. Like my mum.'

Sofia turns and smiles.

'And it was all down to him to keep his daughter safe,' I say. 'It's a protection song, innit?'

Ian glances out the side window and back to the road. 'Well, Ellie believed Gaynor's deception. David's poem might've played a part in that.'

Sofia says, 'It was the "safe underneath Philippa's tree" line thing, wasn't it?'

Ian looks at her for a second, and something's going on. She doesn't notice, coz her head's in a magazine. Ellie's song finishes and nobody says anything for the rest of the journey.

The park is deserted, apart from some kids playing cricket at the far end, well away from the remaining tributes that indicate where Glen's body was found. Ian said witnesses came forward and identified Jon de Vries. We don't know if Glen was killed here or just dumped after de Vries got what he needed out of him. Sofia hands Ian the flowers and he kneels on the grass. Changes his mind about the right spot a few times. He's whispering to himself. A teddy bear has fallen over and he sits it back upright.

He says, 'Glen thought he couldn't help Ellie anymore.' He stands up and looks at the sky. 'But then he goes and does this.'

Sofia turns towards the car. She better not be embarrassed by Ian getting all emotional.

I step in with, 'At the end of the day, he helped, didn't he? Might never have got the truth if he hadn't gone after de Vries.'

Ian puts his arm round my shoulder, as we walk back across the park. 'I'm expecting a lot from you, mate.'

He's got big plans for his online academy, and I know I'll be working hard. I feel like his project. He wants me to achieve.

Suddenly, he jogs up to Sofia and walks beside her. He says, 'The "safe underneath Philippa's tree" line convinced Ellie, did it?'

'Didn't it?'

The conversation feels uncomfortable and I think it would be polite to let them get further ahead of me. But I want to hear, so I stay close enough.

'There was more in Ellie's letter, wasn't there? I know she would have told me more.'

Sofia's shaking her head, turning away from him.

'What did she say?'

She turns back, pushing him in the chest, again and again, until, suddenly, she bursts into tears.

'Did you want to hear that you got it wrong? That she killed herself because of the paranoia you ignored?'

'You –'

'I was looking out for you, damnit! It wasn't your fault, and the guilt would have crippled you.'

Ian pushes her arms away and walks back in the other direction. His face is turned to the sky.

Sofia screams, 'Why couldn't you just come to Rome with me?'

She tries to follow him, but I block her path. It feels like the right thing to do. The least I can do for my friend.

She pushes me.

'It's him or me, Ian. That's it. You can go on... fixing everything for everybody, or you can fix us.'

'That's what it always came down to, isn't it?'

'Ian, I've had enough. You get yourself a proper, normal job, or that's it between us.'

She pulls a piece of paper out of her jeans pocket. Unfolds it and chucks it on the grass. Ian stares at her, then comes back over, bends down, and picks it up. He turns away as he reads. He doesn't want us to see his face.

After a while, he folds the letter back up and walks away.

Chapter Fifty-three

London • December 2019

It's the first time I've spent Christmas with anyone other than Sofia for a long time. I got a real tree. I never saw the need before. When the fake one was covered in lights and baubles you couldn't tell the difference.

'I like that you kept it simple, no tinsel,' Cassie says.

'It only works when it's real,' I say. 'You just embellish the tree, no disguising anything.'

Marlon rolls his eyes, holding a glass of wine he's yet to try. He's spent the past few months working his way up with Steve and gets to handle the desk alone now for the smaller gigs. He was the guinea pig for my online academy. Helped each other out. It's a gradual thing, but the academy's generating more and more interest, especially among the contacts I'm making doing guest lectures at London Met. The old joke is that 'those who can't, teach' but my track record speaks for itself. The global reach the new platform gives me drives my enthusiasm. If only one other young person can achieve as big a sense of accomplishment and satisfaction as I've seen in Marlon, then I'll have done my job.

'For Ellie,' I say, and chink glasses with Marlon.

'And her family.'

I like that. David Beck passed away, peacefully, soon after the public enquiry into the de Vries killings. It was like he'd held on to plead his innocence. I saw him once more before he died. Jamie gave me the heads up that they'd initiated palliative care. I liked to think there was more going on in his mind than his face could express. He's free now, with his little girl again. Gaynor was removed from the police service. It was deemed not in the public interest to pursue a case of encouraging or assisting suicide against her.

'You okay?' Marlon asks.

I nod. He's doing well. Still gets his behind whipped by Cassie from time to time, but never as bad as the day she picked him up from the police station.

'I'm good,' I say. The anxiety attacks diminished soon after my kidnapping, and apart from a couple of fleeting moments, I feel fine.

Marlon's evidence triggered an investigation into Mitchell Henry, who was, just last week, convicted and sentenced to life imprisonment. His DNA matched a sample taken from the scene of Danny's murder. There's an ongoing investigation that's gathering pace into the County Lines network. Regarding the arson at the studio, there was insufficient evidence to secure a conviction against Dexter and Alan. But characters like them don't tend to last too long in that world. Besides, I can live without the studio. I get to handle some mix projects from home, but my passion lies with teaching now. I've found a better way. Things are less important to me than they were – but I still enjoy getting my hands on some of the vintage gear they have at the university.

The doorbell rings, and there stands Sofia.

'Simone wants to know if you have plans for Boxing Day,' she says.

My face must say it all.

'I'll tell her you do,' she says.

She tucks her hair behind her ears. 'Oh, here...' She takes a present from her bag. It's a small box, wrapped with a royal blue ribbon.

I start to untie the ribbon.

'Oh, it's not for opening,' she says.

'It's not?'

'No, it's an empty box.'

'Okay...'

'You said my gift was a symbol of hope until you hurled it.'

'It was.'

'So, keep this one safe.'

Scan here to link to a recording of Ellie's song,
Under the Tree

Acknowledgements

I am indebted to my publishers, Claire Steele and Jill Glenn, for helping me find my voice. Their expertise and boundless enthusiasm made getting to the end an achievable, and even enjoyable, challenge.

For their love and for keeping it real, I thank Kate and Erin.

Finally, my mother, Pat. Thanks for the inspiration, support, and belief.

At ByTheBook, we are dedicated to discovering new creative talent and publishing beautiful books that will find their ways into the hearts of readers worldwide.

BYTHEBOOK.PRESS